The Dead of Winter

No. 1 *Sunday Times* bestseller S. J. Parris is the pseudonym of the author and journalist Stephanie Merritt. It was as a student at Cambridge researching a paper on the period that Stephanie first became fascinated by the rich history of Tudor England and Renaissance Europe. Since then, her interest has grown and led her to create this series of historical thrillers featuring Giordano Bruno.

Stephanie has worked as a critic and feature writer for a variety of newspapers and magazines, as well as radio and television. She has also written the contemporary psychological thriller *While You Sleep* under her own name. She currently writes for the *Observer* and the *Guardian*, and lives in Surrey with her son.

www.sjparris.com

 /sjparrisbooks

 @thestephmerritt

The Dead of Winter

S. J. PARRIS

HarperCollins*Publishers*

HarperCollins*Publishers* Ltd
1 London Bridge Street,
London SE1 9GF

www.harpercollins.co.uk

This collection first published by HarperCollins*Publishers* 2020
1

The Secret Dead first published by HarperCollins*Publishers* 2014
The Academy of Secrets first published in ebook format by HarperCollins*Publishers*
2020

A catalogue record for this book is available from the British Library

ISBN: 978-0-00-841181-7

This novel is entirely a work of fiction.
The names, characters and incidents portrayed in it are
the work of the author's imagination. Any resemblance to
actual persons, living or dead, events or localities is
entirely coincidental.

Typeset in Sabon by Palimpsest Book Production Ltd, Falkirk, Stirlingshire

Printed and bound in Great Britain by CPI Group (UK) Ltd, Croydon CR0 4YY

MIX
Paper from
responsible sources
FSC™ C007454

This book is produced from independently certified FSC™ paper
to ensure responsible forest management.

For more information visit: www.harpercollins.co.uk/green

THE SECRET DEAD

I was eighteen years old and had just taken holy orders the summer Fra Gennaro found the girl. It was not the first time I had seen a naked woman. I had entered the Dominican order as a novice at fifteen, old enough by then to have tasted first love, the sweet warmth of a girl's pliant body in the shade of the olive trees above the village of Nola. A distant cousin, as it turned out; her family were livid. Perhaps that was why my father had been so ready to pay out for my education, though God knows he could ill afford it. Sending me away to the Dominicans in the city was cheaper than a scandal. We were given new names on taking our final vows, to symbolise the shedding of our old selves. I took the name Giordano, though most people just called me Bruno.

Naples in the summer of 1566 was an inferno of heat and noise, dust and crowds; a city of heart-stopping beauty and casual violence. Two hundred and fifty thousand souls seething inside ancient walls built to house one-tenth that number, the tenements growing higher and higher until their shadows almost shut out the sun because land was scarce, so much of it taken up by the vast gardens and courtyards of the palazzos and the religious houses. Tensions in the city

1

streets brewed and boiled like the forces of the great volcano that overshadows them. Even walking from one side of a piazza to the other felt like fighting through the front line of an advancing army: elbows and fists, baskets, barrows and hot, angry bodies jostling and shoving, trampling or crushing one another. Horses and carts ploughed through the heaving marketplaces while the sun hammered down without pity and blazed back from walls of yellow tufa stone or the flashing blades of knives drawn in exchanges of rich inventive cursing. The Neapolitans discharged the tension by fighting or fucking, often at the same time. Soldiers of the Spanish viceroy patrolled the streets, though whether their presence imposed order or fuelled the general air of aggression depended on your view of our Spanish overlords. It was a city stinking of hypocrisy: kissing in public was illegal, but courtesans were permitted to walk the streets openly, looking for business even in the churches (especially in the churches). Blasphemy was also punishable by law, but beggars, vagrants and those without work were allowed to starve in the streets, their bodies rounded up each night on carts and thrown into a charnel-house outside the walls before they could spread contagion. Thieves, assassins and whores thrived and prospered there and, naturally, so did the Church.

In the midst of this simmering human soup stood the magnificent basilica of San Domenico Maggiore, where the faithful could worship the wooden crucifix that had once spoken aloud to St Thomas Aquinas. San Domenico was one of the wealthiest religious houses in the city; the local barons all sent their superfluous younger sons there as a bribe to God, and many of my brothers dressed and strutted like the young lords they still felt themselves to be, keen to preserve the distinction of degree despite their vows. The deprivations of religious life were interpreted here with considerable lassitude; it must have been well known to the prior and his officials that a number

2

of the novices had copied keys to a side gate and often slipped out into the heat of the city streets at night, but I never saw anyone punished for it, provided they were back in time for Matins. Drinking, dicing, whoring – sins such as these were straightforward, easy to overlook in young noblemen with high spirits. It was sins of thought that the authorities could not countenance. In its favour, I should say that San Domenico prized other qualities than birth: it was famed as the intellectual heart of Naples, and a mere soldier's son like me might be admitted at the Order's expense if he showed enough promise as a scholar.

By early September, the city had grown heavy and slow, exhausted by the ferocity of the long summer's heat; people barely made the effort to curse as you pushed past them. There was a sense of apprehension, too; the previous autumn had brought a season of thick fogs off the sea carrying the contagion of fever and the epidemic had infected half the city. I had taken my final vows and been admitted to the Order in the spring, despite some misgivings on the part of the novice master, who confided to the prior that Fra Giordano Bruno had trouble submitting to authority and a taste for difficult questions. During my novitiate I had shown aptitude for my studies in the natural sciences, and the prior had set me to work for a while as assistant to Fra Gennaro, the brother infirmarian, in the belief that vigorous practical tasks – measuring, chopping and distilling remedies, helping to cultivate and harvest the plants used to make them, as well as tending to the ailments of those brothers confined to the infirmary – would occupy my mind and curb my wilfulness. In this he was mistaken; the more I learned about the natural world, its correspondences and hidden properties, the more my questions multiplied, for it seemed to me that our understanding of Creation, handed down from antiquity through the Scriptures and the Church Fathers, did not stand up to the most elementary scrutiny and observation. Fra Gennaro regarded my questions with forbearance and a hint of dry humour; for the most part he proved an attentive, if non-committal, audience while I formulated my doubts and theories aloud and only rarely did he reprimand me when I overstepped the bounds of what he judged a God-given hunger for knowledge. Few of the other friars would have shown such tolerance.

Fra Gennaro had studied medicine and anatomy at the famous medical school in Salerno; he had wished to become a doctor and eventually a professor, but some years earlier his family's fortunes had shifted for the worse, obliging him to leave the university and offer his skills in God's service. It was not the worst blow Fate could have dealt him – he was granted considerable freedom to further his medical knowledge in his new role, though I understood there was some dispute with the prior over the morality of using certain Arabic texts – but it was not the life he had aspired to and, though he never voiced this, I sensed in him a restlessness, a wistful longing for his old world. He was barely forty, but to me, at eighteen, he appeared to possess a wealth of knowledge and wisdom that I yearned towards – and not all of it sanctioned. In his heart he was a man of science, and a Dominican only incidentally, as I felt myself to be; perhaps this accounted for the instinctive affinity that quickly grew between us.

I was skulking through the darkened cloister one starless night in the first week of September, clouds sagging overhead like wet plaster and a warm, sickly wind sighing in off the bay, when I glimpsed him on the far side of the courtyard, his arms bundled full of linen. He was heading not to the infirmary but towards the gardens, in the direction of the outbuildings and storehouses at the furthest extremity of the compound, where the high enclosing wall backed on to a busy thoroughfare. Something in his bearing – his unusual haste, perhaps, or the way he walked with his head down, leaning forward, as if into a gale – caught my attention. Though I risked punishment for being out of my cell at that hour, I called out to him, curious to know what he was about. If he heard me, he gave no sign of it, though I knew my voice must have carried. Instead he kept his eyes fixed on the ground ahead as he hurried through an archway and disappeared.

I hesitated in the shadows, hoping I would not run into the watch brothers. They made a tour of the cloisters shortly after Compline to confirm that everyone was tucked up in his cell and observing silence during the few hours of sleep, then retired somewhere more comfortable until their second circuit just before the bell chimed for Matins at two o'clock. If they knew of the nightly exodus through the side gate in the garden wall, they were practised at looking the other way. But for a friar like me, with no family influence to consider and a growing reputation for disobedience, it would be a mistake to be caught. I could easily find myself a scapegoat for those they did not dare to discipline too harshly.

The air hung close, heavy with the scent of night blooms and a faint aroma of roasting meat from beyond the walls. Through the silence I caught the soft murmur of conversation drifting from the dormitory behind me, the occasional burst of laughter, the chink of Murano goblets. Fra Donato entertaining his fellow aristocrats, I supposed. The wealthier friars – those for whom the Church was a political career built on contacts and greased palms like any other – often held private suppers at night in their richly furnished rooms. As with the nocturnal excursions, the watch brothers remained tactfully deaf and blind to this.

Footsteps echoed behind me on the flagstones across the cloisters, over the low whisper of voices. There was no time to determine whether they were friend or foe; I slipped quickly along the corridor and through the archway where I had seen Fra Gennaro disappear. Here, behind the convent's grand courtyards, the grounds were laid out to gardens with an extensive grove of lemon trees. A path followed the line of the boundary wall, towards the side gate. If you continued past the gate to the far side of the trees, you reached a scattering of low buildings: grain houses, storerooms, the saddlery and stables. Beyond these lay a whitewashed dormitory of two storeys where the convent servants slept.

Without a moon, there was no hope of seeing which direction Fra Gennaro had taken, though if I strained my ears hard, I thought I could make out a distant rustling ahead among the lemon trees. The obvious explanation was that he must be attending to one of the servants who had fallen sick – but my curiosity was still piqued by his furtive manner and his pretence of not having heard my call.

Like every other novice, I had learned to navigate the path from the outer cloister to the gate in pitch-dark, feeling my way and calculating distance from the scents of the garden and the recognition of familiar landmarks under my feet and fingers: the twisted stalk of the vine that grew up the wall at the point where the lemon grove began; the slight downward incline as the path neared the gate. The footsteps persisted at my back, crunching on the hard earth. I moved off the path and into the shelter of the trees as two figures approached, fearing I had been discovered by the watch. But they paused a short distance away and I retreated further into the dark as I caught the wavering light of a taper hovering between them. Urgent whispers followed the scraping of metal against metal; I heard the creak of the gate and a gentle click as it closed again behind them. Novices or young friars heading out to the Cerriglio, the tavern two streets away, for a brief gulp of the city air before the Matins bell called them back to piety. I craned my neck and looked up through the leaves, wishing I could see the moon; I had no idea how late it was.

The gardens were unfamiliar to me beyond the side gate and I stumbled my way through the lemon trees, unsure if I was even moving in the right direction, my arms held up to protect my eyes from the scratching branches. After some while I emerged into open ground and could just make out the bulk of a row of buildings ahead. A horse whinnied softly out of the dark and I tensed; there were grooms who slept above the stables and would be woken by any disturbance. Holding my breath, I edged my way towards the storehouses and stood stupidly, looking around. Had Fra Gennaro come this way? Most likely he was already in the servants' dormitory, tending to some ordinary sprain or burn. How foolish I would look, lurking here in the shadows as if I were spying on him.

Minutes passed and I was debating whether to knock at the servants' quarters when I heard the muted creak of a door from one of the outbuildings behind me. A hooded figure slipped out and set down a pail at his feet. I heard the jangle of a key in a padlock, though it was clear he was trying to make as little noise as possible. A cone of light slid back and forth across the ground from the lantern in his hand. From his height I was certain it was the infirmarian, though I waited until he was almost upon me before stepping into his path.

'Fra Gennaro.'

'*Dio porco!*' He jumped back as if he had been assaulted, stifling his cry with his fingers as the pail clattered to the ground.

'I'm sorry – I didn't mean to startle you.' I moved closer, pulling back the hood of my cloak.

'Fra Giordano?' He peered at me through the darkness,

his breathing ragged in the still air. 'What in God's name are you doing here?'

'I wanted to offer my help.'

'With what?' Now that he had recovered from the shock, I noted the hard edge to his voice. He was not pleased to have been intercepted.

'Whatever you are doing. I saw you in the cloister and you seemed . . .' I searched for the right word '. . . burdened. I thought, perhaps—'

His mouth twitched to one side in a sharp noise of disapproval. 'You should not have been in the cloister. By rights I should report you to the prior.'

I lowered my eyes. We both knew it was an empty threat; I had given him better cause to report me before this and he had not done so. But he wanted me to know that he was angry.

'Forgive me, Brother,' I murmured. 'I was restless and needed a walk. When I saw you, I thought only to offer my assistance. I want every chance to learn. Is one of the servants ill? I could fetch and carry for you, if you let me observe the treatment.'

He did not reply immediately; only watched me with an unreadable expression, narrowed eyes glinting in the flame of the lantern. 'You wish to learn, huh?' He appeared to be weighing something up. After a moment, he stepped forward and gripped my upper arm so hard that I flinched away. His face loomed inches from mine, oddly intent; I could smell on his breath the ginger root he chewed to settle his stomach. 'There is much you might learn tonight, and I could use another pair of hands. But listen to me, Fra Giordano. I have been good to you, have I not?'

I nodded eagerly, unsure where this was tending.

'There are words you have spoken in my dispensary that anyone else would have reported instantly to the prior.

8

Words that would lead you straight before the Father Inquisitor. I have let them pass, because I recognise in you a spirit of enquiry that, while yet undisciplined, is born not of rebellion but of a true desire for knowledge.' He paused and sighed, passing the flat of his hand over his cropped hair. 'In that you remind me of myself. That is why I have not reported you for voicing opinions that to others would fall barely short of heresy.'

I bowed my head. 'And I am grateful for it. But—'

He held up a hand to pre-empt me and lowered his voice. 'Then we are both agreed you owe me a debt of confidence. You could assist me tonight, but you must first swear that you will never speak of what you see to anyone, inside or outside these walls.'

My gut tightened with excitement as my thoughts raced ahead, trying to imagine what kind of medical emergency would demand such a level of secrecy. I stared at him.

'I swear it. On my life.'

He peered into my face with that same fierce scrutiny, still holding my arm so tight that the next morning I would find a ring of violet bruises. Eventually it seemed he was satisfied. He gave a single curt nod and released his grip.

'Wait here, then. I must go to the dispensary to collect my instruments and heat some water. If anyone should come by, make sure they don't see you.'

'Why don't I come with you?' I offered. 'We could carry twice as much between us. Or, better still, they will surely have a fire in the servants' dormitory – could we not heat a pail of water there? It would make sense to be closer to the patient.'

He made an aggressive gesture for me to be quiet. 'The patient is not in there,' he said, dropping his voice until I had to strain forward to catch his words. 'If you are to work with me tonight, Bruno, there are two rules. You obey my every instruction, to the letter. And you ask no questions. Is that clear?'

I nodded. 'But why can't I come with you?'

'*Madonna santa!*' He threw up his hands and stooped to gather his pail. 'Because, as far as anyone knows, you are tucked up in your bed dreaming of saints and angels. Now do as I ask.'

He disappeared into the dark, until all I could see was the small spark of his lantern bobbing across the garden in the direction of the convent buildings. Silence fell around me, punctuated only by familiar night sounds: the snort and stamp of a sleeping horse, the drawn-out cry of an owl, the relentless, one-note song of the cicadas. Further off, a whoop, followed by a gale of raucous laughter from the streets beyond the wall. I pressed myself into the shadows of the outbuildings and waited. Where was this mysterious patient, then, if not in the servants' quarters? I glanced across to the door Fra Gennaro had locked behind him. In the storehouse? Why could he not be treated in the infirmary, like any other . . .

A sudden understanding flashed through me, flooding my veins with cold. This man must be an enemy of the state, someone it would not be politic for us to be seen helping. San Domenico had a reputation for fomenting resistance against the kingdom's Spanish rulers; it was well known that the more rebellious among the Neapolitan barons met regularly in the convent's great hall to discuss the form of that resistance, with the ready involvement of some eminent Dominicans. Perhaps this secret patient was a conspirator who had been wounded in the course of action against the Spanish. That would explain Fra Gennaro's insistence that I ask no questions. Pleased by my own reasoning, I bunched my hands into fists beneath my robe and slid down against the wall of the storehouse to squat on my heels, bouncing with anticipation.

I recited psalms and sonnets to measure the time; another twenty minutes passed before Gennaro returned, with a bundle tied over his shoulder and carrying the full pail of water, steam rising from the cracks in its lid. I leapt up and hurried to take it from him; he nodded and paused to check all around before fitting the key to the padlock. As soon as we were inside, he secured the door again behind us.

He held up the lantern and turned slowly to reveal only an unremarkable room with stone walls and a paved floor. Wooden crates lined one wall; barrels were stacked against the back. A sound of scurrying overhead made me jump; I looked up and a fine dust filtered through between the planks that had been laid over the roof beams to partition the eaves into a loft space. A ladder led up to a closed hatch.

'Only rats,' Gennaro muttered. 'Keep that light over here where I can see it.'

He gestured towards the furthest end of the room. At first I could not make out what he meant to show me, but as I drew closer with the lantern, I saw a wooden hatch set into the floor, the stones at the edges scraped clean where the crates concealing it had been moved away. The hatch was also held fast with a padlock. Gennaro selected another key from his belt, knelt and unfastened it. He paused with one hand on the iron ring and looked up at me, his eyes large and earnest in the flickering light.

'Your oath, Bruno, that whatever you witness here will remain sealed in your heart as long as you breathe.'

I could have taken offence that my oath was not good enough the first time; instead I was too impatient to see what lay beneath the door. Goosebumps prickled along my arms. I swore again, on my life and all I held sacred, my right hand pressed over my heart. Fra Gennaro studied me for a long moment, then lifted the hatch and led the way down a flight of stone steps into an underground chamber.

11

The air was cooler here, with a taint of damp. Though I could see little at first, on peering harder I made out an arched ceiling and walls lined with stone. No sound came from the dense shadows further in, none of the jagged breathing you would expect from an injured man. A cold dread touched me: suppose the patient had died while Gennaro was fetching his instruments and I was waiting uselessly outside? But the infirmarian showed no sign of panic. He closed the hatch and slid a bolt across so that we could not be disturbed. Next he unwrapped an oil lamp from the pack he had brought and lit it carefully from the lantern. In the brighter glow I saw that the chamber was dominated by a sturdy table draped with a thick shroud, under which was laid the unmistakable outline of a human figure.

A strange fear took hold of me, somewhere under my ribs, constricting my breath. Gennaro removed his cloak and hung it on the back of the door, indicating that I should do the same. In its place he shrugged on a rough hessian smock, such as the servants wear, and over this a wide leather apron. Then he rolled up his sleeves, dipped his hands into the steaming water and rubbed them clean before opening the bag he had brought with him. In the lamplight I caught the flash of silver blades. The last item he extracted was a large hourglass, which he set upright on a box beside the table to allow the sand to settle. When he had assembled all the equipment to his satisfaction, he took one corner of the shroud in his hand and glanced at me.

'Ready?'

I tried to swallow, but my throat had dried. I managed a nod, and he pulled back the sheet covering the body.

In the stillness I heard myself gasp aloud, though I had the presence of mind not to cry out. Stretched out on the table was the body of a young woman, about my own age, unmoving as a marble tomb. Her flesh was so unblemished that it seemed at first she might be merely sleeping; indeed, I dared to hope as much for the space of a heartbeat, until I looked more closely and saw in her face the unmistakable contortions of strangulation. It was clear, despite the bulging eyes, the protruding tongue and the discolouration of the face, that she must have been unusually beautiful, not very long ago. Her skin was pale and smooth, her dark hair flowed around her shoulders and her waist was small and neat, her hips narrow and her breasts full. Ripe bruises like shadow fingers formed a ring around her white throat.

'By my reckoning,' Gennaro said, turning over the hourglass, now brusque and businesslike, 'we have about two and a half hours until Matins. There is no time to waste.'

So saying, he took a broad-bladed knife and slit the girl's shift lengthways in one swift movement, from hem to neck, leaving the fabric to fall away either side. I tried to avert my eyes from the dark thatch of hair on her pubic mound, but it was difficult; I had not seen a woman's body in three years. If Gennaro noticed my confusion and the colour rising to my cheeks, he was discreet enough not to mention it.

'Who is she?' I whispered, fixing my gaze on her feet. The soles were bare and dirty.

'Beggar. Homeless. Come, hold that lantern closer.' His reply came just a fraction too quick.

'But – how does she come to be here?' I blurted, forgetting my earlier promise.

'She was found in the street by one of the night patrols and brought to me. They thought they might be in time to save her. Alas, they arrived too late.'

He could see that I did not believe this version of events. I was not convinced that he did either. No Spanish soldier in the city would trouble himself to help a vagrant girl. They were more likely to be the ones who had abused and killed her. At least he had the grace to look away as he said it.

13

'But she has clearly met with a violent death, and quite recently—'

He laid the back of his fingers on the girl's neck, his expression speculative. 'An hour or so, I would say.'

'Then surely we should report it?'

'Fra Giordano, I thought we had agreed no questions?'

I bit my lip. He paused and straightened, his hand hovering over a selection of knives. I could not miss the impatience in his face, though his voice was softer. 'Listen. You told me you have read the work of Vesalius.'

'I have, but—'

'And how did Vesalius come by his knowledge of the human body? Where did he find his raw materials?'

'He stole corpses from the gallows at night.' I felt as if an invisible hand were squeezing my own throat.

'Exactly. And you know he also robbed graves? In the pursuit of understanding, it is sometimes necessary to interpret the law in one's own way.'

'But this girl has been murdered! He may not have got far – someone might have seen something—'

'That is not our concern, Brother.' The sharpness in his tone took me by surprise. He sighed. 'In the medical schools of Europe, professors of anatomy are allocated the bodies of felons for public dissection under the law – as many as four a year in some places.' His jaw tightened. 'I will never be a professor of anatomy now. God in His wisdom saw fit to call me to His service in another way. But that does not mean my desire to learn is any the less.' His tone suggested a degree of scepticism about the divine wisdom in this instance. He planted both hands flat on the table and leaned across the girl to nail me with a fierce stare. 'Listen to me, Fra Giordano. I see in you the makings of a man of science. I mean it. For such as us, pushing the boundaries of what is known, shining the light of true learning into the dark corners of Creation

14

– there can be no higher good. I know you agree.' He jabbed a forefinger into the air between us. 'And do not let anyone make you afraid of God's judgement. All of Nature is a great book in which the Creator has written the secrets of the universe. Would He have given us the gifts of reason and enquiry if He did not wish us to read that book?'

In the soft light, his face was avid as a boy's. I hesitated. Fra Eugenio, my novice master, had taken great pains to impress upon his flock of intellectually ambitious youths that the first and greatest sin of our forefather Adam was the desire for forbidden knowledge. He held firmly to the view that the Almighty intended much of His creation to remain beyond our meagre human understanding. I was of Fra Gennaro's mind, but I was still afraid.

'You mean to anatomise her.' My voice emerged as a croak. This time I did not frame it as a question.

He picked up a long knife and studied the tip of its blade. 'You know as well as I that this city is overrun with indigents.' He gestured with the knife towards the figure on the table. 'She was a street girl, a whore. No one will mourn her, poor creature. If she were not lying here now, she would be on a cart full of corpses heading for Fontanelle. At least this way some good will come of her sad existence before she ends up there. In life she gave her body up to rogues and lechers. In death, she will give it up to the service of anatomy.' He fixed me with a long look, tilting his head to one side as he pressed the knife's point into the pad of his finger. 'You are not obliged to stay, if your conscience advises you otherwise. But think of the opportunity. You are the only one here I would trust to assist me.'

I looked at him. How could I resist such flattery? Even so, in my gut I was deeply troubled by his proposition. In the first place, I did not believe his story about how he had come by the body. There could be no doubt that the girl had been

15

murdered, barely an hour ago, and I feared that in disposing of her corpse – to say nothing of illegally dissecting it – we would be implicated in her death. More than this, though, it was the brutality of what he was proposing that disturbed me. I had read Vesalius's work on anatomy and understood the value of practical experimentation. But this girl had already suffered violence at the hands of a man; whatever she may have been in life, our cutting and probing in the name of scientific enquiry seemed like a further violation. I did not voice any of this. Instead, I said:

'Does the prior know?'

He allowed a long pause. His gaze slid back to the girl on the table.

'The prior has, on occasion, given me permission to examine corpses where it is clear that there would be some greater benefit in doing so. When old Fra Teofilo died last year in Holy Week – you recall? – I was permitted to cut him open in order to study the tumour in his gut. And what could be more beneficial than furthering our knowledge of the female form? You cannot know how rare it is to find such an ideal specimen.'

The gleam in his eyes as he said this verged on lascivious, though not for the girl, or at least, not in the usual way. His desire was all for her interior, for the secrets she might yield up to his knife. From his studied evasion of my question, I took it that the answer was no. He tapped the hourglass with a fingernail. The sand was already piling into a small hill in the lower half.

'Time will not wait for us, Bruno. Go or stay, but make your mind up now.'

'I will stay,' I said, sounding steadier than I felt.

'Good.' Relief rippled over his face. 'And if you think you are going to faint or vomit, give me plenty of warning. We will have enough to clear up without that.'

16

He dipped a cloth in the hot water and wiped it almost tenderly around the girl's chest, along the declivities of her clavicle, the sharp ridges of her collarbones and into the valley between her breasts. 'Note the fullness of the breasts,' he observed, as if he were addressing students in an anatomy theatre, as he marked the place of the first incision in a Y-shape across each side of her breastbone, 'and the enlargement of the areola. If I am right in my speculation, we may find something of unparalleled interest here.'

I concentrated on holding the lantern steady over the table. As if I could have failed to notice the girl's full breasts or large, dark nipples. Perhaps he had forgotten what it was to be eighteen. In his eyes she was simply a specimen, material for experimentation. To me she was too recently living, breathing, warm, with a head full of thoughts and dreams, for me to regard her as anything other than a young woman. I did not dare touch her skin; I almost believed it would still hold some pulse of life. Nor could I look at her face; the terror in those wild, staring eyes was too vivid. I had heard it said that, when a person was murdered, the image of the killer was fixed in their death stare. I did not mention this to Fra Gennaro; I did not want him to laugh at me or take me for a village simpleton.

Any unbidden lustful thoughts shrivelled in an instant as he pushed the blade into her flesh. He made two careful incisions along the breastbone and joined them in a vertical cut that ran the length of her torso to her pubic mound. The sound of the knife tearing through meat was unspeakable, the smell more so. I recoiled, shocked, at the amount of blood that pooled out. Gennaro calmly placed containers under the table at strategic points, and I saw that, like a butcher's block, the surface had channels cut into it that diverted the blood into tidy streams of run-off that could be collected underneath. He folded back the skin on each side of the chest cavity, exposing the white bones of the ribcage. I clamped my teeth together, fighting the rising tide of bile churning in my stomach, reminding myself that I was a man of science. A wave of cold washed over my head and a sudden sunburst exploded in my vision; the cone of light from the lantern slid queasily up and down the wall. Gennaro stopped to look at me.

'You've gone green.' He didn't sound greatly sympathetic. 'Hang the lantern on that hook above me and sit down with your head between your knees. We can do without you passing out on her.'

I did as I was told. I sank to the cold floor at the far end of the room with my back pressed against the wall, clasped my hands behind my head and buried my face in shame. The terrible slicing noises continued, the determined sawing through resistant muscle and tendon, the sucking sound of organs being displaced. I closed my eyes and bent the whole force of my will towards maintaining conscious-ness and keeping my supper down. I could not tell how much sand had slipped through the glass by the time I felt able to stand again, but when I opened my eyes and levered myself to my feet, Fra Gennaro was bending over the girl's exposed abdomen with an ardent expression. His eyes flick-ered upwards to me.

'You're back with us, are you? Come and look at this.' He prodded with the tip of his knife. He was indicating a swollen organ about the size of a small grapefruit, mottled crimson. 'The greatest anatomy theatres in Europe would pay dearly to get their hands on this. It is an opportunity granted to very few anatomists. Providence has smiled on us tonight. Do you know what it is?'

I considered replying that Providence had been less kind to the girl, but I merely shook my head.

'This is the womb, Bruno. The cradle of life. Locus of the

mystery of generation. The source, it is believed, of all female irrationality.' He reached in with bloody fingers and tugged, frowning. 'Hippocrates said it had the power to detach itself and wander about the body, but I do not see how that could occur. This one seems firmly attached to the birth canal.'

He parted the girl's legs and quite perfunctorily inserted two fingers into her vagina, pushing up until he could feel the pressure with his other hand. 'Interesting,' he murmured. 'It seems to me that Vesalius's drawing of the female reproductive organs is seriously flawed . . .

'And now,' he continued, lifting the girl's womb towards him as if he were a street conjuror about to reveal his greatest trick, 'watch closely and learn. For if my guess is correct, you are about to witness a secret that some of the most renowned anatomists in Leiden or Paris have yet to see in the flesh.'

He took a smaller knife and made a precise cut in the outer skin. As it ruptured, a clear, viscous fluid spilled out over his hands along with the blood. Gennaro peeled back the skin and extracted from within the womb a tiny homunculus, no bigger than the span of my hand, but already recognisably human. He laid it in his palm, his eyes bright with wonder.

'Is it alive?' I breathed.

'Not now. You see this?' He nudged with the knifepoint to the twisted white tube that still connected its abdomen with the interior of the womb. 'It can't live without the mother. This is very early gestation, see? A matter of weeks, I would say. But note how you can already make out the fingers and toes.'

The creature had the translucent sheen of an amphibious animal, its half-formed limbs and curved spine so delicate as to seem insubstantial. Perhaps it was his casual use of the word 'mother', but I felt a sudden terrible emptiness, a

19

hollowing-out, as if it were my insides that had been torn away. This homunculus would have grown into a child, if the girl's life had not been cut short by those hands around her throat. I wished fervently that I had never followed Gennaro. I began to fear I lacked the detachment to make a man of science.

Fra Gennaro carefully excised the womb and the tiny foetus, severed the cord that bound them, and placed each into a large glass jar he had brought in his bag. 'But where does it *come* from?' he muttered, as he sealed the jars.

'From the man's seed.' I was unsure if he was addressing the question to me, nor even if my answer was correct, but I needed the distraction.

'Ah, but does it?' He looked at me, seemingly pleased. His cheek was streaked with blood where he had touched it. 'Opinion is divided. There are those who say the womb is merely the field of Nature in which the seed is planted, and others who think there is some additional element contributed by the woman, without which the seed cannot germinate. What think you?'

'I imagine these elements are so small as to be invisible. So that we can only study the effects and must work backwards to infer the cause.'

He nodded and wiped his hands on his apron. 'It may be that we will never unravel the mystery of conception. But that does not mean we should not try, eh? I shall study this further.' He patted the sealed lid of the jar containing the foetus. I had to look away.

From somewhere beyond the thick stone walls of our underground mortuary came the distant tolling of a bell. My head snapped around and I met Fra Gennaro's eye. Neither of us had noticed how long ago the sand had run through the hourglass. I glanced down at myself; my habit was daubed with the girl's blood and God knows what else.

20

Gennaro pulled his apron over his head. 'I need fresh water and new candles,' he said, decisive. 'I will tell the prior you are taken sick and unable to attend Matins. Close the hatch and draw the bolt after me and do not open the door to anyone until I return. I will give three sharp knocks.'

Before I could object, he was gone. I climbed the stairs and slid the bolt across, shutting myself in with the girl. She lay splayed out like a carcass at the butcher's, yellow fat and livid red organs bright against her pale skin. I drew closer to the table, torn between fascination and fear. In Gennaro's absence, I felt emboldened to test the theory of the killer's image by looking into her eyes, but all I saw was naked terror and my own reflection. It seemed apt, in a twisted way; I could not escape the feeling that we were as guilty of her destruction as the man whose fingers were imprinted around her slender neck. I backed away, chilled by an irrational fear that she might suddenly turn her head and fix me with those eyes. I tried to intone the psalms but the words stuck in my throat. Instead, I turned over the hourglass and watched the sand drain through in a fine dust. The minutes that passed until I heard Gennaro's knock were some of the longest of my life.

'We need to dispose of her before first light,' he said, brisk again. 'I will need your help.'

'How?'

'We must take her to Fontanelle.'

'But the city gates will be locked until dawn.'

He slid me a sidelong look. 'They can be opened.'

He crossed to the far side of the room and unlocked a wooden door in the back wall. I had been so intent on the girl I had not noticed it before. A breath of cleaner air filtered through and I saw that the door opened on to an underground passageway.

'Part of the network of tunnels and cisterns belonging to

21

the old Roman aqueduct,' Gennaro explained. 'It links to another tunnel beyond the boundary wall and comes out on the other side of Via Toledo. Here – help me with this.'

From the passageway Gennaro dragged a cheap wooden casket into the room. I grabbed the other end and helped him position it alongside the table. When he opened the lid, I saw that it was lined in oilcloth, and the inside was already bloodstained. He drew out a coarsely woven cloak from beneath the lining, such as the poorest wear in winter. It smelled thickly of decay.

'There is one thing I need to do before we transport her,' he said, draping the cloak over the casket and turning to face me with a stern look. 'You may prefer not to watch this, Bruno. I have to skin her.' He turned back to the table and selected a knife with a thin, cruel blade.

Again, that strange lurch in my gut, as if I had missed a stair. 'Why?'

'So that she cannot be recognised. People may be looking for her.'

'You said there was no one to mourn her.' I heard the accusation in my voice.

'Mourn her, no. But if she was a whore in this neighbourhood, her face will be known. The remains we send to Fontanelle must not be identifiable.'

'It's barbaric.'

He made an impatient noise with his tongue. 'Perhaps. But it is also prudent. What we have done here tonight would be hard to explain to the city authorities. I think you see that.'

I bowed my head. 'Then no one will ever be brought to justice for her murder.'

He laid down his knife and looked at me with an air of incomprehension. 'You think they would otherwise? A street whore?' He shook his head. 'I admire your fervour for justice

22

on behalf of the weak. It is, after all, part of our Christian duty,' he added, as if he had only just remembered. 'But it is not our concern here, Bruno. There will be no justice for her in this life. Pray God grant her mercy, and retribution to those who wronged her in the next.'

With this, he grasped a hank of her lush hair and sliced it through cleanly at the roots, as I turned my face away.

All through the long journey to the Fontanelle cavern, he did not say a word to me, except once, to ask if I carried a dagger. When I said yes, he gave a dry laugh. 'Of course you do. This is Naples. Even novice nuns carry a blade beneath their habits.' I wondered if he was afraid the girl's killer might still be lurking nearby. I tried to shut out the thought that Gennaro knew more about the murderer than he was letting on.

We took turns pushing the cart with the makeshift coffin, the two of us wearing old servants' cloaks with the hoods pulled up close around our faces, despite the warm night, so that we would not be recognised as friars. I could not tell if Gennaro was angry with me for questioning him, or for my squeamishness, or if he was just tired. Reducing the girl to hunks of bloodied meat had not been an easy task. The human body is tougher than it looks; limbs need to be wrenched from sockets, bones sawed through, joints separated with a hammer. Gennaro must have been exhausted, but he did it all alone, while I sat with my back against the wall and my head in my hands, trying to shut out the sounds. What he packed into that box, wrapped carefully in oilcloth to stop the blood dripping through the wood, was no longer human. I stole glances at the casket as he led us through the twisting back streets in the dark, his face dogged and clenched in the light of my lantern.

A couple of times we turned a corner to find a group of

young men staggering home from the taverns, arms slung around one another's shoulders, half-empty bottles dangling from their hands. Each time I braced myself, my hand twitching to my knife in case they should decide to have some sport with us, but they looked at the cart and steered a wide berth around it, their raucous songs faltering away to nothing as they eyed the box. No one wants to be reminded of death in the midst of their revels. I suppose they took us for those men who clear the beggars off the streets. At the Porto San Gennaro I saw the glint in the darkness of coins changing hands as the infirmarian exchanged a few words with the guards, who seemed unsurprised to see him. One of them nodded, before unlocking a small side gate and gesturing us through.

The road began to slope steeply upwards into the Capodimonte hillside. With the incline and the stony track the cart became harder to move, as if it were resisting its destination; we had to put our backs into the work and within minutes I was soaked with sweat beneath my cloak. I had no idea how far it was to Fontanelle – it was not a place I had ever thought to visit – and I did not like to risk Gennaro's anger by asking him. I knew only that it was a great cavern up in the hills, left behind by the excavation of tufa for building. In the early years of the century, the Spanish authorities had begun clearing the city's churchyards to make room for more bodies, and the old remains had been taken to the Fontanelle cave. Since then it had become a dumping ground for the city's outcast dead: those who could not afford or had been denied burial in consecrated ground. Lepers. Sodomites. Suicides. The *lazzaroni* – the nameless poor who died in the streets. Plague victims were thrown in, whenever there was an outbreak. Fontanelle had become a great charnel-house of the unwanted; people said you could smell it from the north gate if the wind was in the wrong direction.

I caught the stench as the incline grew steeper and the track widened out into a plateau; rotting flesh and stale smoke, the kind of bitter ash that hung in the air and worked its way into your nose and mouth as you breathed. A man lurched forward out of the shadows to greet us; again, the chink and flash of money from somewhere inside Fra Gennaro's cloak. A small brazier burned by the entrance to the cavern. In its orange glow, I saw that the man's face was badly deformed, though his body looked strong; his brow bulged low over one side like an ape's and he had been born with a cleft palate. Perhaps this was the only place he could find work. At least the dead would not throw stones at him in the street, or shout insults. He and Gennaro spoke in low voices; I had the sense that they too were familiar with one another. I watched as the man took the cart and wheeled it towards the mouth of the cave, a maw of deeper shadows that swallowed him until he disappeared from view.

I turned to see Gennaro studying me.

'Are you all right?' he said.

Beneath my robe, my legs were trembling as if with cold. I told myself it was the climb. I gestured towards the cave.

'What if he tells someone?'

'He won't.'

'How do you know? Surely you can't see a body in that state and not ask questions?'

'Part of his job is knowing not to ask questions.' Gennaro squinted into the darkness and pulled his cloak tighter. 'Besides, he won't bite the hand that feeds him.'

I did not immediately grasp his meaning, until I thought of the coins chinking quietly into the man's hand, their familiarity. Of course: this would not be the first time Gennaro had brought a dismembered body here for disposal under cover of darkness, no explanations required. I wondered how many other illegal anatomisations he had carried out in that little mortuary under the storehouse, with its convenient tunnel for ferrying bodies out unseen.

The man returned with the cart and the empty box.

'I'll let you know if I find anything suitable,' he muttered, darting a wary glance at me. Gennaro gave him a curt nod and turned again towards the road.

A pale glimmer of dawn light showed along the eastern horizon as we walked back down the track, the city a dark stain below us.

'Does he sell you bodies?' I asked bluntly.

Gennaro looked sideways at me. 'Remember your oath, Brother.'

We walked the rest of the way in silence. Under the cloak I could feel stiff patches on my robe where the girl's blood had dried. I wondered how I would explain that to the servant who came to take my laundry.

'I prescribe a hot bath for this fever that has kept you from tonight's services, Bruno,' Gennaro said, as if he had heard my thoughts. 'I will instruct the servants to fill the tub in the infirmary. Clean yourself well. I will see to your clothes.'

'Will you write about this?' I asked him, as we approached the gate.

He smiled, for the first time since we had set out. 'Of course. This is one of the most important anatomisations I have ever performed. To study a child *in utero* is a rare piece of luck, as I told you.'

Not for the child, I thought. 'But you cannot publish your account, surely?'

'True. At least, not in Naples, and not under my own name. Eventually, however, who knows . . .' His voice tailed off and his eyes grew distant. Perhaps he was dreaming of a book full of his experiments and discoveries.

'But in the meantime – are you not afraid someone will find your notes?'

26

He smiled again, like a child holding a secret. 'I keep them very safe. And I trust you, as I said.'

I forced myself to return his smile, though he meant that I was now as deeply implicated as he was. In ways I could not yet fully comprehend, I felt irreversibly altered by what we had done that night. Despite scrubbing myself with scalding water and a bristle brush until my skin grew raw, I could not erase the smell of blood, nor the memory of the girl's wild death stare. Fra Gennaro made me up a bed in the infirmary, so that I was excused the office of Lauds on account of my supposed fever, but I could not rest. If I closed my eyes I saw her walking towards me with her hands outstretched, pleading, before she reached up and tore the skin from her own face until it hung in tatters from the bloodied pulp beneath.

The following night, I barely waited until the sun had set before slipping out of the side gate and through the alleys to the Cerriglio. I needed company, drink, the easy conversation of my friends. Pushing open the door, I was assaulted by its familiar heat and noise, the animated shouting of a dozen different arguments, its odour of charred pig fat and young red wine and sweat. In the back, someone was strumming a lute and singing a love song; his friends were filling in bawdy lyrics, howling with laughter. I stood still for a moment on the threshold, allowing the tavern's chaos to crash over me, pulling me back to the world I knew. I had not been able to eat all day, and now the smell of hot bread and meat tickled my throat, filling my mouth with salt and liquid.

At least half the Cerriglio's customers were young friars from San Domenico and their companions. Gaudy women moved among the tables, stroking a forearm or sliding a finger under someone's chin as they passed, gauging the response. One caught my gaze as I stood there and I blinked quickly away; when I looked at their painted faces, all I could see was the bone and gristle beneath the skin.

I scanned the room, looking for my friend Paolo. Laughter blasted across from the large table in the centre, where Fra Donato was holding court, as usual. He glanced up and saw me standing alone; his eyes narrowed and he leaned across and muttered something to Fra Agostino beside him, whose lip twisted into a sneer. Neither of them troubled to hide the fact that they were talking about me. I had barely spoken to Fra Donato, but I knew his reputation. His father was one of those Neapolitan barons who had managed to cling on to his land and titles under the Spanish, which led people to speculate about what he offered them in return. But he was a valuable benefactor to San Domenico, and his son was regarded as a prior in the making, despite the boy's obvious distaste for the privations of religious life. Fra Donato was tall and unusually handsome, with the blond looks of a northerner; it was said he was a bastard and his mother a courtesan from Venice, or Milan, or even, in some versions, France or England. Whatever the truth, his father indulged him generously and he, Donato, had certainly learned the trick of buying influence. He was a few years older than me; I had not expected to attract his attention, but recently I had been aware of his scrutiny in services and at chapter meetings. I guessed I had been pointed out to him as a potential troublemaker, and that this had piqued his interest. Now, though, hot with the fear that people could smell the girl's blood on my skin, I could not help but interpret any suspicious glances as proof that someone had seen me last night and knew my dreadful secret. I felt the colour rising in my face as Donato and his friend continued to whisper, their eyes still fixed lazily on me.

'Bruno!'

I whipped around at the sound of my name and saw Paolo at a corner table with a couple of his cousins, a jug of wine between them. He raised a cup and I hurried over, grateful to be rescued.

'I thought you had a fever?' He poured me a drink and handed it over.

'It broke in the night. I'm fine now.'

He grinned. 'Well you look fucking awful. Are you sure you should be out of bed?'

I gulped down the wine, feeling its warmth curl through my limbs. I was about to make some light-hearted comment to fend off any further questioning, when I was prevented by a commotion from behind us. Voices raised in anger; glass shattering, the crash of furniture hitting the floor. I turned, and I swear that, just for an instant, my heart stopped beating.

The dead girl stood in the centre of the tavern, in front of Donato's table. She had knocked over a chair, it seemed, and dashed the glass from his hand. A blood-red puddle spread across the table and dripped slowly on to the floor. She was shaking with rage, her right hand extended, pointing at him. The hubbub of music and conversation died away in anticipation; people always enjoyed a good fight at the Cerriglio.

It was her; there was no question about it. The same glossy fall of black hair, the marble skin, the delicate features and wide-spaced eyes as unspoilt as they would have been in life. The same slender throat, unmarked now. But she had knocked over the chair; how could that be, if she was a spirit? I held myself rigid with fear, my hand so tight around the cup I feared it would crack, though I could not will myself to move. I did not believe in spirits of the dead and yet, buried deep, I had not shaken off the childhood memories of my grandmother's tales, of revenants and unhallowed souls returning to be revenged on the living.

The girl balled her fists on her hips and cast a defiant glance around the room. I froze as her eyes swept over me, but there was no flicker of recognition. If she had come for vengeance, surely I would be her first target? But she turned her blistering gaze once more to Donato, threw her head back and spat in his face.

A cheer went up from the onlookers, all except Donato's comrades. He wiped his cheek with a sleeve, but his movements were those of a sleepwalker. He was staring at the girl with a mixture of horror and disbelief.

'Where is she?'

'Who?'

'You know who!' The girl quivered with rage.

Donato rose to his feet and attempted to recover some dignity. 'You have me confused with someone, *puttana*. I do not think I know you. Unless I was more drunk than I remember last night.'

This won him a smattering of laughter from the crowd. The girl tossed her hair and her eyes flashed.

'Oh, you know me, sir. And I know who you are.'

'So do most of your sex in Naples.' More laughter.

'Have you killed her?' Her voice was clear and strong; she made sure everyone could hear.

Donato paused, as if catching his breath. The mood in the room shifted; you could feel it like the charge in the air before a storm. He leaned across the table.

'I have no idea what you are talking about. But if you accuse me of anything in public again, I will see you before the magistrates for slander. Now get out.' He allowed a pause for effect, before adding, cold and deliberate: '*Jewess*.'

The word hung between them like the smoke that follows a shot. The girl stared at him as if she had been struck. A sharp intake of breath whistled through the crowd, followed by a startled cry; in a heartbeat, the girl was up on the table, silver flashing in her hand. Fra Agostino pushed Donato out of her reach, a lamp rolled to the floor and smashed, someone screamed, and then the doorkeeper they called L'Orso Maggiore (for obvious reasons) shouldered his way into the mêlée and wrenched the girl's right arm behind her back, sending her knife clattering to the ground. She carried on yelling and spitting curses as he dragged her off the table and towards the threshold, as easily as a bear would pick up a rabbit.

'Where is her locket?' she roared, at the door. She repeated the same question, louder, as L'Orso hurled her out into the street. You could still hear her cries, even when the door slammed after her. Gradually, the hubbub of conversation resumed until it drowned her out.

'Donato really should learn to take more care where he puts it,' remarked Paolo, shaking his head as he reached for the wine. 'He'll ruin his father with paternity suits one of these days.'

'Paternity suits?' I turned to look at him.

'Some neighbourhood girl accused him a couple of years ago, threatened to make a fuss. His father had to pay the family off. Sounds like he's at it again.' He gestured towards the door, then glanced at me. His brow creased and he laid a hand on my arm. '*Madonna porca* – are you sure you're all right, Bruno? You're white as a corpse.'

'I need some air,' I said, pushing the table away.

Donato was bleeding from a surface cut on his forearm where the girl had made contact before she was hauled off. His hangers-on fussed around him while the rest of the tavern stared as they exchanged animated whispers. Signora Rosaria, who owned the Cerriglio, was berating L'Orso for not stopping the assault sooner; the crowd pressed in for a better view of the drama. No one had noticed the girl's knife lying on the tiles under a neighbouring table. I ducked down and slipped it into my sleeve on the way to the door.

There was no sign of her in the street. I walked a little way along between the tall houses, towards the corner of the next alley, thinking I had lost her, when I caught the sound of muffled sobs. She was crouched in a doorway, her right arm cradled against her chest. After the initial shock of seeing her in the tavern, my frantic thoughts of vengeful spirits had given way to a more logical explanation, but I was still afraid to speak to her.

Alerted by my footsteps, her head snapped up and she sprang back, her hands held out as if to ward me off. The street was sunk in darkness, except for the dim glow from a high window opposite and the streaks of moonlight between clouds. The girl's face was hidden in shadow.

'I think this is yours.' I offered the knife to her, hilt first. Her eyes flicked to it and back to me; for a long time she didn't move, but I stayed still and eventually she began to approach, wary as a wild dog, until she was close enough to snatch it. She levelled it at me; I raised my empty hands to show that I was now unarmed.

'Who are you looking for?'

'What is it to you?' She bared her teeth. 'I know you are one of them. I have seen you here before.'

'*Them?*'

'Dominicans.' She spat on the ground at my feet. 'God's dogs.'

'You know Latin?' I said, surprised. It was an old nickname for the Order, a pun on *Domini canes*, the Hounds of the Lord, but I had not expected to hear it from a woman, especially one who was clearly not high-born.

'Yes. You think a woman cannot read? Hypocrites.' I thought she was going to spit at me again but she restrained herself. 'Look at yourselves. You take vows of poverty and chastity, and yet there you are, night after night, dicing and whoring like soldiers. And they made you the city's

32

Inquisitors, the ones who decide whether others are practising their religion to the letter, and if they should die for it.' She let out a short, bitter laugh. 'God would spit you out of His mouth.' She was lit up by her fury, illuminated from within, every inch of her taut and quivering. She wanted only the slightest provocation to stick that knife in me, I was sure of it.

'That man you attacked,' I said, keeping my voice steady. 'What has he done?'

Her lip curled; she reminded me again of a dog that knows it is cornered and is readying itself to fight. 'I suppose he is your friend? Did he ask you to make me repeat it, so he could accuse me of slander?'

'He is no friend of mine. I only wanted to help you.'

'Why?' The word shot back, quicker than a blow. She took a step closer, holding the knife out as if I had threatened her.

I shrugged. 'Because we are not all hypocrites.'

Her eyes narrowed; she did not believe me. She was right not to, I reminded myself: I was the biggest hypocrite of all.

'My sister,' she said, in a subdued voice, just as I had assumed she was about to walk away.

'Your twin?' The words were spoken before I could stop them; she stared at me, her mouth open.

'Why do you say that? Do you know her?'

'No . . . I . . .' I blushed in confusion. 'I don't know why I thought that.'

'Yes, my twin,' she said, lowering the knife, as if the fight had gone out of her. 'That friar –' she nodded past me in the direction of the tavern – 'he saw me in the street one day and followed me to our shop.'

'What shop?'

'My father keeps a shop on Strada dell'Anticaglia, off Seggio di Nilo. He is a master goldsmith. That man started coming into the shop to court me. I refused him. I would not be the mistress of a monk, for all his money. I have no respect for your kind.'

'So you have said.'

A muscle tightened in her jaw. 'He would not take no for an answer. Then one day he came into the shop when my father and I were out and found my sister instead.'

'He took her for you?'

'I don't think he cared either way. But Anna was always flattered by the attention of men.'

Anna. I thought of a flayed leg thrown into a makeshift coffin like an animal carcass, stripped to the crimson muscle and white bone. She had had a name. Her name had been Anna.

In this girl's face I saw again the lineaments of her dead twin. A whore, Fra Gennaro had said. Was that his lie, or Donato's? My skin felt cold, despite the warm wind.

'And she went with him?'

'She started sneaking out after dark to meet him. She never told me where she was going, but I followed her one night. She made me swear to secrecy. She knew it would break our father's heart.'

'He would have been angry?'

'He would have killed her.' As soon as she had spoken the words, her hand flew to her mouth. I felt something lurch in the hollow under my ribs, some pulse of hope. The girl's father found out, he killed her in a fit of rage, perhaps by accident; so Fra Gennaro's story could be true. Even as the idea formed, I knew it was absurd.

'I meant only . . .' she faltered, through her fingers. 'He has never lifted a hand to either of us in our lives. But the shame would have destroyed him.'

'Back there, you accused the friar of killing her,' I said. 'Was that a figure of speech too?'

34

She drew her hand slowly away from her face and took a deep breath. It escaped jaggedly, like a sob. 'My sister is missing. She went to him last night and she has not returned. I know she has come to harm.'

'Perhaps she has run away.' As I spoke, I felt as if there was a ball of sawdust lodged in my throat. My voice sounded strange to me.

The girl shook her head. 'She would never have done that. In any case, I followed her last night too. I was afraid for her.'

The ball in my throat threatened to choke me. I feared she could hear the thudding of my heart in the silence.

'To the Cerriglio?'

'No. She went to San Domenico and waited for him by the gate. I saw her go in and she never came out.'

A warm breath of air lifted my hair from my forehead and cooled the sweat on my face. Beneath my feet the ground felt queasy, uncertain, as if I were standing on a floating jetty instead of a city street.

'You must have missed her,' I said, but the words barely made a sound.

'I waited until first light. I could not have our father wake and find us both gone. I would swear she did not leave. Unless there is another entrance. But then, why did she not come home?'

I felt my palms grow slick with sweat at her mention of another entrance. I should have let her go then, but I had to be sure of how much she knew. 'Why do you think he meant her harm, if they were . . . involved?'

'Because she—' Her face darkened and she turned away. 'Her situation had changed. She was going to ask him for something he could not give.'

'Money?'

The slap came out of nowhere; she moved so fast I barely

had time to register that she had raised her hand. Rubbing my burning cheek, I reflected that at least she had not used the hand that held the knife. I stretched my jaw to assess the damage, but she was already stalking away around the corner.

'Wait!' I ran after her, into another, narrower alley. She turned, eyes blazing out of the darkness.

'My sister was no whore, whatever he says.' She paused, and I saw that she was fighting back tears. 'She believed herself in love with him.' She swiped at her eyes with her knuckles. 'What is any of this to you? Why are you following me?'

'If your sister was inside the walls of San Domenico last night, someone must know something.' I was surprised at how level my voice sounded, how carefully I controlled my expression. Only a few months since my vows, and already I had acquired the Dominican talent for dissembling. Though it was a skill that was to serve me well in later years, in that moment I despised myself to the core. 'What is your name?'

'Maria.' Most of the women in this city are called Maria, but she hesitated just long enough for me to understand that she was lying too. 'Yours?'

'Bruno.'

'Well then, Bruno. You know where I can be found. But I will not hold my breath – I know your kind always stick together. Whatever has happened to my sister, he will not face justice for it. Not in this city. A family like mine, against a man of his name?'

I wondered what she meant by that, and recalled the quiet, deliberate cruelty of Donato's last insult to her. 'Why did he call you – that?' I asked.

Her expression closed up immediately. 'I expect it was the worst abuse he could think of.'

We looked at one another in silence for a moment, her eyes daring me to question further.

'What about the locket?'

Her mouth dropped open, the fury in her eyes displaced by fear.

'What do you know of that?'

'Nothing. Only that I heard you accuse Fra Donato of taking it.'

Her hand strayed to her throat; an involuntary gesture, I supposed, as she thought of her sister wearing the locket. I could think only of the bruises around the dead girl's neck.

'If he has taken it . . .' She faltered. I sensed that she was weighing up how much to say. 'It has little value for its own sake. But it belonged to our mother. I *must* have it back.' The note of desperation in her voice told me she was withholding something. She feared that locket falling into the wrong hands – but why?

I stood foolishly staring at her, wishing I could offer some consolation, cursing the weight of what I knew – the truth she would spend the rest of her life raking over and not knowing. Or so I had to hope.

'You know where to find me if you hear anything,' she said again, with a shrug. I was about to reply when, silent as a cat, she turned and disappeared into the blackness between the buildings.

I crashed through the door of the infirmary, careless of the hour, careless of the noise I made. Fra Gennaro was bent over the bed of old Fra Francesco by the light of a candle, applying a poultice to his sunken chest to ease the fluid on his lungs. Gennaro started at the sound of the door, but as soon as he realised it was me, his expression told me he had been expecting this.

I glanced along the length of the infirmary, my ribs heaving with the effort of running through the back streets. Four beds in the row were occupied by elderly friars who wheezed and grunted in concert; they might have been asleep, but they might also have been quite capable of hearing and understanding. It was all I could do not to blurt out my accusations; Gennaro saw the urgency in my face and gestured me towards the dispensary, whispering words of reassurance to Fra Francesco as he stood to follow me.

'She was not a whore, was she?'

He closed the door behind us and set his candle down on the dispensary bench, signalling for me to lower my voice.

'I told you only what was told to me,' he said. His tone was clipped and cold, tight with suppressed anger.

'And you chose not to question it.'

He was across to me in one stride, his hand clamping my arm, face inches from mine.

'As I recall, Fra Giordano, you also swore an oath to ask no questions. Who have you been talking to?'

'I didn't have to talk to anyone.' I dropped my voice to an urgent whisper. 'Tonight her mirror image walked into the Cerriglio and accused one of our brothers of murdering her twin.'

He stared at me, his grip slackening.

'She was never found in the street by soldiers. She died inside these walls, didn't she? That's why you would not speculate on who killed her. Because you already knew.'

He breathed out hard through his nose, his eyes fixed on me for a long pause, as if I were a favourite son who had disappointed him. Eventually he let go of me and rubbed his hands quickly over his face like an animal washing.

'Where would we be, you and I, if we were not here?' he said, looking up.

I blinked at him, unsure whether it was a rhetorical question. He raised his brow and I realised he wanted an answer. 'If you had not come to San Domenico, Fra Giordano, what would you have done with your life?'

'I would have tried to obtain a place at the royal university,' I mumbled.

'Would you? The son of a mercenary soldier? With whose money?'

I looked at my feet.

'My father was well born, but he died desperately in debt to a Genoan banker,' he continued. 'If I had not come to San Domenico, I would most likely have had to beg for a position as a tutor to idle rich boys. And you, Bruno – I doubt you would now be the most promising young theologian in Naples, whatever you claim.'

I said nothing, because I knew he was right.

'We are alike, you and I.' His voice softened. 'Neither one of us, in our hearts, desired the constraints of a religious life. But it was the only door open to us. You acknowledge that, surely?'

I gave the briefest nod.

'Then you also understand that it is not the likes of us who keep San Domenico afloat. Our scholarship may contribute to its reputation, but it is men like Fra Donato, with his name and his father's vast endowments, who ensure its continued prestige and wealth. We are the beneficiaries, and we would do well to remember that.'

'So he must be protected, at any cost. Whatever he does. This man who might be prior one day.' I turned away in disgust.

'What else would you do? Call in the magistrates? Destroy the whole convent and college with a scandal, for the sake of one foolish girl?' He rubbed the flat of his hand across his cropped hair. 'I admire your sense of justice, Bruno, I have already told you that. But you are young. If you want to make your way in this city, you must learn to be a realist.'

I wanted to tell him that folly did not deserve death, that

her name was Anna, and she did have people to mourn her. I wanted to protest that a rich and well-connected young man was not entitled to snuff out a life merely because it had become inconvenient to him. But I could say nothing without revealing that I had been asking questions. My gaze shifted away to the rows of glass bottles and earthenware jars ranged along the shelves. The dispensary always smelled clean, of freshly crushed herbs and the boiling water with lemon juice that he used to scrub down his table and instruments, a contrast to the stale fug of sickness and old bodies that hung over the infirmary. Somewhere in here a tiny, half-formed child was suspended in alcohol, in a jar. Donato's child.

'Suppose someone knew she came here last night, and comes in search of her?'

Gennaro's brow lowered; he fixed me with such a penetrating stare that I almost feared he could see my deception.

'Why should you imagine that?'

'Her clothes did not look like those of a whore. Perhaps,' I added, as if I had just thought of it, 'when you first found her, she was wearing some jewellery that might identify her? If we knew who she was, we might be better prepared to defend ourselves against any accusations.'

He sighed, as if the conversation were keeping him from something pressing. 'The girl came here alone last night. Donato took her into the lemon grove – they argued, and he grabbed her by the neck to frighten her into silence, he said, for he feared she threatened to make a scene and rouse the whole convent. She resisted, and he held her harder than he intended. Her death was an accident.'

'You know that is a lie,' I said, quietly. 'He meant to silence her all right. She must have told him she was with child.'

He brought his hand down hard on the table. 'The business is done now, Bruno. There is no evidence that she was ever here.'

'Did he ask you to help dispose of her?' My voice sounded small and uncertain in the thick silence of the dispensary. 'Did he know what you were going to do?' With every question, I was unpicking the fine thread of trust that existed between me and Gennaro, but I could not stop myself. I wanted the truth. He had brought me into that room with her corpse last night; I felt it was the least he owed me. A sigh rattled through him and he leaned back against the workbench as if he needed support.

'Donato came to me in a blind panic last night, shaking all over. He told me what I just told you – that this young woman had come to the gate, demanding to talk to him. He had taken her into the lemon grove, away from prying eyes, and they had argued, he grabbed her by the throat, she fell to the ground. He claimed he thought she had merely passed out – he wanted me to go with him to see if I could revive her.'

I made a scornful noise. 'He must have known she was dead.'

'Well, he was in no doubt as soon as I saw her. He was on the verge of hysteria – he was begging for my help. She could not be discovered inside the walls, obviously. Our only option was to move the body as far from San Domenico as possible before anyone noticed her missing.'

'But you decided to cut her up first.'

His eyes slid coldly over me. 'It was not my first intention – though I knew it would greatly lessen any chance of the convent being implicated if her body was made unrecognisable. It was only when he mentioned that they had argued over her threat of a paternity suit . . .' He trailed off, tracing one finger along the grain of the table's surface.

'You saw an opportunity that some of the leading anatomists in Europe would sell their own souls for.' I thought of the embryo, silent and transparent in its jar.

That cold sheen in his eyes intensified; he pointed a finger towards me. 'Do not be so quick to judge, Giordano Bruno. The advance of knowledge demands a certain ruthlessness. It is a quality I do not doubt you possess yourself, though you have not yet fully discovered it. I told Donato if he would help me move the body to the storeroom, I would see to it that she was not found anywhere near San Domenico. He was greatly relieved, I think, to have shifted the problem on to someone else's shoulders.'

I said nothing, but I could not look at him. Gennaro folded his arms across his chest. When he spoke again, his voice was kinder.

'The only accusations that can harm us now are coming from your own conscience, which you must learn to silence, or you will put us all in jeopardy. She is no longer your business. Do not give me cause to repent of my belief in you, Bruno.'

I lifted my head and met his gaze. In his stern expression I saw anger tempered by a fatherly concern. I had thought I was being tested, to see how much I was prepared to risk in the pursuit of knowledge. Now I felt deceived; this had not been about the advance of science at all. What we had done was all in the service of protecting a murderer and the name of San Domenico. A murderer who might one day be the head of the most powerful religious house in Naples. I wished bitterly that I had never thought to follow Fra Gennaro last night. Not that my ignorance would have changed anything, but I would have been spared the weight of this guilt.

From beyond the window, the chapel bell struck a long, low note.

'You had better get yourself to Matins,' he said. He reached a jar down from a cabinet to his right, unstoppered it and pulled out one of the ginger and honey balls he kept for

42

throat complaints in winter. 'Here. Take one of these – I can smell the tavern on your breath. And Bruno . . .' he called, softly, as I opened the door. I turned, expectant.

'Remember your oath.'

I nodded. But I also remembered my promise to Maria.

At first light, shortly after Lauds, I crept out of my cell again and crossed the gardens to the lemon grove. I scoured the ground, fancying I could see here or there in the parched earth and scrubby grass some sign of a struggle, but there was nothing conclusive. Nothing to say that the girl had ever set foot here. I searched among the trees for almost half an hour, in vain. Gennaro had deftly ignored my question about jewellery; perhaps he had disposed of the girl's locket in case it should identify her, or perhaps he had never seen it. A necklace chain could easily be broken if you were fighting off a pair of strong hands around your throat.

The bells had just rung for Prime when the sun slipped out from behind its veil of cloud and I caught a metallic glint at the foot of a twisted trunk. I knelt and fished out from among the dried stalks a chain with a gold pendant. An oval, about the size of a large olive, faced with exquisite filigree work and a finely wrought figure of the crucified Christ on the front. I wondered if the girl's father had made it. The chapel bell sounded its sonorous note again and I glanced up to see Fra Donato crossing the grove towards me in rapid strides. With his bright hair lit by the early morning sun, he looked like a painting of the newly risen Christ, if Christ had ever glared at someone as if he wanted to burn them alive with his eyes. I barely had time to slip the locket inside my habit and stand, hands folded demurely into my sleeves, to greet him.

'Brother. *Pax vobiscum.*'

'What are you doing here, Fra Giordano? Shouldn't you

be at prayer?' He had no authority over me, except that afforded by seniority and birth, though he addressed me as if he were the prior himself. His cold blue gaze swept over the lemon trees and seemed to comprehend the scene in a glance. He had come in search of the locket too, I was certain.

'I *am* praying, Brother. I felt moved to speak to God here among the trees, where I can meditate on the wonders of Creation.'

'Perhaps you should have joined the Franciscans.' He left a pause. 'Do you know, they say you are the most promising scholar San Domenico has seen in a generation.' I shrugged. 'They do not say so in my hearing.'

'Well, of course not. They would not want to provoke you to the sin of pride.' He tilted his head to one side. There was an intensity in the way he held my eye that made me under-stand why a woman might fall under his spell. That and the remarkably fine features, the bones that looked as if they had emerged from a sculptor's vision of an archangel. 'I hear you have a prodigious memory too.'

I made a non-committal movement with my head. 'It serves.'

'That is a great gift,' he said, as if he were granting me a rare concession. 'But even with your powers of memory, Brother, certain things are best forgotten. That scene in the tavern, for instance. A woman who believes I slighted her sister or some such thing. Women do not take well to feeling scorned, you know. It can quite turn their wits. They will say terrible things in their fury.'

'I barely recall it,' I said.

He gave me a sliver of a smile. 'Good. It's just that I thought you went out after her.'

'No, Brother,' I said, composing my expression into one of perfect sincerity. 'I had been unwell. I went out because I felt sick and needed air.'

He was watching me carefully, I knew. 'Well, I hope your health is improved,' he said, in a lighter tone. 'We had better not be late for Prime. They also say you show a particular aptitude for your Hebrew studies,' he added, as I turned towards the path. I stopped, remembering his insult to Maria. Was he insinuating something? 'A surprising aptitude,' he repeated. 'Almost a *natural* fluency, apparently. Is there Hebrew blood in your family, Fra Giordano?'

'No.' I regarded him with a steady eye. 'My family has lived in Nola for generations. You may make any enquiries you wish.'

'Oh, I have,' he said, with a pleasant smile. 'Your father is a soldier, is he not? And a soldier for hire at that – not even an officer.' He sounded regretful. 'Still – with the right patronage, a young man with your rare abilities might achieve great things in the Dominican order. You were fortunate to be admitted to San Domenico. Without your place here, I fear your exceptional talents would go to waste.' His eyes skated over me from head to foot as he spoke, as if he were trying to detect whether I was concealing anything.

'I do consider myself fortunate, Brother.' I lowered my gaze to demonstrate deference.

'You might prove it by showing a little less disregard for the rules,' he said. I jerked my head up and stared at him, indignant. He laughed and stretched his arm out to pull down a branch of the tree above us. 'No doubt you think me a hypocrite for saying so. But here one has to earn the right to a degree of flexibility. You are very cocksure for a friar who has barely taken his vows. Not my words, Brother, but those of others who have noted your tendency to pick and choose when to honour the vow of obedience. And I do not believe you have the learning to challenge the authority of Holy Scripture in the way you do. I offer this as a friendly warning. But you should be aware that they are keeping a close eye on you.' He snapped off the twig in his hands and stood there, twirling it between his fingers.

I walked away. I did not know if there was any truth in his words, but the warning itself was not to be ignored. Donato was certainly watching me, and he wanted to be sure I knew he could break my future as easily as that branch. When I reached the far side of the gardens I glanced back to see him under the trees, searching the ground and kicking at the grass with the toe of his calf-leather shoes.

As soon as I was alone in my cell for silent prayer, I opened the locket. The clasp sprung with a satisfying click, to reveal a miniature portrait of a dark-haired woman. It was cheaply rendered; the paint blurred in places so that it was hard to make out her features, though I assumed it must be the girls' mother. I turned the locket over in my hand, perplexed as to why Maria should have been so afraid of losing it. I pictured again the flash of panic in her eyes, the desperate catch in her voice. Perhaps it was more valuable than she admitted, or it was all the sisters had to remember their mother. But I could see that the back of the golden oval was deep and rounded, though the portrait it contained was flat. It looked as if it had been designed to contain something more substantial than a picture. Something concealed behind it, perhaps. Such things were used for smuggling secret communications, I had heard. With this sudden under-standing, my skin prickled into goosebumps. Of course a master goldsmith would know how to work a hidden compartment into a pendant like this. The question was how to find the opening without damaging the mechanism. I worked at the clasp with the tip of my knife with no success, before trying the same trick with the hinge on the other side. I nicked my fingertips so many times the surface and the blade grew slippery with blood, until at last I heard a catch give and the back of the locket opened smoothly. I licked the blood from my fingers, wiped them on my habit and drew out a folded square of parchment.

The writing on it was tiny and densely packed, though neat and precise as if it had been written with a quill as fine as a needle. But my heart was hammering as fiercely as the moment I first saw the girl's body, for the characters written there were Hebrew. I mouthed the first words – *Shema Yisrael* – and realised I was holding a text more dangerous than anything I had read in my life. This was a copy of the Shema, from the Jewish prayer service. Anyone found to possess this would be immediately summoned before the Inquisition, with little hope of a pardon. No wonder Maria was so terrified of it falling into the wrong hands.

Officially there were no Jews left in Naples. They had been expelled in 1541, though a few had chosen to convert and stay. Maria's father must be one such *convertito*, if he was permitted to trade here as a Neapolitan. I had heard that their houses were raided occasionally to ensure that they had truly renounced the faith, but it was rumoured that some had managed to cling on to their traditions in secret. I recalled the deliberate cruelty of Donato's insult to Maria; the way she had flinched as if he had struck her. The insinuations he had made to me – that he could taint me with the same slur if he wished. What did he know of Maria's family history? If the girl Anna had believed herself in love with him, how much might she have confided? To hide the Shema in the locket suggested that, however tentatively, she had chosen to hold on to her identity. Surely she would not have given up such a dangerous secret to a man who belonged among the city's Inquisitors, no matter how strongly she felt for him?

I folded the parchment and replaced it in the locket

with trembling fingers. As I closed the secret compartment, I saw that a drop of blood from my finger had stained the edge of the prayer crimson. I could not think what to do. In my heart I knew I had no choice but to return the locket to Maria; I understood its value now, not least as a memory of her dead mother and her sister. But to return it was as good as confirming that I knew something about the girl's fate, and the bloodstain on the parchment would surely fuel their fears; they would take it for hers. I could not keep it. Fra Gennaro would no doubt see it as more evidence to be erased, so I could not ask for his help. I hid it again inside my undershirt and prayed earnestly for guidance.

Despite Fra Donato's warning that I was being watched, I decided to miss my theology class after the midday meal, asking Paolo to say I was still feverish, and slipped out into the tired heat of the city. With my hood pulled up around my face, I cut along Via Tribunali in the direction of the Duomo. Strada dell'Anticaglia stood steeped in shadow from the high buildings closing in on both sides. Lines hung with washing dripped on me from above as I passed under the ancient arches of the Roman theatre that spanned the street, seeming to hold up the houses. I walked quickly, my head down, scanning the doorways and barred windows for the sign of a goldsmith's. After walking the length of the street, I returned to the only shop that seemed likely, though it had no marker outside, and peered through the small window. Inside, a man stood canted over a workbench with two lamps lit beside him; though it was the brightest hour of the day, the sun would never penetrate to the interior of this little shop in its canyon of a street. He held a thick lens to one eye to magnify his vision as he worked with a delicate, tweezer-like tool. I could see only the top of his head: greying curly hair and the beginnings of a bald patch the size of a communion wafer.

A bell chimed as I entered the shop. The man looked up with a smile that froze on his lips as he registered my habit. He lowered the lens and straightened his back with an air of resignation.

'Have you come to search my home again, Brother? It is barely two months since they were last here.' He sounded as if the prospect made him weary rather than angry. 'We are true Catholics, as we have been for twenty-five years.'

Twenty-five years. He could not be much over fifty; that would mean he had been little more than my age when he had been asked to choose between his history and his home.

'No, sir,' I said, quickly, appalled to have caused him alarm. 'I hoped I might speak to your daughter. Maria.'

His face hardened. 'Neither of my daughters is home at present.' As if to betray him, the ceiling creaked with the footsteps of someone walking in the room above. My eyes flickered upwards; his remained fixed calmly on me. In the light of the oil lamp I saw that his face was drawn, his dark eyes ringed with shadow. One of his daughters had not come home for two days; he must already fear the worst. I wondered if Maria had confided in him about her sister's lover, the pregnancy, or where she had last seen Anna. I doubted it; she had said the knowledge of her sister's affair would break their father's heart. She would want to protect him from the truth.

There was nothing more I could do. Inside my habit, the locket pressed against my ribs in its hidden pocket, but to hand it over would be as good as announcing that his daughter was dead, and implicating myself.

'No matter. Perhaps one day I will come back and buy a gift for my mother.' I turned to leave.

'I should be honoured, sir.' He gave me a slight bow and a

half-smile; despite his understandable dislike of Dominicans, he knew that he needed our continued favour.

I felt a pang of empathy; though I could not imagine the constant threat that hung over this man and his family, no matter how sincerely devout he tried to appear, I already knew what it meant to harbour secret beliefs in your heart, beliefs that could lead you into the flames before the Inquisitors' signatures had even dried on your trial papers. The more I studied, the less convinced I was that the Catholic Church or her Pope were the sole custodians of divine wisdom. I could not tell if it was fear or arrogance that led the Holy Office to ban books that might open a man's mind to the teachings of the Jews, the Arabs, the Protestants or the ancients, but I felt increasingly sure that God, whatever form He took, had not created us to kill and torture one another over the name we give Him. Tolerance and curiosity: a dangerous combination for a young Dominican at a time when the Church was growing less and less tolerant. I nursed my doubts like a secret passion, relishing the shiver of fear they brought. I wanted to tell the goldsmith we had more in common than he realised. Instead I returned his bow and left the shop, the bright chime of the bell ringing behind me.

A few paces down the street I stopped under the Roman arch and tried to think what I might do with the locket. I could wait until the shop was closed and try to push it under the door or through a window, in the hope that Maria would find it. But someone else might see it first, and think to look inside its secret compartment. I could not risk that. I could walk down to the harbour and throw it into the sea, where it could not incriminate anyone. Though I hated the idea of destroying something so precious, this seemed the only safe course, for all of us. I had almost reached the end of the street when I heard quick footsteps behind me, and turned to see Maria running barefoot through the dust.

'I went to Fontanelle,' she announced, pinning me with her frank gaze. I stopped absolutely still. I dared not even breathe for fear of what my face might betray. Every muscle in my body was held rigid. She let out a long, shuddering sigh and her shoulders slumped. 'Nothing. No bodies of young women found in the past two days.'

'Then perhaps she has run away after all,' I managed to say, hating myself for it, though relief had made me light-headed and my legs weak. I leaned one hand on the wall for support.

Maria shook her head. 'I will never believe that. I thought you might have come to bring me some news?'

I hesitated, then reached inside my habit and brought out the twist of paper I had wrapped it in. 'I came to bring you this.'

She tore it open and stared at the locket, her face tight with grief. 'There is blood on it.'

'Mine. I cut my finger on the clasp.' I held it up as proof.

She raised the locket slowly to her lips and closed her eyes, as if in silent prayer. A tear rolled down her cheek. 'Did he take it from her? How did you get it?'

'I found it on the ground.'

'Where?'

Again, I hesitated just a breath too long. 'In the street, outside the gate. She must have dropped it there.'

She shook her head.

'That cannot be true. I have searched the streets around the walls of your convent for the past two days for any sign of what happened to her. I would have seen it. And the chain is broken, as if it was torn from her.' When she saw that I was not going to respond, she rubbed at the tears with the back of her hand and drew herself upright. 'Well. I should

51

not expect truth from a Dominican. But at least I know now that my sister is dead. She would never have willingly let this out of her sight.'

'Very wise. It is a beautiful piece of work. Your father must be a highly skilled craftsman, to have made something so complex.'

She looked at me with a hunted expression as she tried to discern my meaning. 'Did you open it?'

The question was barely a whisper. She knew the answer. She clenched her hands to stop them trembling and her face was tight with fear – the same fear I had felt only a moment before at her mention of Fontanelle. The naked terror of being found out.

'Yes. Is it your mother?'

She nodded, a tense little jerk of her head, her eyes still boring into me.

'She must have been beautiful,' I said. 'But something as valuable as that should be carefully guarded. Others might not be so understanding of your desire to honour your family memory.'

She gave a gulping sob and wrapped both hands over the locket. 'Thank you.' She swallowed. 'Did you show it to anyone? What is inside, I mean?' She glanced over her shoulder, as if I might have brought an army of Inquisitors to hide around the corner.

'No one but me. And I will say nothing.'

'Why?' That sharpness again; the muscles twitching in her jaw. 'Why should I trust you?'

'Because . . .' Because my own secret is far worse, I thought, and it is the very least I owe you for the fact that you will never truly know what happened to your sister. I could not say that. But the answer I gave her was also true. 'Because I believe God is bigger than the rules we impose on one another. I think He does not mind if we find different paths to Him.'

52

'That is heresy,' she whispered.

'So is that.' I nodded to the locket in her hand.

'You are a good man, Bruno,' she said. Unexpectedly, she leaned forward and placed a soft kiss on my cheek, at the edge of my mouth. She stood back and almost smiled. 'For a Dominican.' I could not look her in the eye.

'Wait,' she called, as I began to walk away. 'That man. The friar. Donato, is that his name? Where can he be found?'

'At San Domenico. Or at the Cerriglio, where you found him last night.'

'But he is always surrounded by people. I want to speak to him alone.'

'He would never allow it. Not after your last encounter.'

She shrugged. 'Still, I have to try. For my sister's sake. I just want to know.'

I considered this. 'He is rarely alone, except in his cell. Or perhaps when he takes one of the upstairs rooms at the tavern, to meet a woman.'

She nodded, tucking the information away. 'The cruellest part,' she said, with some difficulty, pausing to master her emotions, 'is that he has stolen from us even the chance to bury and mourn her properly. Whatever he has done with her, I can never forgive him for that.' I watched her teeth clench. She took a deep breath. 'Thank you,' she said, her voice harder this time, determined. 'For what you have done for my family. Perhaps we will meet again.'

'Perhaps.' I bowed and turned away. She would never know my part in what happened to her sister, but I would carry the weight of that knowledge with me always.

September rolled into October, apples ripened in the orchard and mists drifted in from the bay, though without a repeat of the previous year's fever epidemic. Fra Gennaro relaxed around me as he realised that I appeared to have suppressed my qualms and was not going to endanger him with a sudden eruption of conscience; he requested my assistance more frequently in the dispensary, and on occasion confided in me his notes and drawings from previous experiments, as if to demonstrate his trust. He promised to introduce me to a friend of his in the city, an aristocrat and a man of considerable influence as a patron of the sciences. As the weeks passed, I even managed to sleep through the night untroubled by dreams of the dead girl, though not every night.

But in other ways, my fortunes took a turn for the worse. It became clear that I had put myself on the wrong side of Donato, and that was a dangerous place to be. Perhaps he thought I knew too much, or perhaps he just wanted to remind me of his threat. I was summoned before the prior, charged with a series of minor infractions of the rules that he could not have known about unless someone was spying on me. I was given penance and a stern warning not to repeat the offences, as there would be no leniency in future. I lost the small freedoms taken for granted by the wealthier young friars, and found myself reduced to a life of prayer, worship and study – which was, I supposed, no more or less than the life I had signed up to in the first place, but it still chafed. The watch brothers were told to confirm that I was in my cell every night between Compline and Matins. My reading material and my correspondence were subject to unannounced inspections. Everywhere I felt his eyes on me – in the refectory, in chapel, in chapter meetings – and I could do nothing but watch and wait for him to strike. All this petty needling, I felt, was just a prelude. Donato was afraid of what he thought I knew, and he had something planned for me. The worst was not knowing what or when, so that I was permanently on my guard.

Over a month had passed since the night of the girl's death. The season was growing colder; at night, when we trooped reluctantly to Matins as the bells struck two, the air was tinged with woodsmoke and our breath plumed around our faces. I shuffled to my place in the chapel one night in October, stifling a yawn (there was a penance for that, if you did it too often), when I glanced across the choir and noticed the empty seats. Donato, Agostino, Paolo and at least two of the other younger friars had not returned in time for the service. This in itself was unusual; for all his swagger, Donato was careful to make an outward show of obedience. He reasoned that, as long as he was present at each appointed office, no one would question what he did in between. I could see that the prior, too, had noted the absences, though he made no mention of it.

Ten minutes into the service, I heard a disturbance at the back and turned to see Agostino rush in, his face blanched and stricken, the door clanging behind him. With no regard for propriety, he pushed through to Fra Gennaro and whispered in his ear; Gennaro immediately snatched up his candle and followed Agostino out of the chapel. The prior was furious at the interruption, his face slowly turning the colour of ripe grapes, but he mastered himself, exchanged a few words with the sub-prior, and disappeared after the troublemakers. The younger novices were almost bursting with excitement at the unknown drama and the sub-prior had to call us back to order several times. It was a small miracle that we managed to complete the office as if nothing was amiss.

Paolo was waiting for me in the cloister when I returned from Matins. I had never seen him look so shaken.

'Did you hear? Donato is dead.'

'What?' I stared at him. 'When?'

'An hour ago. At the Cerriglio.'

Heedless now of the watch brothers, I followed him to his cell and made him tell me everything.

Donato had taken a room upstairs at the tavern and engaged the services of one of the girls. After she left, he had called for hot water and towels to wash himself before returning to the convent. When the servant took the basin of water up to him there was no answer from the room. She knocked louder and then opened the door, to find him lying on the bed naked with his throat cut. You could have heard her screams at the top of Vesuvius, Paolo said. No one had noticed any disturbance from Donato's room earlier, though one of the other customers thought he had seen a new serving girl, one he did not recognise, loitering on the stairs by the back door shortly before the body was found. But Signora Rosaria had not hired any new serving girls recently, and this man was quite far gone in his cups, so his word was not worth much.

'They brought in the whore Donato was with, of course,' Paolo said, his voice still uncertain, 'though she swears blind he was alive and well when she left him a half-hour earlier. What's more, she didn't have a speck of blood on her, and you couldn't cut a man's throat like that without being drenched in it. I suppose that will not count for much, if they decide to accuse her.'

The strangest thing, he added, was that Donato's purse had been sitting there on top of his habit on a chair by the bed, in full view, and had not been touched. He shuddered. 'Think of it, Bruno. Naked and defenceless. Throat cut right across. It could have been any one of us.'

'Donato went out of his way to make enemies,' I said, carefully. 'I don't think you need to worry.'

'All the same,' he said, rubbing his neck with feeling, 'I think I might give the Cerriglio a miss for a while. Wouldn't hurt me to stay in and pray more often. I could learn from your example.'

'I would be glad of the company,' I said, forcing a smile.

The furore took a long time to die down. Fra Donato's father, Don Giacomo, was almost felled by grief; Naples had not seen such an extravagant and public display of mourning in decades. In return for hushing up the ignominious circumstances of Donato's death, the prior of San Domenico received a handsome donation, for which he was grateful, particularly since he knew it would be the last. Don Giacomo had intended his money to ensure his son's smooth ascent to election as prior one day; now there was no longer any purpose to his bequests. The whore Donato had been with before he died was arrested and quietly spirited away. Some days after the murder, they had found the bloodstained dress of a serving girl stuffed into a well a few streets from the inn, which was considered good enough evidence against the word of a whore. I never learned what became of her; I suppose she was hanged. No one else was ever found guilty of the crime.

The following spring, not long after the Feast of Candelora, as I was crossing Strada del Seggio di Nilo I saw a young woman moving towards me through the mass of people and for a moment my breath stopped in my throat. She carried a leather satchel across her body; a fall of glossy dark hair rippled around her shoulders, burnished in the sun, and she walked gracefully, with an air of self-possession. I withdrew into my hood and turned my face aside as she approached; I did not want to be recognised. If she saw me, she gave no sign of it, but as she passed, a splinter of sunlight caught the golden crucifix locket she wore around her neck, blinding me with a flash of brilliance. When I looked up again, she had vanished into the dust and crowds of Naples.

THE ACADEMY OF SECRETS

Despite what they say about Fra Giordano Bruno in Naples, and the many supposed crimes and heresies that have attached to my name, I would like it known that I was nowhere near Capodimonte that autumn night of 1568 when my brother in Christ met his mysterious death there, and I certainly had no dealings with witchcraft. Of that charge, at least, I am innocent.

I feel the need to say this bluntly because the business touched some of the most powerful men in the city, and the involvement of friars from San Domenico Maggiore in rumours of secret societies, black magic and murder could be catastrophic in more ways than one, if the Inquisition were to catch wind of the rumours.

But I run ahead of my story. Naples is a madhouse, though you'll know that already, my unknown reader, if you have ever set foot here. In case you are a stranger to the city, you need to understand this: Naples is a place of fierce beauty and fiercer tempers. Under the white glare of the sun, two hundred and fifty thousand souls cram together inside the ancient walls, in streets built to hold a tenth of that number. Wherever you walk in Naples, someone and his brother will be always in your face, trying to rob you or start a fight. Arguing keeps us feeling vital, whether it's a fist fight in the market over the price of olive oil, or a disputation about the relative authority of Plato versus Aristotle in the great basilica of San Domenico; the latter has stricter rules, but not necessarily less emotion or violence. Perhaps it's the consequence of living in the shadow of a volcano that could drown us all in fire at any moment. The threat of obliteration means people here live one day at a time, but as insurance they also make great public show of their devotion to the saints whose intercession is all that stands between the city and God's wrath.

When I first arrived in Naples at the age of fifteen, in the Year of Our Lord 1563, I truly thought as I walked under the Porta San Gennaro that I had entered the gates of hell. For a boy from the sleepy town of Nola on the other side of Mount Vesuvius, the heat, dust, crowds, noise, smells and riot were overwhelming; I almost turned and fled back to my father's house, convinced I would never be able to keep a thought in my head in that Babel. But I stayed; I studied; I took my vows as a friar of the Dominican order in the great convent of San Domenico Maggiore, the city's most influential religious house, and by the age of twenty, I couldn't imagine feeling at home anywhere else. Naples gets under your skin; you mould yourself to it. You learn to dissemble, to fight with knives and fists, to haggle, to win at cards by any means, to sing at the top of your lungs on a tavern table, and to jump from a first-floor window when you hear a husband's key in the door – yes, even if you're a Dominican friar. Especially if you're a Dominican friar. Because – let's be honest, for once – we are also a city of hypocrites. The law forbids a man and woman to kiss in the street, but courtesans ply their trade openly in the churches. Blasphemy is punished in public, but child beggars are left to die in doorways. We are all pretending, in Naples. Above all, we pretend to be free, but we are far from it. The Kingdom of Naples is a Spanish vice-realm, and we live under occupation; everywhere you look, there are bands of Spanish troops patrolling the streets, and the viceroy's agents lurk in every tavern, ready to report murmurs of dissent or disrespect among the Neapolitans towards our Spanish overlords.

So being a native of Naples has always meant learning to keep your eyes open, and hide your secrets. I had become skilled at this in my five years at San Domenico, which is why Fra Gennaro trusted me with the Academy.

Fra Gennaro Ferrante was the infirmarian of San Domenico, and his skills were acknowledged far beyond the walls of the convent. He was in his early forties when I first knew him, but as a young man he had studied at the famous school of medicine in Salerno, and would surely have become a renowned professor of anatomy if a decline in his family's fortunes had not obliged him to enter the religious life. But Gennaro was not one to let the strictures of the Church's teachings dampen his quest for knowledge; that was one of the reasons I admired him. He used his position at San Domenico to continue his investigations into the workings of the body, sometimes with the prior's blessing and some-times – as I had learned first-hand – without. But the prior did not like to question too closely how Gennaro's talents were honed, because they brought money and prestige to the convent; no doctor of physick in Naples had his reputation for the ability to remove a tumour, sew a wound, set a bone so the limb was saved, or draw a breech child from the womb without loss of the mother's life. Several times a week, a frantic servant would arrive from one of the city's noble households, begging for Gennaro to attend his master or mistress; if the result was favourable, as it usually was, extravagant bequests and gifts would follow, to show the family's gratitude to God. If there was tension between the Church's teachings on how far medicine might be permitted to intervene in a soul's journey from cradle to grave, the prior trusted Gennaro to act according to his conscience, and did not ask too many questions for fear the income would dry up.

I had been assigned to work as Gennaro's assistant three years previously, as a novice; perhaps the novice master saw in me some glimmer of talent for the natural sciences, though it is likely that he hoped the practical tasks of tending to ailing brothers would concentrate my mind away from the difficult theological questions I was prone to ask. He was mistaken in that regard; working with Fra Gennaro only exacerbated my instinctive sense that there was more to be read in the great book of Nature than the Church was willing to allow. This sounded a lot like heresy, and I was lucky that Fra Gennaro was of the same mind; the Inquisition already had a note of my name, and anyone else would have reported me on the instant for the questions I asked in his infirmary.

Gennaro and I guarded each other's secrets with honour. Two years earlier, I had assisted him in anatomising a corpse that needed to disappear in order to protect the convent's reputation. If that event ever came to light, we would both find ourselves facing public execution; since that night, we had shared an unspoken bond and, on occasion, when we found ourselves alone in the dispensary, he had taken me further into his confidence with details of his medical research into the forbidden secrets of the body's workings. Even so, I was not prepared for what happened on 5th September 1568, when he knocked on the door of my cell half an hour before midnight.

I cracked the door, expecting to find my friend Paolo suggesting an outing to the Cerriglio, the tavern by Santa Maria la Nova where the younger friars gathered at night if they could slip out while the watch brothers were looking the other way. I was ready to turn him down; I had been studying late and, in any case, I had lost my appetite for the Cerriglio after one of our brothers had had his throat cut in its upstairs brothel two years earlier. But instead I saw Gennaro's stern face lit from below by a lantern, his eyes bright beneath heavy brows.

'Are you dressed?' he whispered.

I opened the door further to show that I was still in my habit.

'Good. Come with me.'

'Where—?'

He pressed a finger to his lips and motioned for me to follow. I shot a quick glance back at my writing table, to make sure I had not left out any incriminating papers – I knew that they sometimes searched my cell for indications of heresy when I was out. Necessity had forced me to find ingenious hiding places, and my writings were currently tucked away behind a loose board in the rafters. I pulled the door closed behind me. Gennaro raised a hand and paused for a moment, lowering the lantern and allowing his eyes to travel around the landing, in case anyone should be watching. I held my breath, waiting for his signal. When he appeared satisfied that we had not been observed, he nodded and I followed him to the stairs. We were later to learn that he ought to have looked more closely.

Both the inner and outer cloisters were busy, considering the convent should have been sleeping. But San Domenico was not a typical religious house; the College it housed was the most intellectually prestigious university in the kingdom, and many of the brothers were spare sons of the Neapolitan barons, whose families kept the order's coffers full, so the friars here enjoyed an unusual degree of liberty. Copies of keys to a side gate in the gardens circulated among the younger men, who slipped out at night to the local taverns to compensate for the privations of religious life. Those with money hosted extravagant suppers in their richly furnished rooms, drinking wine from Venetian glass in the light of gold candelabras. The prior turned a blind eye to these minor infractions of the rules, when it suited him. It was intellectual disobedience that he would not indulge, which meant I had to be careful; I had neither a good name nor family money to smooth my path if I crossed him, and I had already been marked as a troublemaker.

So I kept my face hidden beneath my cowl as I followed Gennaro through the shadows, fearful that even the licence the infirmarian enjoyed might not be enough to protect me if I were seen and reported. He led me away from the gate used by the night-time revellers, along an overgrown path through the convent's lemon grove to the stables on the far side of the grounds. Here a boy was waiting with a horse ready saddled; he handed Gennaro the reins without a word and the infirmarian motioned to me to mount behind him. A gate was unlocked and I saw Gennaro lean down and slip the boy a coin as we passed through. 'Keep your hood up,' was all he said to me as we set out into the narrow streets.

'Are we visiting a patient?' I asked, as we wove north-west past Santa Chiara towards the Porta Reale. Torches flamed in wall brackets outside the larger palazzi, and a full moon gave out a pale gleam to light our way. Catches of music and arguments carried from the back streets; Naples was never quiet, even at night.

'That's what I told the prior,' he said. I waited for further explanation, but he fell silent again. The air was warm, but without the heavy, torpid heat that hung in shimmering waves over the city during the day. A night breeze stirred my hair under the cowl, carrying scents of citrus and the sea.

'So – we're not? Seeing a patient, I mean?' I tried again, leaning around his shoulder to gauge his expression.

'Wait and see,' he replied, and his mouth quirked in a half-smile that sent a jolt of excitement and fear up my spine. Whatever we were about to see was clearly illegal or forbidden, if he had lied to the prior about it, and for a young man as determined in the pursuit of prohibited knowledge as I, this was encouragement enough. You might question whether someone so rebellious by nature was suited to the religious life at all, and you would be right to wonder; the obvious answer is that I wanted to study, and since my family had no money to send me to the secular university, my only path to learning was as a monk or a friar. The Dominicans had seen my potential and opened their doors to me, in return for my obedience. It had not taken them long to realise that it could not be bought at the expense of my intellect, and so they kept a close eye on me.

The Porta Reale was locked at that hour, and guarded by soldiers, but I had already discovered that Gennaro was a familiar figure in the night streets of Naples; he dismounted, saluted them, and exchanged greetings in Spanish. I could not hear what was said, but I saw him laugh and clap one of them on the shoulder. Coins changed hands discreetly, and a small door in the main gate opened for us; Gennaro led the horse through and passed me a lantern handed to him by one of the soldiers, before mounting again.

The sound of the gate locking behind us shifted my nervous excitement towards fear. We were in lawless terrain here, outside the city walls; the road sloped steeply up into the hills and the dark pressed in closer. I breathed the scent of night blossoms and listened hard for any hint of danger, either from wolves or bandits, but heard only the hunting cries of owls. To our left, I could make out the fortifications of the Castel Sant'Elmo, black against the sky. We followed the road north towards Vomero; here and there, pinpricks of light glimmered on the hillside showing the few villas built by the nobility to enjoy the view over the bay, away from the stink and heat of the city. I held the lantern awkwardly, but Gennaro seemed to know where he was going without the need for light. I noticed that he had pulled his cloak back to reveal a dagger belted around his waist.

'Will I be back in time for matins?' I asked, after a while, when he had still not said a word about the purpose of our trip. The watch brothers came around with a bell to wake us for the office of matins at two o'clock, and any friar asleep in his cell – or, worse, not in his cell at all – would face discipline. Even the dedicated revellers knew to be back in time, lest they test the prior's patience too far and face a tightening of the rules. Better to turn up and chant the responses half-drunk and smelling of quim than not turn up at all.

'You're excused matins,' Gennaro said, over his shoulder. 'I told the prior I needed you tonight. I assured him that, thanks to my attentive training, you have attained a level of skill that makes you a valuable assistant during difficult operations, which can only enhance the reputation of San Domenico. He seemed reluctantly convinced.'

'And did you mean it?' My pleasure at the flattery was undermined by the suggestion that my mentor had used it as a ruse.

'In a sense.' He was enjoying being enigmatic.

'Damn it, Gennaro – can't you just tell me why you've dragged me out here?'

He laughed. 'All in good time, my eager young friend. Tell me – that memory trick of yours, where you recite a psalm in Hebrew and then recite it backwards – can you do it on demand?'

'Psalm eighty-six. Yes.'

'And you can explain how you do it?'

'Of course. I have been studying the ancient memory systems of the Roman orators, together with the writings of the Spanish mystic Ramon Lull, and I have syncretised them with ideas of my own to form—'

'All right, save your breath. As long as you can articulate your process, if you should be called upon.'

'Who wants to know about my memory system?' I asked, with another flash of alarm. The art of memory had become my passion since my earliest studies of the Roman orators; I was convinced that I could improve on their methods and so learn to carry an entire library of books in my head, but I was well aware that, to the Inquisition, some memory systems danced perilously close to occult knowledge. For that reason, although many of my brothers at San Domenico admired and envied my talent for memorising swathes of scripture or commentary, I had been cautious about who I trusted with my ideas. Why would one of Gennaro's nocturnal patients need to hear me explain how I taught myself to recite the psalms backwards in Hebrew?

The infirmarian didn't answer; instead he pointed ahead. The road wound upwards and narrowed through rocky cliffs of tufa stone, and I could see torchlight in front where a series of terraces had been built into the slopes of the hill. The bulk of an impressive villa was silhouetted against the sky in the distance as we passed high walls and gates.

'Here we are,' Gennaro said, slowing the horse as we rounded the next bend. 'Hold up the light.' He pulled to a stop and dismounted, taking the lantern from me to illuminate a plain wooden door set into the rockface. He knocked twice with the side of his fist; when the door opened an inch, he muttered a word in a low voice and it swung back, though I could not see whose hand had opened it. Gennaro glanced over his shoulder. 'Well, don't hang about there all night,' he said, and entered the doorway.

'What about the horse?' I slid down from the saddle, casting around for somewhere I could tether the animal. Suddenly, a shadow stirred at my side, making me whip around and curse in surprise. A thin, pale man with one hunched shoulder had appeared as if conjured from the air; I could not see if he had come from the doorway or the shadows beneath the cliff, but he merely nodded to me as if our business were agreed, and held his hand out for the reins. I hesitated, then passed them over; there was nothing I could do now but trust Gennaro.

I followed him under the low entrance into a passageway carved through the rock. The door slammed after us with alarming finality, making the lantern's flame shiver in the draught; I glanced back, and hurried after Gennaro. The passage was tall enough to stand upright, wide enough that I could not touch the walls with my arms outstretched; ahead it was illuminated by torches fixed at intervals. As we progressed, the rough-hewn walls of rock gave way to plaster, engraved to give the appearance of *opus reticulatum*, the diamond-shaped brickwork used by the ancient Romans. Niches had been built into the walls at head height, such as you might find in a chapel; they contained statues, though the figures represented were certainly not saints or virgins, but had the appearance of characters from antiquity, from the myths of the Greeks or the Egyptians. After about thirty feet, the tunnel ended in another door. Gennaro knocked, the same sequence; a voice muttered from the other side, he repeated a word in a language I did not recognise, and the door swung open. We found ourselves in an antechamber with a higher ceiling. The wall facing us held another closed door, but that was not its most striking aspect; above this portal, two openings had been cut into the wall, evenly spaced to give the effect of eye sockets, with the doorway as the mouth. From where we stood, I had the impression of looking at a giant skull. *Memento mori*, I thought. Was this some kind of mausoleum? I could hear the sound of running water somewhere. Gennaro gestured to the far wall and I saw an alcove where a spring bubbled up, apparently from the rock itself, then trickled into a marble basin. Beside the fountain, a servant stood looking impassively ahead, white linen cloths folded over his arm.

Gennaro leaned into the alcove and splashed water over his face and hands, washing off the dust of the road; the silent servant handed him a towel, and he motioned for me to copy him.

'Where *are* we?' I asked, pushing wet hands through my hair. 'Those statues – they're pagan, aren't they? Is this – *licit*?'

He laughed and clapped me on the shoulder. 'Since when did you worry about what's licit, Bruno? Come.' He moved towards the door.

'Is the patient through there?' I had concluded by now that we were in a network of passages and chambers beneath some nobleman's summer villa, and that we must be there to perform an operation that demanded utmost secrecy. Gennaro had achieved a degree of skill in assisting women with difficult childbirth, though there were still those who felt that midwifery was women's work and that it was improper for a man to attend a birth, or to interfere if God chose to take the child back before it had even lived. Such niceties would be of no concern to a baron at risk of losing his heir or his lady, but even so, appearances must be preserved. I supposed this to be the reason for our surreptitious arrival.

The servant unlocked the door in the skull's mouth, and I heard the low murmur of conversation from beyond.

'Prepare to have your eyes opened,' Gennaro said. 'And try not to be flippant.'

Before I could ask what he meant, he stepped through, and I followed.

71

My first impression of the room beyond was of the chapter house of a wealthy monastery. It was heptagonal in shape, with a high domed ceiling; columns had been built around the walls, and these were carved with inscriptions of numbers and symbols, as if from a book of alchemical formulae. The floor in the centre was made of mosaic tiles, in the design of a great labyrinth. Banks of expensive beeswax candles illuminated the frescoes on the walls, which depicted curious figures I half-recognised from the little I had read of the religions of ancient Egypt and Babylon. But I had no time to take in the paintings, because as soon as the door closed behind us I found eleven pairs of eyes fixed on me.

The chamber was occupied solely by men, seated in a circle on stone benches built into the walls, as if for a meeting. I was the youngest there by at least a decade; most were in their forties or fifties, at a guess, and three were considerably older, to judge by their white hair and beards.

'Are you bringing children to us now, Gennaro?' One of the grey-beards spoke, holding out a hand in my direction. 'What next – a woman?' A burst of laughter rippled around the group. The tone was good-natured, teasing, but still I bristled; though I did not know yet who these men were, I resented being dismissed for my youth, when I was two years ahead in my studies and could grow a full beard if I chose.

'So this is the young prodigy.' One man rose from his seat and crossed the room. He spoke with a quiet authority, and I could see his clothes were expensive. The laughter died away as he approached me. 'Come here, boy – let me get a better look at you.'

He motioned me to the centre, where a glass lamp hung by a chain from the highest point of the ceiling. In the light he reached up both hands and placed them gently either side of my face. Immediately I knocked his arms away and leapt back, fists raised to defend myself. This caused further mirth among those watching. Let them laugh, I thought; if you are a halfway pretty teenage boy who enters a religious community of men forbidden to touch women, you learn quickly how to fend off the attentions of any older friar who tries to corner you in the bathhouse.

'Peace, boy,' the man said, holding up his hands to show he meant no harm. 'I wish only to read you. Are you not familiar with the science of physiognomy?'

I glanced at Gennaro; he nodded his approval. Against my instincts, I stood beneath the light and let the stranger put his hands to my face again. He closed his eyes as if he were a blind man forming a picture by touch, and I observed him as he pressed his thumbs slowly along my cheekbones, my jaw and the ridge of my brow. His use of 'boy' needled me, since he could not have been above fifteen years my senior, though his hair was prematurely receding and he had shaved the rest close so that his high forehead gleamed in the glow of the candles. He stood a couple of inches taller than me, and had the slim, athletic build and graceful movements of one well-practised in the art of fencing. His face was handsome, in an austere way, with a long, straight nose, deep-set eyes and thin lips barely visible through his neat beard. The rest of the gathering appeared to be holding their breath while they awaited his verdict.

Eventually he opened his eyes.

'A wolf,' he said. 'No, not a wolf – a wolf*hound*. That's what you are.'

'Pardon?' I said.

He laughed. 'Physiognomonics. Cartography of the human body, if you will. The science of reading character – indeed, predicting it – from the outward physical traits. The universe is made up of signs, as you must know, and the human face is likewise a cipher. Men such as you, for example – dark, lean, with a resemblance to a dangerous animal – are likely to end up in prison, did you know that?'

'For what – punching people who insult us?' I said.

The bald man flashed a grin at Gennaro, as if delighted by a new toy. 'So he's a wit too,' he remarked, to his audience, before turning a serious gaze back to me. 'I thought at first a wolf, but you are more of a tracker than a predator. You put me in mind of a dog that will not give up on its quarry, once he has the scent in his nostrils. What animal would you say I resemble?' He took a step back to let me look at him.

I was tempted to make some smart comment, but I remembered Gennaro's warning, and in any case, I was intrigued by his proposition. I considered his face carefully. His eyes were a very light brown, almost tawny; they gave him a feline quality.

'A lynx,' I said. It was the first thing that came into my head. There was a sharp intake of breath around the benches.

His eyes widened further, as if I had said something marvellous.

'Why do you say so?'

'Because of your eyes. I have the impression that you see what others miss. And the lynx is supposed to be the most sharp-eyed of creatures. Plutarch says it can see through rock. But I don't believe any of it.'

He gave an indulgent smile. 'You don't believe a lynx can see through rock, or that I am sharp-eyed?'

'I don't believe that there is any art to read a man's soul in his face.'

He lifted a brow.

'Interesting. You don't agree that a fair appearance denotes nobility of character, and that deformity is a sign of corruption?'

'Not at all.'

'Based on what evidence?'

'My father is a soldier.' I heard my voice grow heated. 'His dearest friend, Tommaso, is hideously scarred. Children cry at the sight of him. By your logic, he should be a monstrous, degenerate person. You know how he came by those scars? His garrison was set alight during a campaign, and he dragged his comrades to safety. He went back four times, saving four lives, including my father's, before he was burned so badly he could no longer stand. It was a miracle he lived at all. So – here is a man so ugly that women cross themselves in the street, who owns more virtue than you or I could ever aspire to.'

'Ah,' said the bald man, nodding, 'but his deformity was due to external causes, he was not born with it. And, tell me – is his character as virtuous as it once was, or has he been made bitter by his change of fortune?'

I hesitated, unwilling to concede the truth of this. 'Wouldn't you be?'

'So you see, then, that it can also work the other way – outward form can affect character. For example, a girl who grows up plain and disregarded and therefore sullen may, on blossoming into womanhood, discover that she is considered beautiful. Being admired instead of ignored might have a transformative effect on her personality – thus beauty can breed generosity and grace. Indeed, I have witnessed this with my own niece. Do you not agree?'

'I have more often seen beauty breed vanity and arrogance. I assure you, the most well-favoured young man I ever met in Naples was capable of brutal cruelty, even murder—' I stopped abruptly; over the man's shoulder I caught Gennaro's glare – that murder was a business about which I had sworn to remain silent. 'Besides,' I added, 'you don't believe your own theories either.'

'Really? Why do you say that?' A smile hovered at the edge of his lips.

'Because you keep a hunchback servant. If you truly thought his deformity denoted a bad character, you would not trust him with welcoming your secret midnight visitors.'

The bald man rubbed his beard and looked around the company, laughing. 'He has a point. Ercole is the best of men, and worth his weight in gold. You give your opinions very forcefully for one so young,' he said, clapping me on the shoulder. 'But I think you were flattering me when you said the lynx. You have read my book, have you not?'

'I don't know.'

'You don't know if you have read my book?' He seemed uncertain as to whether I was toying with him.

'How could I know? I have no idea who you are.'

I had said no more than the truth, but he turned his expression of incredulous amusement on the infirmarian.

'Gennaro, have you really not told this young man what company you have brought him to?'

Gennaro shrugged, but he was also smiling; I had the sense that the joke was at my expense.

'I wanted him to arrive without preconceptions,' he said. 'Don Giambattista, I present to you Fra Giordano Bruno. Bruno, this is Don Giambattista della Porta, the finest mind in Naples, and her most generous patron of learning.'

Porta effected an elegant bow; there was a hint of mockery in it, though I suspected that was partly directed at himself. I stared at him, amazed.

'Della Porta – but – you wrote the book on cryptography,' I blurted. I knew this man by reputation, of course; he was the son of a wealthy nobleman from Vico Equense, further along the coast, and he spent his considerable fortune on the pursuit of scientific enquiry, often – so rumour whispered – far beyond the limit of what was permitted by the Church. It was said that he dabbled in magic. I could hardly believe I was standing in his presence. Suddenly all the Egyptian paintings and alchemical formulae in this underground laby-rinth made sense.

'You've read my book on ciphers?' He looked pleased. 'How did you get hold of that?'

'I . . .' I faltered. Gennaro had a copy among his secret papers; I was not sure that he knew I'd been sneaking in to read it whenever he was out visiting the sick.

'No matter. We have heard great things of you, Giordano Bruno. Your master here tells us you are the most promising young theologian San Domenico has seen in a generation.'

'I thank him for his kindness.' I dipped my head towards Gennaro. He waved a hand.

'I'm not being kind, Bruno. It's the truth. I have told Don Giambattista of your gifts, and he has desired to meet you.'

'Is this what you want, Bruno?' Porta asked, fixing me with that clear gaze. 'To be a theologian? Rise up through the ranks at San Domenico, perhaps become prior some day?'

'No, sir.' I did not even have to think about my answer. 'I could never be prior, I don't have the right family connections. In any case, theology is too proscribed. I want to study philosophy and cosmology. I wish to understand the universe, and—' I stopped, afraid of saying too much. San Domenico may have been liberal in its approach to the vows of poverty and chastity, but the Dominican order provided the city's Inquisitors; we were expected to take our obedience to the Church seriously and could not risk the slightest whiff of heresy ourselves, so I had been obliged to learn how to keep my thoughts private. One careless question could see you denounced. I guessed that this gathering of Porta's would be far from orthodox, but I needed to guard against saying too much, until I knew better who these men were and whether they could be trusted.

'To understand the universe. A modest ambition.' Porta grinned, and surprised me by grasping me in a warm embrace.

'You are among brothers now, my friend,' he said, when he released his grip to hold me at arm's length by the shoulders. 'We are all of us seeking to understand the universe better. Every man you see here brings a unique gift and perspective to his particular branch of learning. All of us pursue wisdom along paths that have not yet been explored, and which few have the courage to tread. Welcome to the Academy of Secrets.'

This was met with a round of applause and murmurs of welcome from the rest of the gathering. I felt a frisson along my spine, and the hairs on my arms stood up. To be admitted to such company was the most terrifying and exhilarating experience I had had since Gennaro and I anatomised the girl two years earlier.

Porta directed me to a seat. 'To become a member of the Academy, you must present to us an original thesis or discovery in some area of study, no matter how arcane. We meet here once a month to share our experiments. To give you some idea of the range of our expertise, I will ask my brothers in learning to introduce themselves and their work. I will begin.'

He sat down, and an expectant silence fell.

'My name is Giambattista della Porta, as you know. I am working on an encyclopaedia of natural magic that will encompass all the hidden properties and correspondences of the material world and the heavens, and teach the adept how to manipulate those properties at will. But I am also conducting research into physiognomy, anatomy, cryptography and memory, among other things. I have built a laboratory and a workshop here in which we carry out practical experimentation.'

He nodded to the man beside him, who announced his name and his field of enquiry – that of optics. He was working with Porta on developing a device that would combine two magnifying lenses in order to see the heavens more clearly. They were some way off a workable prototype, but hopeful of success, and convinced that such an instrument would change the way we were able to measure the stars. I will omit the names of the company, but I was overwhelmed by the breadth of their ambitions to expand human understanding in practical and philosophical directions. There was one who studied hydraulics, another who specialised in the medicinal properties of plants; several whose interests lay in anatomy, in various forbidden forms, including Gennaro, who was intent on unravelling the mysteries of generation; one of the white-haired men claimed to be an adept of the Hebrew Kabbalah, and another had devoted his life to studying the wisdom of the Egyptian sage Hermes Trismegistus. The hairs on my neck stood up as they spoke: questing into the sympathetic properties of plants and crystals may have carried occult overtones, but intimate knowledge of ancient mysticism was unequivocally heretical, highly dangerous, and more seductive to me than any of the pleasures the Cerriglio could offer.

After the introductions, Porta leaned forward in his chair and fixed his lynx-eyes on me.

'Gennaro tells us you have developed, through your own ingenuity, a memory system that allows you to carry encyclopaedias in your head,' he said. 'You will present it to us. But first – some refreshment.'

He picked up a silver bell and rang it; almost immediately the hunchback servant Ercole appeared from the antechamber bearing a tray of glasses in one hand, and a covered iron pot with a spout in the other, from which a curious vegetable smell escaped with the steam. I watched, apprehensive, as he poured a measure of a green liquid into each glass. The members of the Academy sat forward in anticipation; I guessed from their eagerness that this brew was a regular ritual. Porta caught my expression and smiled.

'You're afraid we are going to poison you? That you might wake up naked and strapped to an altar?'

I blinked. 'That had not crossed my mind until you said it. It's only that I know some plants can produce hypnotic or hallucinogenic effects, and I have never tried—'

'Indeed, and as we are men of science, I consider it vital that we learn their properties by experimentation. But you need not fear – this infusion will not produce visions. It comes from the New World – a contact of mine imports the leaves from Spain. They call it *mate de coca*. It's a miraculous brew – it brings mental alertness, aids concentration and staves off fatigue.'

'Every scholar's dream,' I said in wonder, as the glasses were passed around the circle.

'Apparently it is most potent when the leaves are fresh,' he said. 'The natives chew them to suppress the appetite and work longer hours. But to transport the leaves such a distance requires them to be dried, so this tea is the best way of enjoying their benefits. Though I am convinced there must be some means to identify and distil the active ingredients. Something to work on, eh.'

'You would make a fortune,' I said, in admiration.

'The citizens of Naples do not need any more stimulation,' remarked one of the men, and Porta conceded this with a laugh.

'Are we all served? Good. Then, let us offer a toast to Athena, goddess of knowledge and wisdom, in whose service we humbly gather. And now, we will hear young Bruno present his memory system.' He sat back and gestured for me to take the floor.

I drank the tea, grimaced, and stood at the place marked as the centre of the labyrinth. I could have wished Gennaro had given me better warning to prepare for this moment, but that, I presumed, was part of the test. I recited Psalm 86 in

Hebrew, then again backwards, earning nods and murmurs of approbation from around the circle. I could feel Porta's silent gaze on me all through my speech.

When I had finished, I raised my eyes, hardly daring to check his expression. A long silence unfolded; blood beat in my throat as I awaited his approval. Finally, without speaking, he stood and bowed solemnly to me. One by one, the other men all did the same. It seemed I had been accepted into the Academy.

The discussions continued for another three hours, animated by the strange brew from the New World. I will not repeat here the matters that were presented for debate, save to say that I marvelled at the words of every man who spoke; my brain spun with the torrent of new ideas and discoveries that poured forth among them. The hunger for knowledge in that room matched my own, and in every case I sensed that these men pursued wisdom for her own sake, not for vainglory or self-promotion, but out of a genuine desire for the enlightenment of mankind. I felt alert and needle-sharp, though the drink made me garrulous; I argued and questioned and posited theories in a way that would not have been permitted by my tutors at San Domenico, and through it all Porta observed me with an indulgent smile, just as a man who has purchased a new horse will watch it run through its paces with relief that his investment has been justified.

When the meeting drew to a close, he raised his empty glass and proposed a toast to freedom. The others dutifully echoed him, and he allowed his gaze to travel around the room, alighting on each of us as if to impart a hidden meaning. The company broke up after this, the men taking their leave of one another with barely a nod. As I crossed the room towards Gennaro, Porta intercepted me, a firm hand on my shoulder.

'You acquitted yourself well tonight, Bruno,' he said. I

bowed my head in what I hoped would look like humility, but my face was glowing. 'I was sceptical about allowing one so young into the Academy, but Gennaro was right – you do have an exceptional intellect. Your memory system shows great promise – I would like to see you develop it further. But to do that you need to read more widely among authors whose work is not sanctioned by the Church.'

'I wish it were that easy,' I said ruefully. 'I am already suspected of unorthodox beliefs at San Domenico. If I were to ask for books from the restricted section of the library, I would be refused and reported to the Father Inquisitor.'

'Then you must come here and use my library. Come tomorrow afternoon. I am going away for a few days to conduct some research, but Ercole will take care of you.'

'Thank you, sir.' I dipped a bow, hardly able to believe my good fortune.

'Stop this "sir",' he said, smiling. 'We are all equals in the Republic of Learning. And you, Giordano Bruno, are one of us now. Tell me – do you believe in freedom?'

Something in the way he looked at me as he spoke set a warning bell ringing, high and clear, at the back of my mind, but there was only one possible response.

'Of course,' I said. 'Freedom of thought is my greatest dream. A world where we could discuss ideas as we did tonight, but without hiding in underground chambers, as if the desire for knowledge were something filthy and depraved that must not be admitted in public.'

'And what would you risk to secure such a world?' he asked.

'I would fight to the death,' I said with sudden bravado, because I was twenty and full of coca tea and at that moment believed myself invincible.

He smiled again, but his eyes stayed on me, considering. 'Your father is a soldier, you say. Is he in the pay of the Spanish army?'

'He fights for whoever hires him. What else should a mercenary do?'

He arched an eyebrow. 'What about you, and your fighting spirit? Can the Spanish buy you for the right price, or does your Italian blood baulk at that?'

'I have no intention of going to war,' I said, avoiding the question. His lynx-eyes bored into me.

'But we are at war, my young wolfhound, whether you like it or not, and will be until we are free in our own land. Knowledge is power – is it not so?' His grip tightened around my shoulder. 'Why else should we seek to understand the world and its secret properties better?'

Gennaro cut in at that moment, with a hand on my other shoulder.

'I'm afraid I must take Bruno back to the cloister, before too many questions are asked about his absence,' he said. His tone was one of apology, but I sensed he had been monitoring the conversation from a distance and stepped in deliberately to end it. Porta bowed his head, patted me on the back and turned away. I followed Gennaro back along the passageway, my earlier euphoria replaced by an odd, unsettled feeling that there was something vital I had failed to understand.

'Porta took a liking to you,' Gennaro said, on the way back to the city. 'I knew he would.'

'Is he really the finest mind in Naples?' I asked. I was fidgety, my thoughts buzzing wildly like flies against glass.

Gennaro laughed. 'Surely you have learned by now that rich men must be flattered, even in the Republic of Learning. You'll have noted the numbers – twelve members of the Academy, plus our leader – like Christ and his disciples? That's no coincidence. Porta is brilliant, in his way, and willing to take risks, which is essential in a patron. But he's a showman. He loves the kind of experiments that produce a spectacle, and he is easily bored, which is why he must always be seeking the next new discovery.'

'Does no one suspect him or question his activities? From the city authorities, I mean?'

'Bruno, half the men in that room hold positions in government. That is Porta's genius – few people can resist the prestige implicit in an exclusive club. Then, naturally, they are implicated, and their loyalty assured. It goes without saying that you speak to no one of what you witnessed tonight,' he added. 'You perceive the danger.'

'We would be condemned to death for the words spoken in that room,' I whispered. 'If the Inquisition knew.' Now that we were back on the road, in the dark, the whole encounter had taken on the quality of a dream; I had been so caught up in the marvels of the Academy that I had not given a thought to the magnitude of the heresies we had discussed. I had dared to imagine for a few brief hours that we were free.

'Precisely. There were those who opposed my admission at first, convinced that any Dominican must be, by definition, a spy for the Inquisitors.' He shook his head. 'But Porta had heard of my work in anatomy – he was determined I should be a member of the Academy and his will usually prevails. It doesn't hurt to remind him, now and again, that you understand the value of his good opinion. What was he asking you back there, at the end?'

'What risks I would take for freedom. If my father fought for the Spanish. He asked about my Italian blood.'

'Ah.'

There was a long silence. 'He's political, isn't he?' I asked, when it became clear that Gennaro was not going to speak. He sighed.

'We live in an occupied kingdom. Everything is political.'

'That's what I mean. Porta said knowledge is power.' I paused as the import of it struck me. 'He wants to overthrow the Spanish, doesn't he?'

Gennaro threw his head back and laughed so loud it echoed alarmingly off the cliffs above us.

'What's funny?' I glanced over my shoulder; if there were bandits on the road, they would know exactly where to find us.

'You saw our little gathering tonight, Bruno. Three of them are grandfathers. All of us pale as milk, with hands soft as girls'. We are men of libraries and council chambers, better at wielding pens than swords. I have no doubt you can hold your own in a tavern brawl, but the rest of us are revolutionaries only in the realm of ideas. Hard to think of a more unlikely army to rise up against the Spanish.'

'But that's the point,' I said, animated now and leaning forward so that my mouth was almost at his ear. 'If Porta's studies of ancient magic give him access to supernatural powers, we would not need a strong sword arm. That's why he wants to probe those mysteries.'

He reined the horse to a standstill so abruptly that its hooves skidded on the loose stones and I almost flew off the back.

'*Never* repeat that.' He spoke as if reprimanding a child. 'We are not a ragtag of amateur alchemists, dabbling in witchcraft for a hobby. No one is summoning supernatural powers, do you hear me? We are men of science, concerned with natural magic only. We seek to understand better the mysteries of Creation, for which purpose God gave us the faculty of reason and enquiry. I want no talk of demons, or spells, or witches' unguents, or any such wise-woman quackery. Is that clear?'

'But I thought—'

'*Is that clear?*'

'Yes.' I sat back, chastened, and fell silent for a full minute. He nudged the horse with his heels and it resumed its pace with a whinny of protest.

'But think about it,' I said, bouncing forward again to speak in his ear, 'Porta wants to learn how to manipulate and harness the powers of the natural world. Consider Vesuvius, for example, or, or – I don't know – lightning. If, let's say, you could harness the power of lightning – which must be possible – and direct it straight on to the viceroy's palazzo, his entire household would be burned to a cinder in an instant, it would be greater than any cannon—'

'Bruno.' Gennaro sounded weary, but I thought I could see the gleam of a smile in the dark. 'Drink less of the coca tea next time. You talk quite enough as it is.'

A faint glimmer of dawn light showed along the horizon by the time we arrived back at San Domenico. I was not remotely tired – I felt I could have run ten times around the cloisters – but I bounded up the stairs to the dormitory to mull over everything I had heard in the privacy of my cell, before the bell for lauds. I shut the door silently behind me and ripped off my habit and undershirt, then poured water into a basin from the pitcher on my washstand and vigorously splashed my face and neck to sluice off the dust and sweat of the road.

'Busy night?' said a voice, from the shadows in the corner.

I leapt a foot in the air with an emphatic curse, sending the basin crashing to the floor. My eyes had adjusted to the dark well enough to make out a figure lolling on my bed. Fra Raffaele da Monte, propped on one elbow as if he were posing for a painter, just asking to have that knowing half-smile knocked off his face. What animal would Porta identify him with, I wondered, as we stared at one another. Some kind of spoiled, indoor cat, but one with a temper, preening itself while it watched for the moment to scratch your face.

I swore at him again for good measure, my heart thudding against my ribs as if I had run the whole distance back from Vomero. I breathed deep to steady myself; he had me at a disadvantage, but I would only make it worse by reacting without thinking, that was what he wanted. It was then that I remembered I was naked, and grabbed at a linen towel to tie around my waist. He laughed, but there was menace in it.

'How long have you been in here?' We were not permitted locks on the doors of our cells; why would we need them, when the whole point of religious life was that we lived in community, and none of us should have secrets from his brothers? Of course, those with money fitted locks to protect their gold candlesticks and fine jewellery and the senior brothers turned a blind eye, but with my reputation, if I had attempted the same it would have been taken as a sign that I had something to hide.

Raffaele shrugged. 'Since I saw you were not at matins. Where have you been?'

'Whoring.' I turned away to pick up the bowl from the floor so that he would not see my face.

'With anyone else, I might believe that, but we all know you're too good for the girls at the Cerriglio.'

'They are not the only girls in Naples.' It was true that I did not keep company with the Cerriglio whores, though they liked to tease me about it and tried to entice me with special offers, to the frustration of my friends. But my father had told me so many lurid tales of comrades afflicted by the pox that the fear kept me out of brothels for the most part, which I suppose was my father's purpose.

'A lot of us wonder if you even have a taste for girls at all,' Raffaele said, winding a tassel of his belt around his finger. 'Since it's well known you're Gennaro's catamite. I saw you leaving with him before midnight. Does he pimp you out to his rich patients now? I hear some of the barons will pay good money for willing boys from the provinces.'

'That's right. Your father paid me handsomely. He ought to, for the kind of filthy perversion he likes.'

'I should punch you for that,' he said lazily, without troubling to move. I was on the balls of my feet in an instant, fists raised.

'Come on, then.'

He laughed again. 'Calm down, soldier boy. Whatever you've been up to tonight, it's left you very over-excited. I know Gennaro's not interested in your little provincial arsehole. There's something else goes on between you and him – always whispering together in the infirmary. I wonder if it's to do with heretical books. That's the sort of thing that gets you hard, isn't it?' I willed myself not to answer back.

Fra Raffaele did not like me. He was not alone in that; I had acquired a reputation for intellectual arrogance that was, I admit, not entirely undeserved. Even as a novice I had struggled to conceal my impatience with the slowness of my fellow students, and on occasion had found it necessary to correct the teacher when he made a mistake with his Greek or Latin; this, combined with my growing notoriety for unorthodox questions, meant that I was not popular with certain of my brothers. I had bested Raffaele in a debate once when I was still a novice; not merely won the argument, but demolished every one of his points, leaving him speechless with the audience's laughter ringing in his ears. He was five years my senior and had never forgiven me the humiliation.

He swung his legs over the edge of my bed and sat up. He was another in whom good looks had bred superiority rather than decency, I thought. His father was Don Umberto da Messina, a local baron with a prominent seat on the city council, but Raffaele was a bastard, and although his father provided him with a generous allowance, he had not given the boy his name, a slight which Raffaele carried on his young shoulders like the leaden cloaks Dante imagines for the proud in the *Inferno*. Even so, Raffaele considered his father's blood to set him above those of us whose line was not so illustrious, however legitimate. Don Umberto had grown rich from his willingness to support the Spanish, and there were those who feared Raffaele operated as a spy within San Domenico, ready to report any whispers of heresy that could be used against the convent. His eyes and skin were dark, even for a Neapolitan; his full lips and curls led some to speculate that his mother had been a Moorish slave, though anyone who said so in earshot of Raffaele or his friends could expect to go home with a broken nose.

He rested his elbows on his knees, locked his fingers together and looked at me just as the prior did when considering an appropriate punishment.

'You have too many secrets, Giordano Bruno.' He ran his thumbnail along his teeth. 'I suppose you think they give you a tiny scrap of power?'

'My secrets are all in your head,' I said, pretending to occupy myself with tidying the bowl and water jug so I did not have to meet his eye; in my agitated state, I was finding it hard not to rise to his provocations, and I could not risk giving him any reason to report me to the prior. 'Though I am flattered you take such an interest in my activities. I have absolutely no interest in yours.'

There was a pause while he tried to work out whether he had been insulted. 'Tread carefully, soldier boy. Your position here is precarious, for all your supposed brilliance, and you know it. The prior has his eye on you, and so do I.' He pushed himself to his feet. 'No one will care how many psalms you can recite backwards if your name brings San Domenico into disrepute.'

'My name brings nothing but glory to the order.' I assumed the stance of an orator to show that I was not entirely serious, but he did not smile.

'I'm going to find out what you and Gennaro are involved in. Then I'll decide whether to drag your name through the dirt. Remember who and what you are.' He fixed me with his most intimidating stare. I confess; I would have given a great deal at that moment for the ability to direct a blast of lightning at him. Instead I laughed in his face.

'I'm the son of a humble soldier from Nola, Brother, how could I forget? But at least I have his name.'

I thought for a moment that he might hit me, but he mastered himself and shouldered past, snatching the towel from my waist and whipping me around the back of the legs with it on his way. I yelped, and cursed after him as the door slammed. I supposed this was what came of being raised in a community of men; he still behaved like a schoolboy at the age of twenty-five. But I wished I had not attracted his enmity; I did not like the idea that he was watching me, just as I had discovered this new portal to a world of forbidden knowledge. I wondered if I should warn Gennaro.

After Raffaele's threat, I checked carefully when I left San Domenico the following afternoon, but I was certain as I could be that no one had seen me leave. I had asked Gennaro to excuse me from my appointed work with him in the dispensary, and to cover for me if anyone asked. He pursed his lips, but did not argue; he must have guessed at my purpose, and reasoned that he was hardly in a position to stop me, having brought me to Porta in the first place. I did not have permission to borrow a horse from the prior's stable, nor did I have money to hire one, so I walked the long, steep road to Vomero under the relentless sun, one hand on the knife at my belt; the journey took the best part of an hour.

When I reached the door set into the cliff below Porta's villa, I faltered. Was anyone expecting me? If there was no reply, I could hardly present myself at the main door of the house. Perhaps the invitation had been only a courtesy, and not really intended; I feared I might be turned away. But I struck the door with the same pattern of knocks that Gennaro had used the night before, and when it cracked open after a few minutes, I realised I did not know the password.

'I was here last night,' I stammered. 'He told me to come back, to use the library.'

The door opened wide enough for me to pass into the welcome cool of the passageway. The servant Ercole admitted me with a nod, and I followed him through the chambers from the night before, where he offered me the chance to wash my face and hands in the underground spring. He did not speak a word to me as we passed along another network of tunnels on the other side of the meeting room. The final passage ended in a flight of stone steps; at the top he unlocked a door into an unmarked room inside the villa. Looking back, I saw that as he closed this door, it blended seamlessly into the painted wooden panelling of the wall, so that from inside you would never guess it existed.

'Don Giambattista is away,' Ercole said, as he led me down a richly decorated corridor and pushed open another door at the end. 'But he says you may stay in the library as long as you wish.'

I craned my head up to look around the room we had just entered. It was two storeys high with a mezzanine gallery running around three sides, accessed by a spiral staircase, with arched windows at intervals filling the space with light. The domed ceiling was painted with allegorical scenes of the goddess Athena, and every wall was packed with shelves of books and parchments; my mouth hung open as I approached the first stack, hardly knowing where to start. But I was quickly disappointed; there was nothing to see but expensive editions of the most respectable books: Aquinas, Aristotle, Saint Augustine.

Behind me, Ercole gave a discreet cough.

'Upstairs. Come.'

I followed him to the gallery. At the far end, where the window allowed a view over the city and the bay beyond, he reached his hand into a stack of books. I could not see what he did, but I heard a satisfying mechanical click, and the entire shelf stack swung out towards me on a pivot so well engineered that it moved almost silently. I stared at Ercole and he nodded me through the gap that had opened. Here, inside, was a room under the eaves with no windows, containing further shelves of books and a writing table. I blinked, trying to adjust to the gloom. Ercole followed me, and from somewhere in his clothes he brought out a tinderbox and lit a series of lamps in alcoves between the stacks.

'Enjoy your studies, sir,' he said. Like all good servants, he was impeccably polite, and inscrutable. 'There is a jug of fresh spring water on the table in case you are thirsty. Please keep it away from the books. My master has taken the liberty of selecting a few volumes he thinks may be of interest to you. When you have finished here, pull the lever inside the shelf.'

With that, he left me in this darkened cave of treasures and the entrance closed behind him.

I took a long draught of cold water straight from the jug and began to look around Porta's secret library. Here was every volume on the Inquisition's Index of Forbidden Books, a trove of all the authors I had longed to read and feared I might never be allowed to set eyes on. It was only as I spoke the titles aloud, in awe, that I fully understood the weight of the trust he had placed in me. Owning any one of these books would be enough to see him interrogated; even his wealth and family name would not protect him from the consequences of a whole library full, if anyone should report him. I realised again what an extraordinary and dangerous undertaking the Academy was. To have brought together all those like-minded men, each determined to further the boundaries of knowledge in his own field, and maintain their work in defiance of the Church and the Inquisition was no small matter. What might we achieve, through mutual encouragement and challenge? We could become like those adventurers who crossed an ocean, driven only by their faith that there was more to the world than had yet been seen, and were rewarded with new continents! Since my earliest memories I had been consumed by a great hunger to find out what lay beyond the horizon, in every sense. Finally, in being invited to the Academy, I had found a place where that desire was no longer considered sinful, or disobedient, or wrong. Determined to prove to Porta that I was worthy of the confidence he had placed in me, I turned my attention to the pile of books on the writing table, all concerned with the art of memory and its occult uses.

Perhaps half an hour passed; I was so immersed in Cornelius Agrippa's *De Occulta Philosophia*, parsing each sentence twice over so I might have it by heart, that I did not even hear the bookshelf swing open.

'Who are you?' said a woman's voice, sharply.

I jerked my head up, taken aback; she was standing by the entrance to the secret room, like a saint in a painting, her long hair gold in the lamplight. I guessed her to be about my own age, though she moved with a self-possession I could not hope to emulate. Because she was very beautiful, I fixed my gaze on the book to stop myself staring.

'Fra Giordano Bruno of Nola, at your service,' I said, darting a glance at her face. She eyed my habit.

'A Dominican. I did not expect that. I am Fiammetta della Porta. He didn't tell me anyone was here.'

'I'm sorry. Your husband invited me to use the library today . . .' The sentence tailed off as her face softened into a grin.

'My what?'

'Don Giambattista. You are not his – lady?' I could feel the heat rising in my cheeks.

'I'm his niece.' She turned away and idly began to run her finger along the spines of the books in front of her. 'And you are his latest protégé, I suppose.'

'I don't know about that.' The way she said it needled me; I wanted to believe that Porta had seen something special in me, not that I was one more in a line of promising young men he chose to patronise. I wondered if this was the niece whose character had transformed for the better after discovering that she was beautiful.

'Well, he must admire you, if he's let you in here,' she said. 'Not many get to see the holy of holies. What animal does he say you are? No – let me guess.' She came closer and peered at my face. I felt my colour rising under her intense stare. 'Hm. A wild dog, am I right?'

I nodded slowly. It seemed my resemblance to a dog was universally agreed upon. 'He said a wolfhound. He's taught you well.'

'I know what he looks for. What do you think he says of me?' She twirled a full circle on the spot so that I could admire her from all angles. I considered, with a quick glance at the door in the hope that someone might appear and save me from having to answer; there was significant potential to cause offence here. This Fiammetta was small in stature, and slender; her face a pale perfect oval, with a high forehead and pointed chin, her features neat but unremarkable. It was her eyes that gave her face beauty; they were wide and expressive, bright with the promise of mischief, and the same clear tawny gold as her uncle's; I should have spotted the family resemblance straight away. I racked my brains for some creature that would flatter her, when she tossed her loose, curly hair back and breathed impatiently through her nose.

'A horse,' I said, and immediately wished I could take it back.

'A *horse*? Well, *thank* you.' But she was smiling. 'What kind? A carthorse? Or do you mean a mule, perhaps, or a donkey?'

'No, I – I was thinking of a thoroughbred,' I said, desperately trying to retrieve the situation, 'like those Andalusian pure breeds that are taught to dance in the viceroy's processions, they're very elegant—'

'Oh, I'm a dancing horse now? That makes all the difference. You should stop there before you dig yourself any deeper, Brother. What are you reading?'

'Agrippa,' I said, relieved to change the subject, though I expected the name to mean nothing to her.

'Ah. I like Agrippa,' she said, spinning back to me. 'But really you should read Marsilio Ficino, if you are interested in Neoplatonist magic.' She caught my expression and laughed. 'Quite well-read for a woman, aren't I, Giordano Bruno of Nola? Are you impressed? My father finds it disgusting.'

I remembered, belatedly, to close my mouth.

'Your uncle lets you read his books?'

'Of course. Why wouldn't he? My uncle enjoys being unconventional. He doesn't see why a woman shouldn't learn. He's not so broad-minded as to allow me into your little club, mind you, but he lets me indulge my curiosity in here.'

'Do you live with him, then?' I asked, as the blush spread down my neck. I had never met a woman who had even heard of Ficino; I was half in love with her already, just for that.

95

'For now.' She leaned against the book stack. 'I am having a stand-off with my father, so my uncle thought it would reduce tensions if I stayed with him for a while. In fact, it's made things even worse.' She seemed delighted by this result.

'Why? What is the argument?' I could hardly believe my own daring, addressing her like this; I was not used to conversing with aristocratic women, but she seemed to care so little for the difference in our status that she encouraged an unguardedness in me. It was as if the secret library, being so far removed from convention itself, permitted us to talk naturally, as equals.

'I have refused the man he wants me to marry,' she said grandly. 'And now all is in disarray, because neither my father nor my prospective husband imagined that I would want any say in the matter, much less that I would consider their arrangement anything other than a great honour.'

'You wish to marry someone else, then?' I felt obscurely disappointed; I had only met the girl five minutes ago, but already I found myself bristling at the prospect of a rival. I reminded myself sternly that I was a Dominican friar; hardly in a position to be her suitor, even if I were the son of a baron.

'I don't want to marry anyone.' Her lip curled. 'I want to be a doctor.'

'Of what?'

'Medicine. What else?'

'But—' Again, I found all possible responses inadequate. 'You're—'

'A woman?' She smiled again, and her eyes glittered. 'Yes, I had noticed. That is something of a difficulty when it comes to medical school. One day it will be accepted for women to become physicians, I'm sure of it. Until then, I have no choice but to join a convent.'

I stared. 'You want to become a *nun*?'

She shrugged. 'Not especially. But I can't see that it would be worse than marrying some fifty-year-old fool with bad breath just because he has a title, and then pushing out his children for the next fifteen years until one of them kills me in the process. Besides, some of the religious orders allow their women quite a lot of liberty to study. I couldn't qualify as a doctor, obviously, but I could practise as one within the convent, if I learned the skills.'

'But wouldn't you miss—' I had been led to believe that women of good birth aspired to marriage and motherhood as their highest calling. I had never heard a woman express the same ambitions for learning as a man, and I was nonplussed. 'Freedom?' I finished lamely.

She let out a scathing laugh. 'How much freedom do you think I have now? Why did you join a religious order, then, if you see it as such a prison?'

'To study,' I admitted. 'But I would never have chosen the religious life if I came from a family like yours.'

'If you came from a family like mine,' she said, enunciating each word carefully, as if I were slow of understanding, 'and you were the eldest daughter of the eldest son, you would not have even the freedom to choose your own husband. You would be obliged to marry well, for the family's sake.' She rolled her eyes. 'You should understand me better than anyone. You had to take the religious life in order to study because you lack money, and I'll be forced to do the same because I lack a cock. So we are in the same boat.'

I had never met a well-born lady who talked like the girls at the Cerriglio; I hardly knew what to make of her.

'All the same,' I said, aiming for gallantry, 'it would be a terrible waste for you to take the veil.'

'Of what? My mind?' Her expression hardened, and I saw, too late, that what I had intended as a compliment had in fact had the opposite effect.

'You mean of my beauty,' she said, before I could stammer out an answer. 'Don't worry, my mother says the same, as if that is my only worth. You think, I suppose, that it would be a good service to society if all the plain and ugly women shut themselves up in a nunnery, but quite wrong to deprive men of the pretty ones? You are not the first man to express that opinion.'

'I didn't mean—' I looked down at my hands on the table. I was considered skilled at debate among my fellow Dominicans, but I could barely construct a sentence in my defence with this girl.

She glared at me for a moment longer, before relenting.

'How would you feel if someone said you were too hand-some to waste on the Dominicans?'

'It would depend who said it,' I replied, feeling bolder. 'I might feel flattered – if you said so, for instance.'

She folded her arms across her chest and allowed a reluctant smile. 'No one would ever say that to a man, anyway, because a man is allowed to be more than just his face. I'm sure no one assumes that, because you are handsome, you are not also capable of your own thoughts.' She sighed. 'Since I was a little girl, I have watched the women around me and concluded that being a wife and mother would be a waste of my mind, and that would be a greater ingratitude to God for His gifts. I would far rather learn how to deliver a baby than have one myself.'

'You wouldn't get much practice at that in a nunnery,' I said.

She raised a sardonic eyebrow, in a way that reminded me of her uncle. 'You'd be surprised,' she replied. 'This is Naples, after all.'

In that windowless room with Fiammetta, I lost track of time passing. Porta's pile of books sat ignored at my elbow as we talked for what must have been two hours, and I forgot entirely the need to return in time for vespers. I learned some valuable lessons about how to talk to women that afternoon; the more I tried to impress her with my learning and achievements, the more I seemed to elicit a faint smile that hovered between mockery and indulgence. But when I asked about her reading and her interest in medicine, she grew animated; her eyes lit up, her gestures became dramatic, and all her careful poise dropped away as she told me of her frustration at the way the female body and its complaints were dismissed as the business of wise-women and midwives, not the proper province of educated male doctors. She wanted to change this, she said; only think how many lives might be saved and suffering spared if physicians better understood women! Her uncle Giambattista had promised that if he ever had the fortune to anatomise a female corpse, he would allow her to be present. I was amazed that any woman would actively wish to participate in such a gruesome business, but I could not tell her of my own experience in this area; instead I smiled and nodded, which she took for approval of her ambition. The room had grown darker around us as the lamps burned low; finally, one of them guttered out and I jumped up, seized with a sudden panic about the time. She came to stand in front of me, took my hands in hers and placed them either side of her face.

'You have still not guessed correctly what animal my uncle declares me to be,' she said, with a coy smile. 'You must read my face again, properly this time.'

'I do not know the science,' I whispered. Her mouth was mere inches from mine; I could feel her breath on my lips.

'Then you will have to learn by practice,' she said, holding my gaze. So I traced my fingertips gently over her cheeks, her brow, her lips, as she closed her eyes. She must have felt my hands trembling. I had almost summoned the courage to lean in and kiss her, when we heard the click of the secret door and sprang apart. The shelf swung open in a sudden flood of sunlight. Ercole stood in the doorway.

'Pardon me, my lady – I didn't realise you were here.' His face was impassive, though I suspected he had known very well that Fiammetta was in the library. 'I came to see if you needed fresh lamps, sir. And also to let you know that it is almost six o'clock. I have no wish to send you away, but I thought you might have obligations, and it would be best if the Dominicans did not send someone to find you.'

He set the new lamps on the table and took away those that had almost burned out, bowing discreetly to us as he did so. 'I will wait for you outside.'

I turned to Fiammetta in alarm as the door closed behind him. 'I hope he won't tell your uncle that there was anything improper—' I began.

She laughed. 'Honestly, you must relax, wolfhound. My uncle wouldn't care. I told you he keeps an unconventional house. Ercole knows how to turn a blind eye too – and I am not just talking about secret societies of *great learned men*.' She said the last three words in an affected voice, in case I was in any doubt about what she thought of that concept. 'I can see you need further lessons in the art of physiognomonics. Come back tomorrow – my uncle is away for the next couple of days in Capodimonte, and I get bored with no one to talk to.'

'What is he doing there?' I asked, intrigued. He had mentioned research, but there was nothing on the hill of Capodimonte, as far as I knew, except a great forest, and Porta did not strike me as a man dedicated to hunting.

'Experiments, as always. Something to do with caves. He had the servants rounding up stray dogs before he left.' She reached into the shelf and pulled the lever. 'Until tomorrow, wolfhound.'

*

I had missed the evening meal, and my absence had been noted. Gennaro came to find me in the cloister before compline, furious.

'The prior was asking for you – I had to tell him I had sent you to our illustrious patient from last night with an emergency remedy,' he hissed, shaking me by the shoulder. 'Listen, I don't care how much time you spend in Vomero, but get yourself back here for the offices so I don't have to lie for you. The last thing we want is anyone investigating your disappearances. The Academy has placed great trust in you, Bruno, and you need to repay it with discretion, not by drawing attention to yourself.'

I bowed my head, chastened.

'I'm sorry. Will you excuse me my duties in the infirmary tomorrow afternoon, though?'

He twisted his mouth in disapproval, but gave a reluctant nod. 'If you swear you will be back for vespers.'

I was so grateful I clasped him by the shoulders and kissed him on both cheeks, just as Raffaele passed by on the other side of the cloister, noting us with a wry look. I decided not to tell Gennaro of his threats, in case the infirmarian forbade me from visiting Porta's villa. All through the service of compline, I was aware of Raffaele's eyes on me, his smirking and raised eyebrows. He walked close behind me when we left the church, all the way to the dormitory. At the door of my cell, I turned abruptly.

'What do you want?'

'Mind your manners, little soldier. I merely wanted to wish you pleasant dreams. You must be very tired.'

I looked at him. What was he insinuating? Did he know that I had walked to Vomero and back, or was it a reference to my being out the night before? My best course, as always, was not to rise to it.

'Thank you, Brother. The same to you.' I slammed the door

in his face. Let him sit on the landing all night watching my cell; there would be nothing for him to see.

I should have been more careful, of course. I should have heeded Gennaro's warning, or taken Raffaele's spite seriously. But all I could think about was seeing Fiammetta again. The next day, as soon as the midday meal was over, I made my way to the side gate, meaning to slip out unseen, but I was intercepted by my friend Paolo da Rimini, racing up behind me with his habit hoicked above his knees as he ran.

'Hey!' His freckled face creased with mock-hurt. 'Were you going without me?'

'*Merda*. Sorry.' I realised, belatedly, that we had a lesson with our Hebrew tutor that afternoon at the Augustinian convent of San Giovanni a Carbonara in the east of the city. Those of us studying for our theology degrees were sent for tuition with the leading experts in different disciplines at other religious houses in the city, to broaden our knowledge. 'Listen, I have to go somewhere. Can you make an excuse for me? Tell him I'm ill.'

Paolo frowned. It was not unusual for any of us to skip our lessons now and again, using our licence to leave the convent as a cover for more entertaining pursuits, but I had never played truant without Paolo; he and I had been novices together, looked out for one another, lied our way out of trouble for each other countless times. When I was accused of blasphemy by another novice for mocking his terrible poem about the Virgin, it was Paolo who defended me to the prior with such passionate testimony to my pious devotion that the matter had been dropped. I knew he would do anything for me, and I hated having to lie to him.

'You've been elusive these past couple of days,' he said, trying not to sound wounded. 'I called for you the other night, but you weren't in your cell, and you weren't at the

102

Cerriglio either. And yesterday afternoon you vanished. Is it some business to do with Gennaro?'

I hesitated. I trusted Paolo implicitly, but the Academy was not my secret to confide, and I could not risk him guessing at anything to do with it.

'No. It's . . .' I leaned in closer and whispered. 'A woman.'

His eyes lit up and he slapped my arm lightly. 'You sly dog! You could have told me. A courtesan, is she?'

I shook my head. 'I can't say. You understand.'

His expression grew solemn. 'Ah. She's married.'

'Exactly. Her husband is away this afternoon.'

'Well.' He tilted his head to one side and grinned. 'All right for some. I'll get you out of Hebrew this time if you come for a drink tonight and tell me all the details.'

I half-ran the whole way uphill to Vomero. Ercole let me in with barely a word and led me to the library. She was waiting for me in the secret reading room, dressed in a white linen gown with a loose, jewelled girdle, her hair tied back with a blue ribbon. She greeted me with a warm smile, and nodded towards the entrance. 'I've told Ercole I will call him if we need anything,' she said, with a meaningful look. 'He understands that we would prefer to study undisturbed.'

'What are you reading?' I gestured to the book open on the table.

'This is my uncle's encyclopaedia – have you not seen it?' She offered the volume; I opened it to the frontispiece and read the title: *Magia Naturalis*. Beneath the author's name was a drawing of a lynx. That explained why he had thought I was trying to flatter him.

'We are not allowed such things,' I said, turning the pages in wonder. 'But – he said he was working on an encyclopaedia of natural magic – I didn't realise he had already written one.'

'He published this ten years ago, when he was not yet twenty-five,' she said, her pride evident in her voice. 'There are editions in five different countries. Now he means to expand it from four volumes to twenty. But he was questioned by the Inquisition about some of the contents – he will have to be more careful this time.'

It was hard to tear myself away from Porta's book; I would have given much to spend an afternoon immersed in it, not least to discover what the Inquisition had found to object to; the thought that Porta had already attracted their attention troubled me. But Fiammetta had her bright, mischievous eyes fixed on me, a secret smile playing around her lips, and the look she gave me suggested that reading was not her first priority that day.

We did not talk of medicine and natural magic. I put my hands to her face again, guessed a falcon, a dolphin, a doe – any animal I hoped might possess sufficient grace and beauty not to insult her. It was all prelude to the inevitable. Laughing, she shook her head at each suggestion, and then she kissed me. Her skin smelled of rosewater and her mouth tasted faintly of salt. She wrapped her fingers in my hair and arched her head back to let me kiss her throat, and I wondered if she had done this before, with other protégés of her uncle, or if some quality in me had proven irresistible.

She let me unlace her bodice and kiss her small breasts, but she could not let me take her virginity, she explained candidly, since that was all she had to barter with over her future. Without it, she would be worth considerably less to the nuns or to a prospective husband, but there were other things we might do to bring each other pleasure. I did not ask how she knew of such matters. Instead, I let her show me, and I learned much in that hot, windowless library as the lamps burned low. It was not my first time with a woman, but my previous attempts had been rushed, clumsy affairs

104

by comparison. Fiammetta taught me to take my time, as well as introducing me to new aspects of the female anatomy that I could not have learned from any textbook. If I felt a twinge of guilt, it was only over the books Porta had set out for me, abandoned on the table as I explored other avenues of forbidden knowledge.

'I must not miss vespers this evening,' I whispered afterwards, as we lay on the Turkish carpet, breathing hard, sweat slick on our skin in the lamplight. 'There's enough suspicion of me already – I can't lead the Dominicans to your uncle.'

'Go, then,' she said, leaning forward to gently bite my lower lip. 'But come back tomorrow.'

I promised I would, though that evening I scrambled into vespers a minute after the prayers had started; my late arrival occasioned a stern glare from the prior over the rim of his lectern, a furious scowl from Gennaro and a narrowed, knowing look from Raffaele. But the next day, giddy and reckless with desire, I returned to Vomero. Fiammetta met me herself at the door in the cliff, and led me through the underground tunnels to a different exit, through a grotto in the gardens.

'I thought it might be pleasant to be outside,' she said, slipping her arm through mine as she led me along a path through a grove of lemon trees, away from the villa. I darted an anxious glance over my shoulder.

'Where is Ercole?'

'Indoors, I expect. He won't bother us.'

'You're sure he won't say anything to your uncle?' I had the impression that, beneath his veneer of spotless civility, Ercole disapproved of me, and I could not help but worry that my place in the Academy might be at risk if Porta thought I had taken advantage of his generosity to despoil his niece. I did not want to have to choose between them.

Fiammetta laughed, but there was a note of melancholy

in it. 'I told you, my uncle would not interfere in my business unless he thought I was in danger. This' – she stretched out her hand to encompass the villa and its extensive grounds – 'is the only place I am really free. No one expects anything of me. My uncle treats me as a person, not an ornament to be traded, or an inconvenience to be dealt with. But, alas, he returns tomorrow.'

'You seem sad. You are not looking forward to seeing him?'

She sighed. We had reached a bower of tangled vines that formed a shady arch with a stone bench beneath; she motioned me to sit.

'I am, of course. I miss his company. But the day before he left, a letter arrived from my father. I have been in Naples three weeks – my father says he has indulged my games long enough, and I must return home or he will come to fetch me. Uncle Giambattista said he would reply when he came back from Capodimonte.' She made a face. 'He will not throw me out, but he doesn't want to antagonise his brother. I have known all this week that I must face my choice about whether to join a convent or marry a disgusting old man.' She reached for my hand and twined her fingers with mine. 'And then you appeared.'

I did not know how to take this. 'So I am, what? A rebellion? A test, to see if you would miss the temptations of the flesh?'

She shook her head. 'No, neither. Or perhaps both. I saw you come in with Ercole that first day. I liked the look of you, so I followed you to the library. I suppose I was feeling angry, and reckless – I thought if I must become a prisoner of one kind or another, I might at least enjoy my last days of liberty. Does that shock you?'

'No . . .' If I sounded uncertain, it was because I had never heard a woman talk of desire as something she might own

106

and act on. The girls at the Cerriglio were loud and brash and full of lewd jokes, but it was all commerce to them. As a youth, the wisdom I had gleaned from my father was that men desired and women resisted; if you wanted something from them, you would have to learn to cajole and persuade to get past their natural aversion to the act. Later, when I joined the Dominicans, I was told that women were the instruments of Satan, inflamed with lust and determined to lure men away from reason and into sin. It had never occurred to me that a young woman might see a man and want him, purely for her own pleasure. 'But you are saying I could have been any one of your uncle's associates who happened to cross your path?'

She smiled. 'Not at all. Have you *seen* most of my uncle's associates?' She laid her head on my shoulder. 'I wish we could go on like this for ever. Sometimes I think all I ask from life is to carry on living here, working as my uncle's assistant. That would be enough to make me happy – as long as you came to visit.' She squeezed my hand. 'I know Giambattista would agree to it – he likes the company. But my father would never countenance such a thing.'

'Your uncle has no wife or family?' I had noted on all my visits how quiet the villa seemed, for such a large place, with few servants to be seen apart from the faithful Ercole. Fiammetta gave me a sidelong look.

'I don't think finding a wife has ever been of much interest to my uncle.'

'Ah.' I nodded, taking her meaning.

'My father urges him to, for convention's sake. There is enough malicious talk about Giambattista as it is.'

'Why, what is said of him?'

'You must know? That he is a magician, that he dabbles in witchcraft and conjures spirits, that he is hostile to the Spanish. None of that does my father's position any good.

107

But Giambattista says he will not make some poor woman's life a misery to spare his brother from gossip. People will say what they want, regardless. The great good fortune of being the second son, he says, is that he is not obliged to fill the world with more della Portas.' She laughed, and settled comfortably against me.

'You are fond of him,' I murmured into her hair, smiling.

'He is the best of men.' She twisted her head to kiss my neck. 'And you are the best of men outside my own family. Let's pretend we can go on like this indefinitely.' She guided my hand beneath her skirts and tipped her head back as I began to move my fingers. An instant later she snapped upright, her eyes open, casting wildly around.

'What was that?'

I had heard nothing, but her fear made me tense and strain to listen.

'There was a noise, from the trees over there.' She pointed. 'Go and look.'

Obediently, I stood and surveyed what I could see of the terrace. I caught a faint rustling from the undergrowth along the boundary wall, but could see nothing amiss.

'A bird in the bushes, probably. Nothing to worry about.' I sat beside her and attempted to resume, but the disturbance had made her skittish.

'You're sure no one followed you here?'

'Of course not. I would have noticed.' But her words planted a seed of anxiety. *Would* I have noticed? I had been in such a rush to see her – perhaps I had not watched as carefully as I should when I left San Domenico, or on the road out of the city. Still, I could not believe I had been so oblivious that anyone could have followed me all the way to Vomero without my being aware of it.

She seemed to accept my protestations and returned to my arms, but we both remained a little distracted, alert to any unexpected sound and not quite so abandoned to our pleasures as we had been the day before. I found myself wishing we had stayed in the privacy of the secret library, especially since this might be our last afternoon together. When the time came to leave, I felt oddly melancholic, conscious that I had not been the liveliest company. Fiammetta showed me out of a gate in the garden wall that opened on to the road.

'Forgive me,' she said, as if reading my thoughts. 'My mind was elsewhere today, it was not your fault. I was jumping at shadows – I even started to fear that my father had sent someone to spy on me and report back to him – isn't that absurd? I'm sorry. Will you come again tomorrow?'

'Won't your uncle be back?'

'If you come a little earlier, to this gate, we might steal an hour together to say goodbye before he arrives. If he sees you, he will want to tell you all about his caves and we would never get a moment of privacy. Say you will?'

How could I refuse her? I covered her face with kisses and slipped out of the garden into the shining heat of late afternoon. Several times on the road back to the city, I stopped, reaching for my knife, convinced I had heard footsteps behind me, but each time it was only a labourer or a trader leading a donkey; I sheathed the knife quickly and muttered a blessing as they passed. I congratulated myself on arriving in good time for vespers, though my relief was short-lived; Raffaele came into the church immediately after me and seated himself on the opposite side of the nave, so that he could stare at me throughout the service. His look was one of such undisguised triumph, like a fox in a henhouse, that I began to fear he had found out my secret.

But he said nothing, and by the next day I had persuaded myself that I had been worrying unduly; Raffaele simply enjoyed tormenting me. I decided to skip the midday meal;

I asked Paolo to tell the prior I was taking an extra Hebrew tutorial across town. This would be my last visit to Porta's villa, I told myself, at least for Fiammetta's sake; after today, I could leave it a while until any suspicion about my absences had been forgotten, but I was determined not to disappoint her. It was a day of fierce heat; I had asked for a skin of fresh water from the kitchen, which I slung by a leather strap around my chest, and I had almost reached the side gate in the gardens when the prior stepped out from among the trees and greeted me with a forbidding smile, his hands folded into the sleeves of his robe. Behind him stood two of the convent servants, tall, strong young men who worked in the grounds. I knew then that I was discovered.

'You are heading the wrong way for the refectory, Fra Giordano,' the prior said, pleasantly.

'I have been obliged to move my lesson at San Giovanni to an earlier hour, Most Reverend Prior. I had arranged to send my apologies.' I bowed.

'You know that you are obliged to seek permission in advance if you wish to miss mealtimes or services,' he said, in the same light tone. 'You are making quite a habit of failing to do so.' He nodded to the water-carrier. 'You seem prepared for a longer journey.'

'It's a hot day, Most Reverend Prior. I did not want to arrive with my throat parched and unable to speak.'

'Hmm. Walk with me, Fra Giordano.'

It was an order, not a request. He set off back towards the cloisters, and I had no choice but to fall into step beside him. The two burly servants followed.

'As you know, since you are one of our most promising scholars, I have been pleased to encourage your theological studies with the best masters in the city, in the belief that your achievements will bring greater glory to San Domenico.

But it has been brought to my attention that you have been abusing the liberty we give you.'

I did not reply. He meant that someone had informed him of my absences, and that could only have been Raffaele. I wondered how much either of them thought they knew. The prior placed a hand on my shoulder.

'As Dominicans, we do not believe that men of God should be shut off from society, and for this reason I do not keep a closed order. But we need to cultivate a strong will to be *in* the world, yet not *of* it. I understand how easy it is for a young man to be dazzled by the distractions of a city such as Naples. And so I feel that, to keep you on the correct path, a period of silent prayer and penitence is in order. After that, I will consider whether your devotion is strong enough to allow you to leave the convent.'

'No, please, Most Reverend Prior – I assure you, my faith and my will are as solid as Mount Vesuvius—'

He gave me a shrewd look, as if judging whether I was being facetious. 'The most volatile mountain in the kingdom, you mean?'

'That was a bad example. You may trust me, I swear – I have no interest in the city's temptations, only I must not be late for my tutorial—'

He had heard the note of panic in my voice; his grip on my shoulder tightened. 'Silent prayer and penitence, Fra Giordano. Humble yourself before Our Lord, and then you may make your confession.'

He led me into the shadow of the cloister, towards the Oratory. Silent prayer and penitence was the prior's euphemism for detention. The Oratory was a cell, barely large enough to be called a chapel, with no windows save a narrow slit high up in the wall, no furnishings except a crucifix and an altar, and a door that, once locked, could not be opened from the inside. It was, in effect, a prison, and a period of

111

solitude in that dismal place, with no food, was intended to encourage a wayward friar away from thoughts of disobedience.

'I implore you – I will take my punishment as you command, Most Reverend Prior – only let me start it this evening. Don't make me miss my tutorial this afternoon – it's very important—'

He unlocked the heavy door of the Oratory, and I could see by his expression that my protestations were only making him more suspicious.

'Prayer is no punishment, Fra Giordano – unless you count it a hardship and not a blessing to spend time undistracted in the presence of Our Lord. Do you?'

'No.'

'I thought not. I'm sure with a mind as sharp as yours, it will not take you long to catch up on whatever you have missed in your lesson today.' He pushed open the door and held it for me. I glanced back; his enforcers blocked the path. I had only two choices: I could go inside, or I could be forced in with a punch to the gut.

I bowed to the prior as I ducked through the low doorway into the stale air of the Oratory. It smelled of piss from the last disobedient wretch incarcerated here. 'How long?' I asked, as he shut me in. There was a grille in the door with a panel that could be opened to communicate with the prisoner. His bony face appeared in the gap.

'Until you have a better sense of your duty, my son,' he said, with a grimace. 'But overnight, I think. *Pax tecum.*' The panel slid shut.

I waited until I heard the key turn, and cursed him colourfully under my breath. A bar of light slanted across the top of the wall from the tiny window. The painted Christ above the altar looked reproachfully at me from beneath his thorny brow.

'Come on, then,' I muttered to him, 'you're the one who

knows how to get out of sealed caves. What's your trick?' He did not grant me an epiphany. I sat on the floor with my back against the altar to avoid his gaze, furious with myself for getting caught. Not only had I ruined my last chance to see Fiammetta, but I would be leaving her with the impression that I was the kind of man to abandon a girl with no explanation. I had enough experience of women to know that they did not respond well to being slighted; I feared that if she was upset or angry, she might speak ill of me to her uncle when he returned, and that could jeopardise my place in the Academy, or my chance of seeing his secret library again.

After I had passed ten minutes in futile recrimination, the panel in the door opened. I whipped around, hoping the prior had changed his mind, but instead I saw Raffaele's face through the grille.

'Come here,' he said, imperious as ever. Reluctantly, I moved closer. 'You're much safer in there, Bruno,' he said, unable to keep the delight from his expression. 'That road to Vomero can be very dangerous. And the della Porta place even more so – you know he practises black magic? Well, of course you do. That's why you go there, isn't it? I'm doing you a favour, Brother, protecting your reputation.'

I was tempted to spit in his face, but restrained myself; I did not want to make things any worse. So he had followed me after all; this, too, was the result of my own stupidity.

'Did you tell the prior I was there?'

The smile curved like a knife. 'Not yet. I'm deciding what to do with that information. It's a shame you won't be able to meet your little vixen, though. Think of her there, all hot and ready, waiting for a friar to satisfy her filthy wanton appetites. I wouldn't like her to be disappointed, so I must be on my way. Don't let me interrupt your devotions.' He made to slide the panel shut.

'Don't even think about going near her,' I hissed, through my teeth. 'Or God help me, I will kill you.'

He laughed. 'Don't you think the girl would be better served by a man who is her equal in status? I'm sure your peasant rutting is all very well, but she'd probably appreciate a little finesse.'

I slammed my hand against the bars. 'I'm warning you—'

'What will you do? Fell me with one of Porta's magic spells?' He lolled against the door, as if the whole business was a tremendous joke. 'Keep your voice down, Bruno – we don't want the prior knowing you've been spending your time with that sodomite and his heretical friends, do we? The Inquisition might want a word if they knew. So let's keep that between ourselves until I've shown the girl what a man of quality can do for her.'

I was still cursing uselessly after him as he shut the window. I shouted myself hoarse, but no one came; I paced the cell, impotently furious, even punching the door at one point, though I quickly realised that crippling myself would not help Fiammetta. I thought of her, trustingly waiting for me at the garden gate. Raffaele must have followed me the day before and spied on us; the thought made my skin crawl. She would open the gate to him, in that deserted part of the gardens; she would see a figure in a Dominican's robe, and open her arms . . . She would almost certainly have told the few servants to stay away, so we could be private. No one would hear her protests as he pushed her to the ground beneath the lemon trees . . .

I had worked myself into a frenzy by the time the panel was opened a second time. To my amazement and relief, I saw Paolo's anxious eyes through the grille. I flung myself against the window like a caged animal, so that he stepped back in alarm, even though the door was between us.

'Thank *God*. How did you know I was here?'

114

He made a face. 'I presented your apologies to the prior at dinner, as you asked. He thanked me, and said he was well aware of your *extramural activities*, as he put it. His tone made me realise you'd been discovered. And now he has me marked as your accomplice. Not for the first time.'

'Sorry. I'll make it up to you. Listen, I really need you to get me out of here.'

He held up his hands. 'I brought you a bread roll and some figs – that's the limit of what I can offer. How could I get the key – the prior has it on a ring at his belt.'

'There's a spare. He keeps it in a cupboard in his office – if you wait until he's in church for nones, you could slip in and borrow it.'

He shook his head, laughing. '*Madonna porca*, Bruno – I'm already in trouble for you, and now you ask me to miss the service, break into the prior's office, steal a key and help you escape punishment? They will kick me out when we're caught, and you know what that means – I'll be sent to some godforsaken monastery at the other end of the kingdom to do menial work for the rest of my miserable life. Can't you just take your punishment this time? It's only till the morning – I'll bring you food.'

'It's not that.' I hesitated. 'It's the woman I told you about. I'm supposed to meet her this afternoon, up in Vomero. Raffaele made sure I got locked up so he could go there instead. I'm afraid he's going to force her.'

'Oh.' His eyes darkened; he despised Raffaele as much as I did. 'Well – that's different. That entitled little prick. Could you get there in time to stop him?'

'I don't know. I think he's already left – I can only try, as long as you help me.'

He turned to look across the cloister at the clock on the wall. 'Ten minutes till nones. I'll do what I can. You owe me.'

115

A half-hour passed. I tried to measure time by reciting psalms, but I was too agitated. What was keeping him? When at last I heard a key in the lock, I half-expected to find the prior outside, ready to throw Paolo in with me; instead I saw my friend, furtive in the doorway, hurrying me out.

'You're in luck,' he whispered, casting his eyes from left to right to make sure no one was watching. 'The prior has gone out to a meeting across town. I need to get this key back before anyone notices I am not in church. Hurry – I hope you're in time.'

'Lock that behind me,' I said, kissing him on both cheeks. 'Let them think I can walk through walls. You have my undying devotion.'

I raced off to the stables, where I sought out the boy who had provided Gennaro with the horse the other night, and told him that the infirmarian had sent me. He stammered something about needing permission; I insisted it was an emergency, I was acting on Fra Gennaro's instructions, and lunged at the first horse I could see. Cowed, he saddled it for me and I had spurred it on in a cloud of dust before he had even fully opened the gate. I knew the boy would be punished, Gennaro would be furious with me, and Paolo would also find himself in serious trouble when my flight was discovered. But none of that seemed as urgent as the need to stop Raffaele thinking he could do what he liked with Fiammetta.

I made the journey to Vomero in half the time on horseback, urging the poor beast around sharp corners and up the hill at breakneck pace, several times almost colliding with carts coming down to the city, earning furious curses and fist-shaking from those I nearly trampled. When I reached Porta's villa, I hammered on the garden gate until my knuckles bled, but there was no response. I strained to listen, but could hear no sound of struggle, or protest. Perhaps he had dragged her to some remote part of the grounds – or perhaps I was so late that he had already finished his business with her and left. But then, I reasoned, I would have seen him on the road here. I tethered the horse to a tree, knotted my habit above my knees and shinned up the wall, dropping down the other side.

The terrace was deserted. I scoured the ground around the gate for any sign of violence, but the earth was baked hard from weeks without rain, and the marks in the dust could have been anything. I stood, helplessly looking around, when my eye was drawn by a splash of colour. I bent and found the blue ribbon from Fiammetta's hair caught in the grass at the foot of a tree. Had she dropped it there as a sign to me? Or had it been torn from her? I set off along the path through the lemon grove, my heart pounding in my throat. Ahead, the villa's tiled roof was visible over the trees, and eventually I found my way to the grotto where we had emerged from the underground chambers the day before. I tried the entrance and was surprised to find it unlocked. But once below ground, I realised I had lost my way; the interlinking passageways all looked the same, and I had been too distracted by Fiammetta the last time to have properly mapped it in my mind. I navigated by instinct, taking a left branch and then a right, until I heard footsteps coming the other way; I was reaching into my habit for my knife, when Ercole rounded the corner with what looked like a winding sheet in his arms.

'Ah. Good afternoon, sir.' He seemed entirely unruffled to find me there. 'You were not expected today, I don't think?'

'I—' I stared at him. He was impossible to read. Surely he knew I was meeting Fiammetta, that I had been all week? 'Fiammetta?' I asked, too anxious to dissemble. 'Is she—'

He dipped his head. 'The lady Fiammetta is quite well. But her father has sent servants to accompany her back to Vico

Equense. She is packing for the journey and I'm afraid is unable to receive visitors today.'

I could fathom nothing from his expressionless face. I wanted to shake him.

'But she's not – he didn't hurt her?'

His eyebrow raised a quarter-inch. 'Who, sir?'

'A man – you didn't see him? A Dominican?' I gestured to my own habit, as if he might not know how to recognise one.

'There have been no Dominicans here today, sir, except yourself. But I must tell you, my master thinks it would be wise if no one from your order is seen here for the next while. He sends his apologies, and trusts that you will understand the need for discretion.'

'He is back, then? From Capodimonte?'

Ercole gave a patient smile. 'I'm afraid I must show you out now, sir, we're extremely busy.' He took me gently but firmly by the elbow and steered me along the passage until we reached the meeting chamber of the Academy.

'You promise me Fiammetta is unharmed?' I said, as he took me to the door.

'I assure you, sir, no one in this house would allow a hair on her head to be touched. We are all extremely vigilant where she is concerned.' He glanced down at my hands as he said this. If he noticed the ribbon I had wound tight around my finger, he did not mention it.

'I can't say goodbye to her?' I knew what his answer would be, but I had to try.

He bowed his head in apology. 'Best not. She will understand. We will see you here again before too long, sir, I'm sure of it,' he added, as he opened the door in the cliff and left me there in the road, like Adam shut out of Paradise, unable to make sense of what had happened.

*

The stable boy told me no one except the head groom had noticed the horse missing, and he had managed to spin a tale that was more or less believed; I promised I would give him money if he kept his mouth shut. I slipped through the grounds unseen and rushed straight up the stairs to the infirmary. Gennaro looked up from the bedside of an elderly brother and swore vehemently at the sight of me.

'I thought you were locked up?'

'I am. I was. I need you to put me to bed here and tell the prior that when you came to bring me water, I was running such a fever you feared for my life, so you made the decision to countermand his authority and bring me here for treatment.'

'*Dio cane*, I will give you reason to fear for your life if you keep putting me in this position. What has happened now?'

I told him I would explain everything in due course, but I could not let Paolo get into trouble for letting me out. He shook his head and muttered at me, but pointed me to an empty bed at the far end of a row. 'As long as you have not endangered the Academy?' he asked, in a low voice, as he bent and tucked a sheet around me. I hung my head.

'Raffaele knows I've been going to Vomero, to della Porta's house,' I whispered in his ear. 'He says he hasn't told anyone, but I don't know if I believe him. And if he hasn't yet, he certainly will after today.'

'What happened today?'

'I don't know exactly. But I think he was thwarted, and that will make him all the hotter for revenge.'

He straightened up and folded his arms, his eyes cold with fury. 'Giambattista was right,' he said, through his teeth. 'You are too young and foolish to be trusted with something like the Academy, for all your brilliance. I was the one who persuaded them to accept you. Now your recklessness will bring us all to ruin.'

I called after him, but he strode away. I passed a wretched few hours, tormented by unanswered questions. I knew I had put Fiammetta in danger, exposed the Academy, and left Gennaro, Paolo and the stable boy to be punished for my carelessness. Late in the evening, I heard the prior's voice; he and Gennaro argued outside the door of the infirmary, though I could not hear what they were saying. I half-opened my eyes to find the prior standing over my bed, and feigned delirium; I heard Gennaro assuring him that my condition was serious, and though I guessed he trusted neither of us, he left without insisting I be moved. When he had gone, Gennaro sat heavily on the edge of my bed, with an air of defeat that was unlike him.

'Pompous old fool,' I said, propping myself up on my elbow. I expected Gennaro to agree; instead, he reached out as if by reflex and cuffed me around the head with the back of his hand.

'*Ow*! Well, he is.'

'Pompous he may be,' he said, 'but he is no fool. He's a very shrewd politician. You can't see it because you're twenty and all you can think about is where to put your rod next. You should know that the Spanish would love to get rid of our prior and replace him with someone more biddable, and your antics may just have given them the excuse.'

I sat back, stung. I had never heard such quiet anger in his voice. 'Why do they want to get rid of him?'

He sighed. 'Do you really not know this? The Spanish want to introduce their version of the Inquisition here, with their own people. San Domenico has been instrumental in resisting that, largely thanks to our prior.'

I grunted. 'Only because he doesn't want to give up the power that comes with appointing Inquisitors himself.'

'Partly that,' Gennaro conceded, 'but it's also because he has a sense of justice. The Spanish Inquisition makes our

120

Neapolitan version look positively forgiving. Our law at least requires two witnesses to any charge of heresy – under the Spanish Inquisition, anyone can be arrested and interrogated on the basis of a single accusation. Do you understand what that would mean for someone like Porta? Or you, or me? Or anyone whose neighbour or jealous wife has a grudge against him? One vindictive accusation, and any of us could be tortured until we confess to every crime under the sun.' He passed a hand over his forehead; I could see his perspiration gleaming in the candlelight. 'If Raffaele goes to his father, who is in the pocket of the viceroy, with reports that friars from San Domenico are close associates of Giambattista della Porta, they could use that to depose the prior and put in one of their own puppets. Then we could all say goodbye to the limited freedom we enjoy now.'

'I'm sorry,' I said, chastened. 'I didn't know.'

'No. You didn't think. You need to open your eyes, Bruno. Everything is political, whether you like it or not. Now – drink this.'

That night, as if by some divine joke, I did develop a strange fever, which left me drifting in and out of troubled dreams for hours. At one point, I thought Paolo was sitting beside my bed, saying something about Raffaele disappearing; later, I opened my eyes to see Gennaro laying a cold cloth on my head, telling me I had been shouting in my delirium. By the time the fever broke, I had no idea how many days had passed.

'You're back with us, are you?' Gennaro said, tipping a cup of cold water to my lips. 'You've been sick for two days. You've missed all the drama.'

I narrowed my eyes at him. 'Did you give me a dose of poison?'

He didn't answer; only crossed to the window and stood with his back to me. The infirmary was empty apart from one elderly brother at the far end, snoring like the beginnings of an earth tremor.

'What drama?' I asked. 'Was Paolo here? He said something about Raffaele—'

'Raffaele is dead,' Gennaro said, not turning around.

'What?' I scrambled to sit up. 'How?'

'No one knows. Sometimes God calls His servants home in the flower of their youth. Not for us to question His ways. Pray for your brother's soul, Bruno.'

Raffaele had been found at dawn, two days earlier, lying beneath the shrine of Santa Maria delle Grazie in Capodimonte, an unlit candle in his hands. The two widows who had come to pray thought he was asleep at first, he looked so peaceful; there was not a mark on his body, except three faint scratches on his cheek, which might have been made by an animal. When his corpse was brought back to the city, Gennaro examined him and found nothing to suggest how he had died, certainly no evidence of foul play or assault. Raffaele's father, Don Umberto, mistrusting the Dominicans, had his own private physician carry out a further examination of the body, but he too could see no obvious explanation. Gennaro offered to anatomise him, in order to confirm or deny fears of poisoning, but Don Umberto was a superstitious man and could not countenance the thought of his son being butchered before burial, even if he was only a bastard.

It was concluded, therefore, that Fra Raffaele da Monte, while making a pilgrimage to offer his devotions to Our Lady, had been taken by some unexplained seizure or heat-stroke, may God have mercy on his soul. Inevitably, there were rumours of witchcraft, but no one seemed to know quite where to direct them. Raffaele's friends knew, of course, that he had made me his enemy, but it was also well known that I had been laid up in the infirmary with a severe fever at the time, so how could I have any connection with his death? I waited, sick with anxiety, for questions, but after a week had passed and Raffaele had been buried, with a great show of mourning, I gradually allowed myself to believe that he had told the truth about not mentioning Vomero to anyone.

I was careful, for a while. I observed the rules, stayed in my cell at night, turned up punctually for the holy offices and applied myself diligently to my studies and my duties; I gave no one reason to criticise me. But I felt the prior's eyes on me in church and in the refectory, as if he were weighing me up. I wondered if he felt Raffaele's death had liberated him, or compromised his position further, but I could not ask, and I was relieved when he did not mention the dead man to me. But as September passed into October, despite everything, a murk of suspicion about Raffaele's death hung in the air of San Domenico like the autumnal mists off the bay, and seemed to concentrate around me.

I did not leave the convent at night again until the next meeting of the Academy. Porta greeted me warmly, but gave no indication that he knew of anything that had passed between me and his niece; I wanted to ask after her, but he moved briskly on to speak to others. When the coca tea had been served, he took the floor, eager to share the results of his latest experimentation.

'As you know, gentlemen, our part of the world is always teetering on the edge of apocalypse. The mountains all around the Bay of Naples rumble with volcanic activity – this is the background to our lives. But my curiosity was piqued by rumours of an unusual cave in the hills of Capodimonte. It's famous among the locals – the goatherds especially – for killing dogs.' He glanced around the company, eyes bright with excitement, but his gaze skated over me. 'If a dog runs into this cave, they told me, within a few minutes it will collapse as if it has fallen suddenly into a faint. If you catch the dog in time, and throw it into a stream or pool of cold water in this state, it will revive. But if you leave it, after a few minutes more it will be stone dead. Why?'

There was a chorus of theories from the benches around the wall, mostly to do with noxious fumes from the volcanic rock.

'Exactly.' Porta was fairly dancing on tiptoe in his enthusiasm. 'Some invisible poison enters the dog's body – either through its eyes or ears or mouth – that snuffs out its vital spirits. And not just dogs – I learned a tragic tale from a few years back, of two beggar children who sought refuge in the cave during a storm and were found dead there in the morning, looking for all the world as if they were merely sleeping, not a mark on them.'

I glanced at Gennaro and caught his eye; he looked away.

'But what, precisely, is taking away the life force?' Porta continued. 'There is nothing visible in the cave, no smoke or gases to be seen seeping through the rock, as we might see from volcanic fissures. And whatever it is does not take effect if the dog is near the mouth of the cave, close to fresher air – he must be led further in. I'm afraid we got through rather a lot of dogs in the course of my experiments, though they were mostly old and lame strays we had rounded up. Those died much quicker than strong, healthy dogs, which leads me to conclude that—'

'Would it work on a man?' I interrupted. Everyone turned to look at me. I cleared my throat. 'Would it be strong enough to kill a grown man, this invisible poison?'

Porta pretended to consider. 'Well,' he said, pulling at his beard. 'I can say from my own experience that you begin to feel faint and nauseous after a few minutes, and at that point you rush for the entrance to gulp down the air outside. So in theory, I suppose a man *could* die, but it would take a good deal longer, and he would almost certainly note enough warning symptoms to escape first. Which leads me to suspect this poison possibly enters the body through the breath, since I found I was able to stay in for much longer with a wet cloth tied around my mouth and nose—'

'So for a young, healthy man to die in this cave, he would have to be held there against his will?' I persisted. Gennaro gave a warning cough, but Porta only smiled.

'That would be the logical conclusion,' he said. 'But I haven't progressed to that level of experimentation yet. It's hard to find the volunteers.'

A ripple of indulgent laughter passed around the room, and I fell silent.

I hung back after the meeting was over, hoping to speak further with him. He placed a hand on my shoulder.

'No more questions about caves, Bruno, understand? Not all secrets are meant to be uncovered. By the way, you must come back and use the library again, when things are a little less . . . heated at San Domenico. I understand you didn't get much reading done last time.' He winked. I blushed to the tip of my ears.

'You're not angry?'

'Why should I be angry? My niece is a young woman who knows her own mind and can make her own choices. I would only be angry if a young man felt he was entitled to her, regardless of what she wanted.' His mouth tightened and for a moment he struggled to master himself. In that fleeting expression, I saw that, for all his geniality, Porta could be ruthless. I wondered if those blazing lynx-eyes were the last thing Raffaele saw in that cave, before he fell into his final sleep.

'I have something for you,' Porta added, before I could

ask any further questions. From his sleeve he drew out a folded paper. I turned it over to find it sealed with red wax.

'She used one of my ciphers,' he said, quietly proud. 'Even so, you should burn it after reading.'

Holed up in the infirmary, I borrowed Gennaro's copy of Porta's book on ciphers and painstakingly decoded the letter.

My dear wolfhound,

By the time you read this, I will be preparing for my wedding. I'm sorry we didn't have the chance to say goodbye that last time; I understand that you were unavoidably detained. The man who came to tell me so did not have your gracious manner, I regret to say. Fortunately, like most girls, I have learned how to fight like a vixen, as my uncle calls me (did you guess at last?). He says my face denotes strength, stubbornness and force of character; he predicts an unsettled future for me, which I suppose at least would not be boring.

It was equally fortunate that day that Ercole keeps a closer eye on me than I realised; suffice to say, I fought, I shouted, and I go to my marriage bed with my honour intact. I think it unlikely that that man will try to force his attentions on any other woman in future.

If you are wondering about my wedding, I gave the matter long reflection and concluded that, while religious vows are for life, marriage is at best temporary, particularly if one's husband is getting on in years and has a growth in his nether parts. (I have this on good authority from our family physician, who heard it from another physician, who heard it from the man who attends my future husband – apparently such growths, untreated, do not predict long life.) So perhaps, in time, I may find myself widowed – widowhood being, as I'm sure you know, the most desirable state a woman of my birth can aspire to: all the respectability of marriage without the burden of a husband. I feel certain that we will meet again; but I shall never forget how you sweetened my days of indecision. Think of me next time you go to the library – but not too much, because you must read Ficino, and all the rest. I expect great things of you, wolfhound. My uncle predicts that, one day, your name will be known in Rome, and Venice, and even in the northern lands of the Protestants – the very height of fame! – and his predictions are almost never wrong. I pray that all your studies in the art of memory will teach you not to forget me.

Your vixen, F

I held the letter to the candle flame when I had finished reading and found myself hoping, in a most un-Christian way, that her husband would not last long. The blue ribbon from her hair was hidden in the rafters, along with my secret writings. The prior still watched me with the sharp eyes of a raptor (with his black-and-white robe and his hooked nose, he would be a magpie, I decided, in Porta's scheme of physiognomy), but it seemed that Fiammetta's letter turning to ash in my hand marked the end of the business.

In that, I was mistaken. Two months after Raffaele's death, I was summoned to the prior's chamber. I knocked and entered, to find the prior behind his wide desk. He seemed unusually apprehensive.

'A visitor for you, Fra Giordano.' He nodded to his right.

In a chair by the hearth sat a stocky man with a bulbous nose and thick brows fixed in a permanent scowl. His complexion was choleric and tufts of hair sprouted from his ears; a wart protruded from his left cheek. I knew who he was; I had seen him at Raffaele's funeral, where he had worn exactly the same expression of indignation. Looking at him close to, I could only think that Raffaele's looks must all have come from his mother.

'You can go now,' he said to the prior, as if dismissing a servant.

The prior bristled.

'Don Umberto – if you wish to speak to one of my friars in my convent, I must insist that I am present—'

'He can speak for himself, can't he? I thought he was famous for it, this one. Or don't you trust him?'

'Naturally, but I—'

'Then leave us,' Don Umberto growled. I had never seen the prior subservient before, and I would have enjoyed the novelty if I had not been so terrified. The prior hesitated, then gave me a quick, curt nod and left the room. He would not have given in so easily, I was certain, if he had not been afraid he was on shaky ground with Raffaele's father.

The baron heaved himself up from the chair and crossed the room to the cabinet where the prior kept his decanters of Venetian crystal. I watched him, the way you watch an unpredictable dog. He was a short man, with a squat torso running to fat now, but I guessed that in his prime, when it was all muscle, he could have bested men a foot taller in a fist fight.

'Your father is Giovanni Bruno of Nola?' he said, his back to me.

'That's right, my lord.'

He lifted the stopper from one bottle, sniffed the wine, made a face and poured some anyway.

'I could have him sent to put down the Morisco rebellion in Granada,' he said, off-hand, swirling the liquid in his glass. 'The Spanish need reinforcements, those Moors are vicious fuckers. You'd likely never see him again.'

128

I swallowed.

'Why would you do that, my lord?'

'Because I can. I have the viceroy's ear.' He turned to face me, his mouth a snarl. 'Why was my son in Capodimonte?'

I took a breath and concentrated on keeping my voice level. 'I understand he was offering prayers to the Virgin, my lord.'

He grunted. 'You and I both know Raffi might have climbed a hill if he thought there was a virgin at the top of it, but not that kind. And since it's a long way from any brothel, I have to ask myself, what was he doing there?'

I didn't know what to say. A silence unfolded. He pointed a hairy forefinger at me.

'And now I'm asking you.'

'I don't know why you think I would know, my lord. He didn't confide in me.'

'No. He didn't like you. Thought you were too clever. Was he right?'

'I don't know how one would measure an excess of cleverness, my lord.'

'See, that's the sort of thing, right there.' He jabbed the finger in the air. 'Answering back. Too clever to know your proper place. Raffi said you were a troublemaker. He said your memory games rely on black magic.'

'That is untrue, my lord. The art of memory comes from our illustrious forebears, the Romans, who used—'

'All right, I don't want a lecture. There's nothing illustrious in your ancestry, boy, I've checked. You've been up before the Inquisition already, haven't you?'

I bowed my head. 'Once, but they found nothing—'

'You don't want to be hauled in front of them again, then. They don't ask nicely the second time.' His mouth twisted into a malicious smile.

'My lord, I have done nothing wrong.' I tried to keep the

fear from my voice, but I could feel a line of sweat trickle between my shoulder blades; this man was a bully, as his son had been, but he had even greater power to make my life, and my family's, miserable for his own amusement, if he chose.

'Raffi may have been a bastard, but he was useful. I was fond of him, in a way. And I don't believe he died of heat-stroke. This place' – he waved his glass in the air, indicating the room; the wine sloshed over the rim and on to the prior's good Turkey carpet – 'is too pleased with its power. Your prior thinks he can't be challenged.'

'That is not my fault, my lord.'

He stomped across the room to me, lip curled back over his teeth.

'Someone in this convent knows the truth about my son's death. And every one of his friends says he talked of you as his greatest enemy. He was obsessed with you, apparently.'

I lowered my eyes again; it was hardly worth telling him that was not my fault either.

'Did you kill him?'

'What?' I snapped my head up and stared at him, so taken aback that I forgot the correct address. 'No. I was sick with a fever at the time – I was in the infirmary. There are witnesses.' Whatever Gennaro had dosed me with, it had been a stroke of genius, though I wondered again at his foresight; had he already guessed that Raffaele would need to be silenced, if he had made a connection between me and della Porta?

'Convenient. But you wouldn't have needed to leave your bed, would you?' He narrowed his eyes.

'I don't understand, my lord.'

'Not if you killed him with witchcraft. They say a magician can send his spirit out to commit murder while he stays home with his feet up.'

I gaped at him like a landed fish, but could find no words

130

in my defence. My hands had begun to shake; I had to tuck them into the sleeves of my habit so that he wouldn't see. His accusation was outlandish, but it could find purchase. This was a superstitious city, and public opinion was everything. If he repeated this belief that I killed his son by witchcraft enough times, in the right ears, he would need no evidence; the rumour alone would be sufficient to frighten the prior, who would sacrifice me in a heartbeat to save San Domenico's good name. My reputation as a rebel, my previous appearance before the Inquisitors, would all count against me. Naples may not have the Spanish version of the Inquisition yet, but the word of someone as powerful as Don Umberto could see me arrested and interrogated; he could easily find some other friar who disliked me enough to bear false testimony against me. Even so, through my fear, I registered that he had not mentioned della Porta. This could only mean that Raffaele had not told his father about my visits to Vomero either, otherwise Don Umberto would surely have stormed up there with his accusations.

'I have never practised witchcraft,' I managed eventually, dry-mouthed. 'My lord. I am a student of theology.'

'We'll see.' He threw back the last of the wine and wiped his chin. 'Raffi said he thought you'd end up on the pyre, through your own stubbornness. Said you were the type.' He poked his finger into my breastbone. 'I *will* find out what happened to my son. And I will have justice for him, one way or another. You'd better learn to keep eyes in the back of your head, Giordano Bruno. I'll be watching you.' With that, he flung the empty glass into the fireplace for dramatic effect, and blazed out as it shattered.

Perhaps Raffaele was right; perhaps I am the kind of man whose stubbornness will take him to the pyre. It seems to me that I am always half-listening for the knock on the door that announces the Inquisition. I make an outward show of obedience, but when I kneel to pray, I am hoping fervently for a time when men – yes, and women too, why not? – who seek knowledge and truth do not have to hide underground in fear of despots who cling to power by keeping people in the dark with their lies and worn-out superstitions. I pray I live long enough to see it.

A CHRISTMAS REQUIEM

Naples, December 1569

When they told me the Pope wanted to see me, my first thought was that it must be a joke. My second was that it must be a trap.

'For God's sake, Giordano Bruno.' The prior paced the good Turkey carpet in his study, hands clasped behind his back, black-and-white robes whisking about his legs so that he resembled a giant magpie. I knew then that the matter was serious; only extreme frustration could provoke the prior to take the name of Our Lord in vain. It happened a lot when he dealt with me. 'Can you not comprehend what an honour this is for our convent? That His Holiness should condescend to show interest in a friar from San Domenico Maggiore – and you only twenty-one years old, and from a family of no distinction? It's a mark of God's favour, and your reluctance is nothing short of disobedience.'

He stopped and fixed me with his corvine glare. I avoided his eye and looked instead at the hard December sky over Naples through the windows behind him.

'Call it prudence, Most Reverend Prior,' I said. 'I can't help wondering how His Holiness knows of me, and what he might have heard to prompt his interest.'

'Oh, there is no mystery there,' he said, resuming his steady steps. 'Fra Agostino da Montalcino has the ear of one of the cardinals. It would seem you made a great impression on Fra Agostino during his recent visit to Naples, and he has been mentioning your name all over Rome. Word reached the Holy Father, and now here is your official invitation. I'm surprised you are not more animated by the prospect – I had thought you an ambitious young man.' He arched one thin eyebrow as if challenging me to deny the charge.

'Fra Agostino hates me,' I said bluntly. 'If my reputation in Rome is built on his reports, I'll be walking straight into the arms of the Inquisition. And everyone knows Pope Pius V is . . .' I let the sentence fall; even I had the sense not to insult the Pope to the prior of the most prestigious convent in Naples.

'Zealous in his pursuit of purity,' the prior finished for me. 'Yes. Before he ascended the throne of St Peter, he was Grand Inquisitor. They say he still wears a hair shirt under his robes.' The way he pursed his lips suggested that he considered such practices primitive, though he would never say as much. 'And Fra Agostino did not *hate* you. He found you irritating, I grant, but he is hardly alone in that. It is entirely possible for someone to recognise and admire your intellectual gifts, Fra Giordano, even while finding you most infuriating in person.'

I sensed we were no longer talking about Fra Agostino, so I changed the subject.

'I had hoped to visit my family for the Octave of Christmas.'

He made an exasperated noise and crossed to his desk, where he picked up and brandished the letter I had not been allowed to read.

'This is not a suggestion, Fra Giordano.' He flicked it with

136

one finger. 'It's a summons. Pope Pius wants you to demonstrate your memory system. You are expected at the Vatican in time for the Christmas Masses. That is the end of the discussion. Your family will still be there next year in whatever godforsaken village you crawled out of when you joined the Dominican order.'

'Nola,' I muttered, drawing myself up. The prior, like all the senior brothers at San Domenico, was the younger son of a baron, raised in a palazzo until he exchanged the rich silks and servants of a nobleman for the rich silks and servants of a wealthy churchman. My hometown on the other side of Mount Vesuvius may have been small and rural, but it riled me to hear it insulted by a man who would never set foot there. 'Makes the best olive oil in the kingdom.'

He almost smiled. 'I never heard of a village that didn't claim that distinction. But you have left that life behind. Tell me – do you not wish to see the glories of Rome, make an impression on the most powerful men in Christendom?'

I dipped my head in acknowledgement. 'If I could be sure they were not going to burn me.'

The prior rolled his eyes. 'I would not send you if I thought that were likely,' he said, smoothing the folded letter to a crisp edge between his fingertips. 'Apart from anything else, it would reflect very badly on me. Just try not to do anything stupid.'

I ran straight across the cloister to the infirmary in search of the wisest man in San Domenico. Fra Gennaro Ferrante was bent as usual over the workbench in his dispensary, mashing herbs to make a purgative for one of the elderly brothers whose kidneys were failing. At the sight of my face, he dismissed the young novice who was assisting him, as I once had, and wiped his hands on his apron.

'But Fra Agostino hates you,' he said, when I told him my

news. 'You made him look a fool in front of the entire convent by contradicting him in public.'

I leaned back against the bench. 'He made himself look a fool with his idiotic arguments. I merely pointed that out, in case anyone had failed to notice.'

'Yes, and you had a church full of friars laughing at his expense. The head of the Dominican convent in Rome, Bruno, twenty years your senior, honouring us with an official visit, and some young upstart makes him a laughing stock in the middle of his sombre address?' He shook his head. 'If you did that to me, I would not respond by recommending you for preferment to the Pope.'

'Perhaps Fra Agostino is a man of greater Christian charity than you, despite his stupidity.'

'I doubt it. I saw his face when he stormed out.'

'Then you agree that it must be a trap? I shouldn't go?'

He lifted a shoulder. 'I don't see that you have a choice. You can't turn down the Holy Father. But you should not go alone. If you think religious politics in Naples is a nest of vipers, wait till you walk into the Vatican.'

'You'll come with me?' I grasped at his sleeve, delighted; the prospect took on a different hue if Gennaro would be my companion. I had been to Rome only once, as a boy, and had hardly allowed myself to admit how much I wanted to see the Eternal City again, with its ancient ruins and new wonders of art and architecture. The prior was right; I was ambitious. But my ambitions did not tend in the right direction for a career in the Church. In Italy, it was acceptable to lust after wealth and power, even under such an austere pope as Pius V. What was not condoned was a desire for knowledge, for exploring beyond the limits of what the Church permitted us to know about the heavens, the earth, the human body, and my refusal to accept that the old ideas were true simply because it had always been so had already brought me the unwelcome attentions of the Inquisition.

Gennaro laughed, and gestured to the tools of his trade lying on the workbench.

'The prior would never allow me to go – I am needed here. But leave it with me. You will need powerful friends in Rome, if you have powerful enemies. I have an idea.'

Two days later, the prior called me back to see him. He seemed less agitated this time; instead of pacing, he stood by the tall arched window in his office, looking out over the rooftops of the city towards the bay, while I hovered by the empty fireplace, uncertain as to whether I should sit without an invitation.

'Do you know of Giambattista della Porta?' he asked, turning swiftly to watch my reaction.

I composed my face into what I hoped was a blank.

'I have heard the name,' I said carefully. Was this a trap? But if the prior had any reason to confront me about my association with della Porta, he could have done so long before now, I told myself. I clasped my hands together inside my sleeves to hide any tell-tale trembling.

'Hm. Yes, he has a certain . . . *reputation* in Naples,' the prior said, his lips tight. 'But he is also a most generous benefactor to this convent.'

'I – had no idea,' I said. This, at least, was the truth.

'Don Giambattista della Porta donates lavishly to San Domenico because we are the city's Inquisitors, and for someone like him, it makes sense to keep the Inquisition on his side. Not that we can be bought, of course,' he added quickly. 'You know what is said of him, I presume?'

His eyes fixed on mine; I gripped my hands tighter and fought not to swerve from that searching gaze.

'I understand he is a patron of learning and a great collector of books.'

The prior grunted a reluctant acknowledgement. 'Many of those books forbidden by the Holy Office. He has published writings on natural magic and cryptography which brush too close to occult knowledge, in my view. But he has the patronage of Cardinal Luigi d'Este, so who am I to argue?'

I said nothing, wondering where the conversation was tending. If the prior knew or suspected that I belonged to the Academy of Secrets, Porta's underground society for the advancement of scientific knowledge and the sharing of banned books, he would surely have produced some evidence by now. Even so, I felt a trickle of sweat run down my neck, despite the chill of the room. Merely the rumour of such a society's existence could be enough to warrant interrogation by the Father Inquisitor, and we all knew what that involved.

'Della Porta writes to tell me he has heard of your invitation from His Holiness, and since he plans a Christmas visit to Rome to see his patron, he offers to take you in his coach.' He pressed his hands together as if in prayer and touched his forefingers to his lips. 'This would be extremely convenient for me, as it would save us the expense of your journey, and the trouble of sending servants to accompany you. On the other hand, I am not persuaded that della Porta is at all a suitable acquaintance for a young friar so prone to questioning authority as you, Fra Giordano. Two days of travelling with him and God knows what heretical notions he might fill your head with.'

I lowered my eyes and strove to contain my excitement. 'Most Reverend Prior, you said yourself that this invitation from His Holiness is a sign of God's favour. Perhaps, like Our Lord, I must face temptation along the way. If you pray for me, I am certain that my faith will remain strong enough to resist.'

He blinked. 'Are you comparing yourself to Christ, Bruno?'

'No. I – that is . . .' I could not tell if he was mocking me. 'Besides, heretical ideas are to be found everywhere.'

'That much is true. And you have distinguished yourself from your earliest novitiate as one with an appetite to seek them out. I shall pray on the matter.' He turned back to the window. 'Della Porta says he will introduce you to the cardinal. Este would be a useful man to know, I must say. His family is one of the most influential in Italy, and he is celebrated for his generosity. If you impress him, it would reflect well on San Domenico.' Though he had his back to me, I could almost hear the clicking of the abacus in his head as he calculated the possible value of these contacts against the potential dangers.

'Then surely it is to the glory of our convent that I make this journey in such company, Most Reverend Prior?' I asked, all innocence.

He shot me a knowing look over his shoulder and folded his arms. 'See – I said you were ambitious,' he murmured, with that not-quite smile.

So it was that on the twenty-third of December 1569 I found myself rattling along the Via Appia northwards, wrapped in a wool cloak against the December chill, marvelling at receding vistas of hills ridged with lines of cypress trees and fortress towns. Occasionally I stole a glance at the sharp profile of my companion, who kept his head bent over a book for the most part; he was a seasoned traveller, for whom the journey held few novelties. I had known Giambattista della Porta a little over a year, and was still in awe of him, in the way that a young man looks up to an older one who seems to embody all the virtues and accomplishments he himself aspires to. Porta was the second son of a wealthy nobleman; at only twenty-three, he had published a four-volume encyclopaedia of natural magic,

141

which had been reprinted five times in Latin and translated into Italian, French and Dutch. Now, in his mid-thirties, he was cultivating an international reputation for his poetry and plays, and his treatises on optics, cryptography and the art of memory. His book collection was the envy of universities and religious houses across Naples, but only a select few of his most trusted confidants knew of his secret library and its treasure of occult learning, hidden in a specially constructed inner room lest the Inquisition take too close an interest in his business.

'First time outside the Kingdom of Naples?' he asked, turning to me with an indulgent smile, taking my frequent gasps for expressions of amazement, when more often they were reactions to the lurching of the carriage. For all its obvious expense, it was spectacularly uncomfortable, its bone-shaking jolts made worse by the state of the roads.

'My father brought me to Rome once as a boy, though I don't remember much. You visit often, I suppose?'

'I used to. Though I haven't been for three years – not since Pope Pius was elected. I wonder if they are any closer to finishing the great basilica of San Pietro. I doubt it. Since Michelangelo Buonarroti died there is no one worthy to take over the work. It will be a miracle if the dome is on before the Second Coming.' He leaned back in his seat and crossed one leg over another. 'Rome is a remarkable city for studying the art of geometry in architecture. The Florentines think they invented the rebirth of the classical style, but their inspiration came from the imperial ruins in Rome, and Rome perfected it. Oh, and you must see Buonarroti's frescoes in the Sistine Chapel before you leave. An artist whose genius will not be seen again in Italy. Not under this pope, anyway – a man with no vision except to castigate everything that brings pleasure or enlightenment.' His lip curled. 'You know that Pope Pius was a goatherd until he joined the Dominican order at fourteen? No wonder he has so little refinement or feeling for beauty.'

'I was also running about the hillsides until I joined the Dominicans,' I said, somewhat defensive. 'Growing up in the country does not in itself confer narrowness of mind. That's a flaw that afflicts people of all stations.'

'True.' He bowed his head by way of apology. 'I have known plenty of men raised in grand palazzi among all the advantages of art and learning, with less wit to appreciate them than that horse.' He gestured out of the window, where his bodyguard, Tito, rode alongside the carriage, with three other armed men under his command. 'And Pope Pius has had fifty years of immersion in all the scholarship of the Dominicans, and still he thinks only of purging heresy – and by heresy, he means anything he can't understand. Watch your step with him.' His face grew serious, and his golden eyes darkened. 'When he was head of the Inquisition in Como, he had to be recalled for being too enthusiastic in his persecution of miscreants. He's executed bishops before now. He will know exactly how to trip you up, if he has a mind to it.'

'I heard he made the Jews in Rome wear badges to mark them out,' I said.

He grimaced. 'And he has sodomites burned alive in the public piazzas. Often on no more than hearsay.' He fell silent and turned back to the window. I knew it was whispered of him, a man of his age with no wife or children, though I had never dared ask if there was truth in the rumours. I wondered if that was what had kept him away from Rome for so long.

'Still,' he continued, 'from what I hear, Pius is too busy worrying about Elizabeth Tudor to spare much thought for your misdemeanours.'

'Who?'

He laughed. 'The queen of England, Bruno. You must

143

know that her father broke from Rome and declared himself head of his own Church, and Elizabeth – who is considered a bastard by the Catholics – persists in his heresy. I heard the Pope is considering a bull to excommunicate her, which would as good as give her Catholic subjects licence to regicide.'

I did not see the relevance. I could barely have pointed to England on a map; in my limited knowledge, it was a miserable, bitterly divided country of never-ending rain, constantly burning its subjects every time it switched religion, and whether its sovereign was excommunicated was of little interest to me. It was not as if I had any intention of going there.

A sickly smell of decay began to seep through the gaps in the carriage windows. We had experienced this before along the Via Appia, but now the smell had intensified. Porta took out a scented kerchief and pressed it to his nose and mouth; then, seeing I had none, offered it to me.

'The perfume of the Eternal City,' he remarked, nodding to the window. I peered out, counting the corpses lying at the roadside, fly-blown and hacked apart by carrion birds.

'What happened to them?'

He shrugged. 'Malaria. Bandits. Or someone wanted to be rid of them and preferred the body not to be found inside the city walls. Same as happens everywhere.' He gave me a knowing look. 'What a waste, eh.'

I breathed hard through my mouth and nodded. He did not mean of human life; he meant of available bodies. Fra Gennaro, along with other members of the Academy, would have given anything to get his hands on this many corpses for anatomising, but in Naples the prohibition on such things was so severe that bodies had to be acquired on the black market, with all the risks that entailed.

'We could take a few home as a gift,' I suggested, half-smiling, glad again of Porta's armed outriders, and the fact that I was not facing down bandits alone on this road with only the convent servants for company.

He laughed. 'You'll have to get your own coach for that, I'm afraid. Now – let us talk of happier things. Cardinal d'Este wants you at his Christmas Eve feast tomorrow night. He's going to be delighted with you – and so are his unmarried sisters.' He winked. 'The cardinal likes to fill his house with artists and musicians, especially during the festive season, and he keeps the best table in the Papal States. Now *he* is a man with an insatiable curiosity for the new learning – quite the opposite of the Pope. There are few in his position would be bold enough to give patronage to someone like me.' He caught my expression. 'What's funny?'

'Nothing. Only – it seems strange to me that you would need patronage.'

'Because I am rich, you mean?'

'And you have a family name.'

'Those things will only protect you so far. And they are better protection against the law than against the Church. I could more easily buy my way out of a murder charge – hypothetically – than one of heresy. For that, it is useful to have a cardinal who will speak for you. Este would be a valuable friend to you too, if you mean to pursue your studies outside the confines of what your order permits. He will want to hear about your memory system.'

'But I'm under strict instructions from the prior to go straight to Fra Agostino at Santa Maria sopra Minerva,' I said, despondent. 'I would need his permission. He is to be my guardian while I am in Rome.'

'Your—' Porta let out a bark of laughter. 'For God's sake, Bruno – does your prior think you are a virgin girl, who must be chaperoned everywhere?'

'He thinks I am susceptible to getting myself into trouble.

He fears that in your company I will have my head turned by new ideas.'

'Let us hope so. The only chance for humanity is men who are prepared to risk new ideas, and there are few enough of those in Italy. Even fewer inside the Vatican.' He slapped a hand on my leg for emphasis. 'Your Fra Agostino will not dare defy a cardinal, if he has any care for his position in Rome.'

'Is everything a matter of political manoeuvring here?' I asked.

Porta laughed, but there was a weariness in it. 'Not just in Rome,' he said, turning back to the window. 'But Rome is the worst – always has been. In fact – I have an early Christmas gift for you. I thought you'd be better off having it now.' He reached into the bag at his feet and drew out a short knife with a silver handle and a sheath of soft black leather.

I turned it over in my hands, admiring the work, and looked up at him. 'It's beautiful. But – I am a friar. I can't go about armed.'

'You can in Rome,' he said. 'Even cardinals keep a weapon up their sleeves. Now – behold what remains of the greatest empire in history.'

He pointed to the window. I tried to crane out to see the two crenellated towers of the Porto San Sebastiano as we approached, but it would not open far enough. Seeing my efforts, Porta rapped on the roof for the coachman to stop.

'Appearance is everything in this city,' he said, affecting seriousness, 'and arriving in stately fashion in a well-appointed carriage is vital to making an impression. However – if you don't care about any of that, you are welcome to sit up front and see the sights.'

I did not need further encouragement; I sprang out and clambered up to join the driver, pressing a sleeve over my mouth to keep out the dust of the road. I could hardly stop myself exclaiming with wonder as we passed under the archway of the great stone gatehouse and along a straight, paved road that led through an extraordinary kind of wilderness; a vast, parched field scattered with fallen stones. Majestic arches, half-ruined walls, and columns jutted from the undergrowth like broken teeth; to our right, the remains of a giant circular amphitheatre could be seen in the distance.

'*Dio mio!*' I shouted, half out of my seat, so loudly that it startled the horses. 'This must be the Forum! Porta' – I leaned down and banged my fist against the side of the carriage – 'Cicero himself spoke to the crowds here! Can you believe it?'

Over the rattling of the wheels I heard him chuckle. 'Quite something, isn't it?'

'I never want to leave!' I yelled back, laughing with delight. 'And look – that must be the Colosseum! Where they held the chariot races – can you picture it, before it was all overgrown with trees? If only we could step back in time and see it! Shame it's no longer in use.'

'Don't worry, Bruno,' Porta said cheerfully, from inside the carriage. 'They still throw people to the lions, if that's what you want.'

'Fra Agostino is occupied with his duties at present,' said the young novice who showed me to my cell at the convent of Santa Maria sopra Minerva, puffed up with the importance of his task. 'He will see you after vespers.'

I thanked him and set my bag down on the narrow bed. No apology from my host, then. The slight was deliberate, but I was determined not to rise to it; I needed to nurture Fra Agostino's goodwill, at least until my audience with the Pope was over. I had been reluctant to say goodbye to Porta when he dropped me at the door; now I was alone, and at the mercy of a man who, as Fra Gennaro had pointed out, had every reason to resent me.

Santa Maria sopra Minerva, being the headquarters of the Dominican order in Rome, was hardly austere, but I had been lodged in a sparely furnished room, with little by way of worldly comforts except a thin mattress and thinner blankets, and a heavy crucifix glowering from the wall. It looked like the sort of cell a brother might be put in while doing penance, to concentrate his mind on humility, not somewhere for an esteemed visitor set to dazzle the Holy Father. This, too, I suspected to be deliberate. Perhaps it was meant to spare me the sin of pride. At least I had Cardinal d'Este's Christmas Eve feast to look forward to the following night, I consoled myself, although I wondered if Porta might have over-praised his patron; I was dubious about the degree of entertainment one might expect from some elderly cardinal and his spinster sisters.

'What time is supper?' I asked the boy. I had not eaten since midday and my stomach was cramping with hunger. He stared at me as if I had uttered an outrageous blasphemy.

'It is the Christmas fast, Brother. Surely you know that? There is no supper tonight. We are supposed to spend the time in prayer.'

'Already?' I almost swore, but thought better of it; there was every chance this sententious boy was a spy, sent to report my every careless word to Fra Agostino. At San Domenico, our tradition was to fast after the evening meal on the twenty-third of December until the celebration of Christmas Eve; I had hoped for one last supper in Rome before the enforced deprivation. As a young man of vigorous appetites, I had never found that abstinence from food focused my mind on holy things; quite the reverse. Once, after a day of fasting as a novice, I had contemplated an image of poor San Lorenzo being griddled over the fire and found myself salivating at the thought of roast meat. On reflection, perhaps that should have been a sign that I was not suited to religious life. 'Then I shall begin my period of prayer this minute, if you would be kind enough to leave me.'

He hesitated, which only confirmed my suspicion that he had been instructed to observe me, but I fixed him with such a stern glare that eventually he withered under the force of it – he could not have been more than sixteen – and backed out of the room, saying he would fetch me for vespers.

When the boy's footsteps had receded along the passageway, I took a purse of money from my travelling bag, wrapped my cloak around my shoulders and closed the door of my cell silently behind me. I was prepared to deliver some excuse about wishing to pray in the chapel if I should run into any of the brothers on my way out, but the convent appeared to be deserted; perhaps they were all solemnly at their devotions, as the novice had suggested. The only living soul who saw me leave was the old servant at the gate who had admitted me only a quarter hour earlier; I nodded to him, but he asked no questions and I stepped through into the streets of Rome, giddy with a sense of freedom.

The hour was just past four, the winter sun low over the rooftops, gilding red tiles, white marble churches and the pale stones of ruins. The whole city clamoured for my attention. In the streets behind the convent I found the Pantheon and a temple to Hadrian, and marvelled at the craftsmanship that had endured centuries; further afield I stumbled on ancient columns and sunken gardens with the remains of baths and water conduits. I wandered south through narrow streets of artisans' shops – crossbow-makers, milliners and tailors beginning to pack up their wares as the light faded – and emerged into a small piazza with a busy market and taverns around its perimeter. I stopped at one – the Taverna della Vacca – to buy bread and porchetta with a cup of spiced wine; the girl who served it told me the place was called the Campo dei Fiori, this tavern had once been owned by the Borgia Pope's mistress, and I should come back on a Monday or a Saturday for the horse fair if I really wanted to see it looking lively. I didn't linger; for all its bustle and festive crowds, there was no escaping the sight of the tall pole erected in the centre of the square, a pulley fixed to its cross-beam, instantly recognisable to anyone who has witnessed *il tormento della corda* – the torture that hoists a victim aloft by his wrists tied behind his back, then drops him in a series of sharp jolts so as to dislocate his shoulders. It was a favourite method of the Inquisition, and the thought of the cheerful little market transformed into a place of public execution cast a chill over my mood. I left the Campo dei Fiori and resolved to take a different route back.

At length I passed a grand palazzo and there before me was the open vista of the river. I had a clear view across to the forbidding walls of the Castel Sant'Angelo, the papal prison, and the famed basilica of San Pietro, greater even than in my childhood memories, the drum of its dome towering above the rooftops of the Vatican palace, though it was encased in scaffolding and the dome itself remained unfinished, as Porta had said. My breath caught in my throat; it seemed absurd that in two days' time I would stand within those walls, presenting my memory system to the most powerful man in Christendom. It was – as the prior had made sure to remind me – a singular honour for the son of a mercenary soldier from the unremarkable hillside town of Nola, and the potential ramifications seemed suddenly overwhelming. If I were to succeed here – if I could impress His Holiness enough to secure his patronage – my future in the Church could be made. After all – if a goatherd could rise through the Dominican order to become cardinal and then pope, why not a soldier's son? But that path had never interested me; the religious life had only ever been a means of gaining access to learning. I had not yet finished my theology degree and already the constraints of the Church's teachings were chafing at me. Over the past year, I had come to feel only truly at home in Gennaro's dispensary or during the monthly meetings of Porta's Academy of Secrets, as we argued and encouraged one another to greater daring in our pursuit of new understanding in science and philosophy.

And there was still the question of Pope Pius's interest in me. Now that I had been treated to Fra Agostino's pointed coldness, I found it harder still to believe that he could have spoken so highly of me that the Holy Father had felt compelled to see my brilliance for himself. Fra Agostino, I was certain, was so concerned with his own reputation that he would only ever remember me for the way I had publicly contradicted him, and had the whole congregation of San Domenico laughing in his face. And wouldn't that be the ultimate revenge – to summon me here so that he could watch me humiliated in turn before the most important men in the Church?

I leaned against the wall of a house and peered out across the Tiber at the seat of power as the sun dipped red and gold towards the jutting supports of the dome, thinking with a shudder of the torture device I had seen in the Campo dei Fiori.

Naturally, I got lost – which, I acknowledge, does not say much for my celebrated powers of memory. I navigated my way uphill away from the river by the setting sun, but the back streets all looked the same. On occasion, I had the unsettling sense that I was being followed; a prickling at the nape of my neck, as if someone's eyes were on me, but though I spun around every time I felt it, I could see no one who was not simply going about their business, and convinced myself that my fears were only the result of the gathering dusk and my general apprehension about being in Rome. All the same, I was glad to feel Porta's knife at my belt, hidden under my cloak.

By the time I found my way to Santa Maria, I was late for vespers. I circled the church, hoping I could slip in a side door and hide myself in a back pew unnoticed, but all the smaller entrances appeared locked, so that I had no choice but to push open the great main door, which crashed shut behind me, causing every head in the congregation to snap in my direction. Fra Agostino, poised in front of the altar, glowered down the aisle at me with his small eyes, as if he expected no better. I mouthed an apology; he puckered his lips tighter and pointed to a seat close to him, meaning I had to walk the length of the nave in the echoing silence with every friar looking on in judgement. I spent the rest of the office with my gaze firmly fixed on the bright frescoes over-head to avoid eye contact with anyone.

'So – you do not observe the Christmas fast, Brother?' Fra Agostino remarked, afterwards, when I was seated opposite him by the fire in his study.

'What makes you think that?'

'You have crumbs all down your habit.' He flicked his fingers impatiently to indicate.

I looked down, and brushed away the evidence with a mea culpa grin; he did not smile in return.

'You should have asked permission before you decided to go promenading around the town indulging yourself,' he said.

I looked at him, not quite believing he was serious. 'Fra Agostino – I only went for a walk. I am a man of twenty-one.'

'You are a man in holy orders, Fra Giordano, and I have personally assured your prior that while you are in Rome, you will answer to my authority and I will take it upon myself to keep you out of trouble. This city is full of temptation.'

'I don't doubt it. But in this instance, the only pleasure that seduced me was gazing on the beauty of San Pietro.'

'That, and the porchetta,' he said drily, gesturing again to my habit.

I let him have that, reminding myself that I needed to show deference to his rank, even if the man himself hardly merited it; he was twice my age and it was true that I was obliged by the rule of my order to submit to his authority. Fra Agostino looked as if a bout of fasting would do him no harm; he was fleshy, though it did not sit comfortably on him, as it can on men who have acquired substance through pleasure in good living. Agostino's bulk seemed a burden to him; he shifted constantly in his seat, and pulled with a finger at his collar, which appeared too tight around his thick neck. His skin had an unhealthy pallor; a mole protruded from his right cheek with a bush of wiry black bristles sprouting from it, the only stubble on his smoothly shaved face. The more I told myself not to stare at it, the more my eyes seemed drawn back by an irresistible force.

'Well, it seems you are to be granted further opportunity to resist temptation while you are here.' He held up a piece of paper between his finger and thumb. 'A messenger came this afternoon from the Este household. The cardinal requests your presence at his Christmas Eve celebrations. Very grand connections for a boy like you.'

'I am honoured.' I bowed my head so he wouldn't see the tension in my jaw.

'Don't be.' His lip curled. 'Luigi d'Este is like a child in his pursuit of amusement. You will be this week's novelty, and by St Stephen's Day he will have forgotten you and moved on to the next musician or poet he has been told is marvellously gifted. Don't expect consistency from an Este.'

'I'm not expecting anything from him.'

'You know, I'm minded not to let you go at all.' He tilted

153

his head back and looked along his nose at me, enjoying his small moment of power. 'Some of the artists under his patronage are of questionable morals. And he shows off with his food and drink in a way quite unseemly for a churchman. I've heard more than one person say they have never seen such displays of over-indulgence.'

Suddenly I wanted to go to Cardinal d'Este's party more than anything; the prospect of all that food might just get me through a night and day of fasting.

'My prior is keen that I make his acquaintance,' I said, offering a winning smile.

'Hm. On the other hand . . .' His expression grew calculating. 'My patron, Cardinal Rebiba – who has so kindly brought you to the attention of the Holy Father – is frequently at odds with Cardinal d'Este. They hold quite different views on many points. Rebiba understands that a cardinal's principal concern should be with virtue, not beauty.'

'May one not appreciate both?'

'I don't want a theological debate, Fra Giordano – I recall very well how you conduct yourself in those.' He fixed me with an icy glare just long enough for me to understand that I was not forgiven. 'But Cardinal Rebiba would no doubt welcome a pair of eyes and ears inside the Este household. You may go tomorrow night, on the condition that you make yourself useful. Provide the cardinal and me with a full report of who was there, what was discussed, if anything was said against the Pope or the other members of the Sacred College. Any debauched behaviour you witness among the guests.'

'You want me to spy on my host?' I stared at him.

'I simply ask you to give an account of the evening to my patron – who is the reason you're here at all. It would be a fitting way to repay him for his exceptional generosity to you, and you have no loyalty to Cardinal d'Este – unless there is something you haven't told me?'

154

I shook my head, dismayed; he smiled without showing his teeth, one finger absently toying with the bristles on his cheek. 'You can go now. No doubt you have much to prepare before your audience with His Holiness.'

I pushed back my chair, unsure of how to respond. Gennaro and Porta were right; I was up to my neck in a nest of vipers. Less than four hours in Rome and already I was being used by one cardinal as a weapon against another.

'May I ask you something, Fra Agostino?' I said, as I stood.

He looked up from his papers, irritated to find me still there. 'What?'

'Why am I here?'

'Is that a metaphysical question?'

'I mean – I know that you are angry with me for the way I spoke to you in Naples. And rightly so,' I added quickly, lowering my eyes. 'I was disrespectful. So I don't understand why you would have recommended me to Cardinal Rebiba, when it's clear that you have no liking for me.'

He stroked the bristles on his face and considered how to answer.

'Put it this way,' he said, after a moment. 'If I had a dog that had been taught to perform tricks, I would want to show it to my neighbours. It does not follow that I would allow that dog to sleep in my bed.'

'I was not expecting to sleep in your bed, Brother.' I aimed for a light-hearted tone, but he merely looked at me with even greater disgust.

'You are right to think that I dislike your manners. I find you uncouth, arrogant, wilful, disobedient and too pleased with the sound of your own voice. Because you are clever, you think yourself above the normal rules of deference and respect that apply to the rest of society, and particularly the Church. You have an abundance of self-regard and none of the humility befitting someone of your years and background.'

'But apart from that, I'm exemplary,' I said. His expression remained stony. I needed to stop trying to win him with humour; it was not working.

'And you are also flippant and trivial. But apart from *that*, you are undeniably gifted. I recall the afternoon at San Domenico when you recited psalm after psalm with no notes, in Latin, Hebrew and Italian – any psalm people requested, and sometimes backwards – though I felt that was an unnecessary flourish which provoked too much mirth among your brothers at the expense of the holy scriptures, and added nothing to our understanding. I was more impressed that you had great swathes of St Thomas Aquinas by heart.' He folded his hands together. 'The art of memory has always been one of the strengths of the Dominicans, though other orders try to claim it as their tradition. But it is we who refined it. I felt that a talent as exceptional as yours should not be hidden away in Naples, but used to reflect greater glory on our order. His Holiness Pope Pius V, though he condemns frivolity, is always pleased by men who will use their abilities to further our understanding of God's truth, particularly when they come from his own order.'

In other words, he thought I might be a useful passport into the Pope's favour; if I met with approval, he and his Cardinal Rebiba would take all the credit.

'As long as you remember not to answer back, and don't try to be funny, I'm sure the Holy Father will see the gold in the dross,' he added, drawing his thick brows together. 'Of course, I need not elaborate what the consequences will be if you do or say anything to bring me, the cardinal or this convent into disrepute.'

I was about to come back with a witty response, but thought better of it, and closed my mouth.

*

156

Cardinal d'Este's palazzo, off the Piazza Navona, was so vast it would have taken me twenty minutes of walking around the perimeter walls to find the entrance, if Fra Agostino had not instructed one of the convent servants to show me the way. I noticed the man carried a thick wooden stave at his side, and I was glad of it, since I had left Porta's knife in my cell, thinking it might be unwise to turn up armed at a cardinal's party. Fra Agostino, it seemed, was attentive to the safety of his performing dog. Or his spy; the weight of that commission sat heavy on my shoulders as I was shown into a cavernous entrance hall and had my cloak lifted from me by a swarm of attendants. I wondered what harmless lies I might invent that would satisfy Fra Agostino and Cardinal Rebiba without making Porta feel I had betrayed him and his patron in any way.

I was led along a carpeted corridor bright with banks of candles, up a wide flight of stairs and into a chamber grander than anything I had seen in Naples. The ceiling must have been two storeys high, the walls faced with red and cream marble and every surface painted with frescoes of heroic scenes in scorching colours: rich cobalts, vermilions, ochres. The place blazed with light, as silver candelabra the size of cartwheels swayed from the roof beams. Branches of stone pine, laurel, juniper and winterberries had been wreathed into garlands to decorate the window embrasures for the Christmas season; at one end of the room, a trio of musicians with pipe, lute and viola de gamba played a lively dance tune. Overwhelmed by so much magnificence, I hovered in the doorway, feeling conspicuous in my Dominican habit. I was by no means the only man there in religious robes – I thought I glimpsed the scarlet of a cardinal's skirts whisking through the crowd – but it was the costumes of the women that dazzled the eyes. So many women! In silk and brocade; cascades of lace and embroidery; jewelled

157

sleeves, pearl headdresses and glass beads that caught the light, faces glowing as they tilted back their heads to laugh at a suitor's joke, falls of gold or chestnut hair rippling as they moved. I found myself sincerely hoping that Fra Agostino had been right in his predictions of debauchery.

By twenty-one I was not a stranger to women, despite my vows. At San Domenico, the prior picked his battles shrewdly and had evidently decided that the rule of celibacy was not one he was prepared to expend much energy enforcing; as long as no brother was foolish enough to get himself caught up in a paternity suit or attacked by a wronged husband, a blind eye was generally turned if young men slipped out through a garden door at night to visit local taverns like the Cerriglio, whose upper rooms served as a brothel. My experience in that regard was not so extensive as some of my brothers; my father's stories of the horrors he had witnessed among his fellow-soldiers on campaign had instilled in me a healthy fear of the French pox, so I had generally kept away from professional women. The year before, I had imagined myself briefly in love with Porta's niece, Fiammetta, though I had not seen her since she had left Naples to be married. But I had never, before that night, been in a room with so many beautiful and expensively dressed women; I cast my eyes around the party, mute with amazement at the bare shoulders and low-cut bodices, and noticed a few coquettish glances directed my way. It occurred to me that a number of these women might be courtesans, and I hoped I could get through the evening without making a fool of myself in front of Porta and his cardinal. I began to understand now why Fra Agostino and his patron disapproved of Cardinal d'Este, and found myself all the more disposed to like the man.

A servant dressed in Este colours pressed a silver goblet of spiced wine into my hand and melted away; at the same time, I saw Porta weaving through the crowd, his arms outstretched in greeting, a broad smile on his face.

'Here he is! The talk of the town. Come – let me introduce you to the cardinal.' He took my arm and marched me the length of the room; as the crowds parted, I saw a group of people seated near the great fireplace.

'Am I really?' I asked, as Porta strode towards them. 'The talk of the town?'

He laughed. 'Well. Not yet. But you will be. People here love new blood.'

This did not sound especially reassuring, but before I could ask any more, he thrust me forward into the presence of the seated group and the young man in scarlet at its centre sprang to his feet and held out his hand to me.

I stared at him, briefly confused, but recovered myself quickly enough to drop to my knee and kiss the ring on his proffered hand. The only cardinal I had seen in the flesh was an old greybeard, and so I had pictured all churchmen of his rank to be well advanced in years, but I remembered now that many were significantly younger, thrust into the Sacred College by ambitious families to further represent their interests.

Cardinal d'Este could not have been much over thirty; he had a full head of dark hair swept back from a high forehead, and eyes that gleamed with mischief as he gestured impatiently for me to rise. He gave the appearance of being a vigorous young nobleman who had dressed up as a cardinal for a game – which was, perhaps, not so many miles from the truth, except that the game was deadly serious.

'So this is your young genius from Naples, Porta?' He clasped me by the shoulders and looked me up and down. 'You're here to astound the Holy Father, I hear?'

'I intend to do my best, Most Reverend Lord Cardinal,' I said, bowing my head.

'Give us a taste of it, then. Porta says you can do the psalms on request.' He looked over his shoulder to the seated company. 'What would you like to hear, Sisters?'

I followed his gaze to the two women he had addressed; they too were around the cardinal's age, and not the elderly spinsters I had anticipated. Both were strikingly handsome, with the same dark hair and long, straight nose as their brother, their gowns exquisite confections that shimmered in the light. Though they looked so similar, there was a marked difference in their manner; the one on the left, in a low-bodiced dress of deep red velvet with a collar of rubies at her throat, looked directly at me from under her painted brows with a mix of amusement and knowing. The other, in gold-veined white silk, her shoulders and décolletage covered more modestly with a silver shawl, sat back in her chair and regarded me as if reserving judgement.

'Come, Lucrezia,' the cardinal said, with a teasing smile, 'you are renowned for your devotion to studying the holy scriptures – you must have a favourite psalm?'

The woman in red threw her head back and let out a pleasingly unrefined laugh. 'I prefer the Song of Solomon, Brother,' she said, giving me that same direct look; I felt the blood rush to my face. 'You had better ask Leonora – she's the one who should have been an abbess.'

Her sister raised her eyes briefly, as if this were a joke grown old, and turned her thoughtful gaze to me.

'Psalm 140,' she said.

'Which language, my lady? Latin, Greek, Hebrew, Italian?'

Cardinal d'Este laughed. 'We'd better have it in Italian, or my sister Lucrezia will lose interest.'

Lucrezia leaned forward. 'Oh, you're wrong, Luigi – I feel sure I could listen to this pretty friar all evening, in any language.'

I blushed deeper, but I did not miss the way the young

man standing behind her tensed at her provocative tone, and his knuckles whitened as he gripped the back of her chair. I glanced at him; a youth a few years older than me, with light brown hair and a smooth face, his mouth pressed tight, green eyes alight with anger. Porta had said the cardinal's sisters were unmarried, but this young man's possessive manner suggested he was a suitor, or believed he had some claim on her. I had no wish to make further enemies in Rome, so I directed my gaze politely to the other sister, Leonora, as I recited Psalm 140 from memory.

When I finished, Porta clapped his hands in delight at the cardinal's evident approval and cried, 'Now backwards, Bruno!' So I obliged by reciting the psalm backwards, which drew astonished exclamations from the onlookers. Hearing their gasps, more spectators gathered around to listen, until I was the centre of a considerable crowd.

'Bravo!' said the cardinal, regarding me with the open pleasure of a child watching a dancing puppet; I recalled Fra Agostino's snide warning about his appetite for novelty. 'What about Psalm 86? Give us that one in Latin, for my learned fellow clerics.' A couple of older men in religious robes standing by laughed at this, and so I obliged; by now the audience had the hang of the game, and people started shouting out numbers of psalms to test me. I was glad I had barely had time to touch the wine; on my painfully empty stomach, even a glass would have blunted my ability to remember. I complied with each request, sometimes speeding up my delivery to impress them further, until eventually Lucrezia d'Este interrupted with a loud yawn.

'Very clever of you,' she said, toying with her necklace, 'but can you parrot anything other than the holy scriptures? Which I must suppose you have been learning since your cradle.'

'Come now, Sister – I will not have that!' Cardinal d'Este

rose gallantly to my defence. 'I was raised for a life in the Church since the nursery too, as you know, and my memory is like a sieve – I count it an achievement when I can remember the whole Pater Noster. Fra Giordano is unquestionably a prodigy – he appears to carry the entire bible in his head. Even you, with your jaded taste for marvel, must acknowledge you are impressed.'

Lucrezia did not appear willing to concede anything. Perhaps she had thought to make me look foolish, but I merely bowed and asked if she would care to hear some Petrarch. She sat up then, and favoured me with a cool smile.

'Petrarch? You think, I suppose, that all women are set a-flutter by a sonnet of love?'

'I wouldn't know, my lady. I have no experience of setting women a-flutter.' I met her eye and saw the corner of her mouth twitch, amused. 'I can give you some Cicero, if you prefer?'

'God, no. It's a party. Let's have the Petrarch, then.'

She gestured for me to begin, and I launched into some verses; she kept her gaze on me in a way that began to make me feel distinctly uncomfortable, until I faltered over the words. The room appeared to be growing hotter. She noticed my stumble, and I could see she was pleased by the effect; I was almost relieved when I was interrupted by the sudden crash of a tray of drinks smashing to the floor as the young man by Lucrezia stepped backwards into the attendant carrying it.

'My apologies,' he muttered, smirking at me, as the servant scrambled to pick up the fallen goblets, red-faced in front of his employer, while the women shrieked and lifted their feet lest their velvet slippers be splashed with wine. Cardinal d'Este took the opportunity to grasp me by the elbow.

'Thank you for a most entertaining performance,' he said. 'Let us take some air together. Porta, join us.'

He led me through to an adjoining room, equally breath-taking in its decoration; here the servant trotting before him opened a door and I followed Porta and the cardinal on to a wide loggia that ran the length of the building, above an inner courtyard. Away from the heat of the fire and the press of bodies, the sharp December air was as welcome as a draught of cold water and I felt my head begin to clear.

'So, my friend,' said the cardinal amiably, draping an arm around my shoulder. 'What are you going to tell Cardinal Rebiba about me?'

I stared at him. 'Your Eminence, I—'

'No need to be coy, Bruno – that snake Agostino da Montalcino will have asked you to spy on me tonight, I'm not a fool. Don't worry, it doesn't offend me. You're not the first. I feel sure that between us we can concoct a few stories that will have the venerable Rebiba reaching for his sal ammoniac.'

'You are not afraid of him?' I realised as I spoke how naïve the question was. What must it be to come from a family so powerful that you never needed to fear what was said about you behind your back?

The cardinal gave a mirthless laugh. 'There's not much he can do to me for now, I have enough allies in the Sacred College. But you should certainly be afraid of him.'

'Your Eminence—' There was a warning in Porta's voice.

'He needs to know, Porta. Listen.' He leaned against a pillar and folded his arms, fixing me with a serious look. 'Cardinal Rebiba is a dangerous enemy.'

'But he's not my enemy,' I said, glancing at Porta in alarm. Cardinal d'Este laughed again.

'He's certainly not your friend, whatever Fra Agostino has told you. Scipione Rebiba is as obsessed with purging heresy as Pope Pius himself. It was Rebiba who introduced the

Roman Inquisition to Naples, nearly twenty years ago. And your convent, San Domenico Maggiore, resisted.'

'I didn't know that.' A chill began to seep inside my robes; I could not tell if it was the air or the story he was about to unfold.

'San Domenico is a rich convent. It had a comfortable relationship with the city authorities and the barons, with plenty of money flowing in for indulgences – the prior who was in place at the time didn't want to be the one responsible for interrogating people for heresy all of a sudden. He feared it would affect those lucrative connections. So Rebiba contrived to have him replaced with someone more malleable.'

'How do you know all this? You must have been a child at the time.'

'My uncle Ippolito is also a cardinal. He's told me all about it.'

'My father remembers it too,' Porta cut in, his expression grim. 'The fear that spread through Naples when the Inquisition arrived. Suddenly anyone with a vendetta could accuse his neighbour of heresy, and see him put on trial and possibly tortured. The Dominicans were hated for a long time because of it.'

'The prior that Rebiba installed died a few years later, and your current prior is showing himself increasingly reluctant to persecute heresy with the fervour that the Pope and Rebiba would like,' Cardinal d'Este said. 'The word here is that heresy is allowed to flourish in Naples because your prior is too liberal – including with his own friars. And the Spanish want to use that as an excuse to introduce their version of the Inquisition to Naples, which is even harsher than ours, and would clearly undermine Rome's authority in the kingdom. Naturally, Cardinal Rebiba takes all this very personally. And he is not to be underestimated, Bruno.' He exchanged a glance with Porta.

164

'Ten years ago, when the previous pope was elected, he ordered Rebiba and another cardinal arrested, because they had opposed his election,' Porta said. 'They were both imprisoned in the Castel Sant'Angelo. The other cardinal was strangled one night in his cell. No trial, no repercussions – but clearly on the then pope's orders. Some weeks later, Rebiba was released without charge – but can you imagine what those weeks did to him? Lying awake night after night, waiting for the footstep in the dark? It has made him utterly without mercy.'

'Not even cardinals are safe,' Este said, touching a hand tenderly to his own throat.

'Oh God.' I leaned on the balustrade and looked down over the courtyard, feeling faint. I could not even enjoy the prospect of amusing my friends in Naples with the idea that anyone could consider our prior too liberal. 'Then I am walking into a trap.'

'Well.' The cardinal rested his back against the stone pillar beside me. 'It is certain that Fra Agostino was sent to San Domenico to report on anything that could be used against your prior. A young man of prodigious – one might almost say *unnatural* – gifts is going to be an object of interest. And I have not studied the art of memory the way either of you have, but I have read enough to know that it draws on occult philosophies and magic.'

'Every book Bruno has used in developing his memory system came from my secret library,' Porta said, lowering his voice. 'And every one is on the Inquisition's Index of Forbidden Books. If he should be tortured, that would give them enough to take me in as well, and cast suspicion on you, Your Eminence, as my patron.' He nodded to the cardinal.

'I wouldn't mention either of you,' I said fiercely, but my stomach had clenched tight at the prospect and I feared I might retch. In truth I had no idea what I might be capable of, faced with the prisons of the Inquisition, and whether any of my principles or loyalties would survive. Like most healthy young men, I tried not to think about death at all if possible, and only as something that happened to other people.

'Oh, I'm sure you wouldn't,' Porta said smoothly, patting my arm. He seemed remarkably sanguine, though I knew he had been bred to hide his feelings under a mask of courtliness. 'All the same, it would be well to make sure nothing you say to the Pope about your memory system gives even the slightest hint of unorthodox reading.'

'Make sure you give all the credit to St Thomas Aquinas,' Cardinal d'Este added. 'He was a good Dominican, and a student of memory – they can't find fault with him.'

'But if I have been brought here so that they can use me to attack the Prior of San Domenico, they will find something else to fault.' I turned to face him, and my legs buckled under me; whether it was fear or hunger, I couldn't say. The cardinal reached out and caught me by the arm. He had heard the panic in my voice.

'Let's get this young man something to eat, and hear some Christmas music, and we'll have no more talk of the Inquisition,' he said, with deliberate good cheer. As we paused for the servant to open the door from the loggia, he laid a hand on my shoulder. 'Speaking of danger,' he said in a low voice, and my heart froze, though he was half-smiling. 'Watch out for my sister Lucrezia. She's taken a liking to you, and she's a young woman who is used to getting what she wants. Well – not so young any more,' he added wryly. 'She will be thirty-four soon. High time she was married off, and put an end to all the gossip.'

'Was that her betrothed, the man who knocked over the drinks?' I asked as we stepped back inside. 'I don't think he took a liking to me.'

'Ha! No, he wouldn't. That's Renzo Arduino. Don't worry about him. He's nobody – just a bastard nephew of the Prince of Piombino that my sister keeps on a leash to amuse her, in lieu of a lapdog. He'll yap at anyone who comes near, but he has no claim – the family would never let him marry her, though he can't seem to get that through his head, and hangs around in the hope that one day she'll take his suit seriously. If he gives you any trouble, just tell me and I'll have his arse kicked out of Rome faster than he can scatter a tray of drinks. But I'm serious – mind Lucrezia. If you've been tasked with spying on me tonight, you can be certain that others here will have the same commission. And since you are to appear before the Holy Father tomorrow, it would be wise if you kept yourself free from any taint of gossip. Don't give them any more ammunition to use against you.' He slapped me on the back as we approached the press of guests. 'Now – let us celebrate the Nativity of Our Lord with some decent food and a dance. I want you to hear my new singer from Brescia.'

The cardinal's Master of Ceremonies rang a bell and led the guests through to a high banqueting hall, its ceiling painted with scenes from the lives of the saints, the walls hung with rich tapestries. A long table had been set down the centre, with embroidered cloths, silver plates and goblets, gold candelabra and more Christmas garlands; the air was rich with the scent of pine and spices. All around me, people had grown animated and louder with the wine, jostling and pushing for seats closest to the cardinal and his entourage; in the press, I became separated from Porta and decided that, instead of running after him like a child who has lost his mother, I would do better to grab the nearest seat, in case I should find myself without one at all. I stood, looking around for an empty chair, shoved on all sides, when a hand closed over my sleeve. I turned to see Lucrezia d'Este smiling at me with a wolfish glint.

'Sit by me,' she said, pulling me after her. 'My brother will have kept seats.'

It was not a command I could refuse, as she well knew. The crowds parted respectfully before her and she gestured me to a chair at her side, across the table from the cardinal, who glanced from me to his sister and raised a wry eyebrow, as if to say I had been warned. Leonora sat opposite me, next to her brother; she also regarded me with a tight-lipped smile, as if she felt her thoughts were best kept to herself. Further down the table, a fight had broken out; Renzo Arduino, Lucrezia's lapdog, who had missed out on a seat close to his lady, was trying to force his way in several places down, near enough that he could at least skewer me with a glare of such fury that I felt compelled to move a candelabra so that it obscured his face.

The din of chatter died away as Cardinal d'Este stood to give thanks for the birth of Our Lord, the obedience of His Holy Mother, and the blessing of the Christmas season. A pious 'Amen' echoed the length of the hall, before the double doors at the end were flung open to admit a small army of servants bearing silver trays and platters with an array of delicacies beyond anything I had seen, even at the grandest feast days at San Domenico. There were stews of boar, beef and venison; plates of fish and shellfish; fresh pasta stuffed with cheeses and pine nuts; pies and pastries; roasted game birds and song birds in thick sauces of cream and herbs; seven different kinds of bread. I had only to set my glass down for a moment and a boy in Este livery would appear silently at my elbow and refill it. Musicians and singers accompanied the meal with motets composed for the season, though they could barely make themselves heard over the noise. I saw what Fra Agostino had meant about the luxury and indulgence of the cardinal's table, and how it might scandalise anyone who believed the religious life should be one of abstinence and self-denial, in imitation of Christ. For myself, in a short while I was too drunk to give much thought to such theological questions. I ate, laughed and joined in the bawdy jokes, told stories of my own youthful adventures in Naples, and was persuaded by Lucrezia to teach her one of the filthiest army songs I had learned from my father; wine continued to flow and the laughter around us grew wilder and more raucous. Occasionally, I caught Porta's eye across the table, though my head was too muddied to understand the import of his glance. When Lucrezia slid her hand up my thigh under the table I barely even noticed at first, though Renzo Arduino certainly did.

After the meal, when the guests were sated and the singers brought in, I excused myself and stumbled out to the staircase, pausing to ask a servant where I might go to piss. He pointed me down to a rear courtyard where animal troughs had been filled with sand for that purpose, and when I had relieved myself I adjusted my habit and leaned against a pillar for a while, hoping the night air would straighten my head. I still possessed enough clarity to realise that I was far too drunk to think of going back to Santa Maria yet; if Fra Agostino should accost me on my way through the door, I was in no state to offer him any useful account of the evening, and my obvious indulgence would only confirm his low opinion of me and the convent I represented. I tilted my head back to look at the upper balconies of the palazzo; the pillars around the loggia all appeared doubled. I pressed one hand over my left eye and squinted until they steadied. If I could find a place to rest for an hour or so, I reasoned, I might yet be able to creep back to Santa Maria after matins, and avoid Fra Agostino until breakfast, by which time I might be in better shape. To my drunk mind, this seemed in the moment a foolproof plan. I was looking for the entrance when a drawling voice spoke from the shadows behind me.

'What do you think you're doing?'

I turned. Renzo Arduino stepped into the torchlight. His right hand rested lightly on the sword at his belt.

'I'm having a piss. Did you want to watch?'

'Do you think the lady Lucrezia is a common whore?' He drew himself up, his chin tilted at me in challenge, but he was swaying on his feet, and there were wine stains down the front of his fine silk doublet. I realised he was as drunk as I was.

'What?' I had to narrow my eyes to focus. 'Of course not.'

'No? You're acting as if you think she's for sale. I saw you groping her under the table all through dinner.'

I had enough of my wits about me to realise that it would be unchivalrous to protest that it had been the other way around.

'I think you must be mistaken.' I tried to move past him, but he shoved me hard in the chest; I stumbled and he took a step towards me. I realised then that he had come for a fight and, much as I would have liked to oblige, it would not help my reputation or that of San Domenico if I were to appear before the Holy Father on Christmas day with a black eye and bruised knuckles.

'Do you seriously think,' he said, through his teeth, his hand back on his sword hilt, 'that she would be interested in fucking a dirty little Neapolitan peasant like you? How do you dare have the temerity even to look at her?'

He was almost vibrating with rage. I suspected he knew as well as I did that the lady Lucrezia had made it clear that she was extremely interested. I had done my best to ignore the slow, stroking motions of her fingers at the top of my thigh, and her murmured innuendoes in my ear; it was fortunate that the wine meant my response was muted. But I had

170

met too many men like this Renzo in my own order – bastard sons of noblemen, obsessed with the distinctions of rank because they were so acutely conscious of their own tainted status – to take the insult with grace, especially in my cups.

'What are you, her bodyguard?' I stepped up to face him, my hand sliding around my back, under my cloak, before I remembered that I had left Porta's knife behind.

'I am going to be her husband, you dog.' He was taller than me, but I was riled enough not to be intimidated.

'Ah. She forgot to mention your betrothal. I'll be sure to pass my congratulations to His Eminence, her brother. He'll be surprised by the news, I imagine.'

'It's not official,' he blustered. 'But I will have her eventually. I haven't spent this long courting her for nothing. I am of the royal house of Piombino, you know.'

'Mm. Though that's not really official either, is it?'

At that, he moved to draw his sword, but the drink had made him clumsy; it stuck in the scabbard, and as he fought to free it, I could not think of any way to stop him except to land a hard punch in his gut. He doubled over, coughing, and I ducked past him towards the door leading into the palazzo.

'I'm going to make sure you end up at the bottom of the fucking Tiber,' he shouted after me, when he had recovered enough to speak. 'In so many pieces your whore bitch mother will have to spend the rest of her worthless life fishing for them. Memorise *that*, you Neapolitan cunt! Good evening, Your Grace,' he added, with an unsteady bow, as an older man in bishop's robes passed me in the doorway, looking from one to the other of us with consternation.

The night air and the confrontation had sobered me somewhat; I realised with a jolt of fear that I had narrowly avoided a brawl in the cardinal's house, which might have ended in serious injury for one or both of us, and would not have

171

helped my standing in Rome, or Porta's. I congratulated myself again on having the foresight to leave the knife behind. I needed to get away before anything worse happened. I also wanted to make sure I avoided any possibility of the lady Lucrezia propositioning me directly; I did not think she would react well to an outright rejection, but the alternative would place me in an equally dangerous position. Cardinal d'Este, tolerant as he was, would be unlikely to forgive such a breach of etiquette.

I decided to find Porta and ask him to make my excuses to the cardinal. I also wanted to ask if he could spare one of his bodyservants to accompany me to Santa Maria; I was not convinced that I would find the way back easily in my present state, and although Renzo was loud and arrogant and I did not take his blustering threat literally, it was possible that he was angry enough to follow me into the streets and teach me a lesson on the way. That odd, unsettling sense of being stalked earlier in the afternoon also came back to me. Perhaps I had imagined it, but in the light of what Cardinal d'Este had told me about Rebiba and the Pope, it did not seem impossible that someone could have been set to spy on me while I was here. In the dead of night, half-drunk, my fears swelled and loomed like distorted shadows in candle-light; I did not relish the thought of walking through Rome unarmed in the dark.

In search of Porta, I soon realised I had taken the wrong staircase. I could hear the hubbub of music and conversation but I seemed to be moving away from it with every twist of the corridor. My head had begun to spin again and I felt a sudden need to sit down. To my right, I noticed a door that had been left ajar; a light flickered from within and I pushed it open to find a small chamber with a cheerful fire blazing in the hearth. Chairs had been pulled close and empty glasses lay abandoned beside them, but whoever they belonged to had disappeared. Against one wall there was a day bed piled with cushions and velvet throws. I stood by the fire to warm my hands, and decided to pause for a rest before finding Porta.

I had only intended to close my eyes long enough to clear my head. Instead, I fell into strange dreams, and when I half-opened them I believed for a moment that I was in the kitchen of my childhood home in Nola, with my head in my mother's lap, her strong fingers raking with a soothing rhythm through my hair. I blinked hard and my vision cleared to show the lady Lucrezia stroking my head, a knowing smile playing over her lips.

'Very ungallant of you to fall asleep on me, my little Dominican,' she chided, running a forefinger down my cheek.

I scrambled to sit up. We were alone in the small chamber, the door shut fast, the fire and the candles burning low. I had no idea what time of night it might be, or how long I had slept. The sudden movement had set my head pounding.

'Forgive me, I – I have to get back,' I stammered. But she was perched on the edge of the day bed, sitting on my habit; I could not move without physically pushing her, and she knew it.

'No rush,' she said, placing her hand on my chest. 'No one is going to come looking for us.'

I glanced at the door. This was not true; I was certain that Renzo Arduino was, at this very moment, urgently searching every room in the house for us, ready to defend his lady's honour. I was more worried about my own.

'My lady.' I tried subtly to move, only to find that my belt had been unfastened. 'I'm sorry, but I'm expected back at Santa Maria. I am in holy orders,' I added, unnecessarily, indicating my habit.

She let out that raucous laugh that sounded as if it should belong to a tavern-keeper and not a noblewoman. 'Yes, I had noticed,' she said. 'I never met a churchman who let those vows bother him unduly. Do you know how many mistresses my brother has? And he's a cardinal.'

'Well, exactly.' I tried to sound deferential. 'He is senior enough that such things would not damage his prospects. Whereas I am merely a humble friar—'

'There's nothing humble about you,' she said, toying with the collar of my habit. 'I watched you tonight, showing off your memory tricks. You're very sure of yourself and your own brilliance. It's an attractive quality.' She leaned closer; I pressed myself back against the wall. 'Tell me,' she said, 'what do you think are *my* attractive qualities?'

I let my gaze flicker downwards and noticed that she had loosened her bodice. 'Um.' My mouth dried. The pain in my head felt as if it were bulging outwards through my eyes. 'You are a very beautiful woman, my lady. But His Eminence the cardinal is my host, and I would not for all the world insult a lady as noble as you by even daring to look—'

She made an impatient noise. 'I'm not offering to *marry* you, boy,' she said. I wondered if she actually remembered my name. 'And His Eminence the cardinal is my little brother, who has not dared argue with me since he was a toddler in napkins. Please don't worry on his account. His only concern is for my happiness. Which I believe you could enhance tonight.' She unlaced her bodice all the way and let it fall open, then reached for my hand and placed it decisively on her small, firm breast.

I stared at her, my eyes locked on hers, frozen for several moments as if my brain could not quite process what was happening. My body caught up quicker than my thoughts; as she slid a hand up my leg and bent her head to kiss me, I knew I had to move before my natural responses rendered me helpless. I sprang from the bed, snatching the hem of my

174

habit out from under her as my belt fell to the floor, and backed towards the door.

'My lady, I can't – I must stay pure. I am to see the Holy Father tomorrow.'

Her smile vanished. 'Pure. *Please*. Who would know?'

I gestured to the ceiling. 'God is watching.'

'He's seen worse.' She stood and advanced towards me, but there was no honey in her expression now; she looked at me as if we were circling one another in preparation for a duel, and I realised that the conquest had become a matter of saving her pride. For the space of a heartbeat I considered giving in; she was, after all, a good-looking woman, standing before me half-naked, the firelight playing pleasingly over her skin. It would have been no hardship to give her what she wanted. But in the same moment I realised the price would be too high; to make an enemy of her brother the cardinal, on whose goodwill Porta depended, as well as that hot-headed thug Renzo, would not be worth a few minutes of pleasure that I was fairly sure I was not sober enough to appreciate. The insult to her vanity would be brief, and I could take comfort in the knowledge that I had done nothing deserving of reproach.

'Forgive me,' I stammered again, fumbling for the latch, and fled before she could lunge at me, leaving her staring in disbelief and fury as the door swung shut. I ran for the nearest set of stairs, tore along an empty corridor and found myself in an outer courtyard by the stables, where boys were saddling horses by torchlight, ready for whenever the last guests chose to depart. The sounds of music and singing carried from the house behind me. My breath steamed in the air; I glanced up to see stars pin-bright in a clear sky. I shivered, realising I had forgotten to collect my cloak, but I did not dare return to the main entrance in search of it. I had lost my belt too, and had to hitch my habit up to keep it off the frosty ground.

175

The thought of it in the lady Lucrezia's hands, as evidence, gave me a cold sensation in my stomach, as if I were the one with something to feel guilty about.

'You look frozen, Fra Giordano,' said a woman's voice softly, behind me. I jumped, turning with my hands up in defence; the Ferrara accent was so like Lucrezia d'Este's that I feared she had followed me. But when the figure stepped forward from the shadows, I saw that it was her sister, the lady Leonora. She was wrapped in a heavy cape of fur, with matching mittens on her hands.

'I left my cloak,' I said, with an anxious glance at the house.

'I came out to escape the noise,' she said, by way of explanation. 'I like to look at the stars. I find them reassuringly indifferent to our petty concerns, don't you?'

I nodded, with a shiver, though in that moment my concerns seemed far from petty; I had insulted the sister of a cardinal, whose suitor had threatened to kill me, and the next day, on no sleep, I was to appear before the Pope, who was apparently planning to trap me into condemning myself and my convent for heresy.

'Do you ever imagine what it would be like to fly among the stars?' she murmured, her head tilted back. 'Your friend Porta told my brother he is working on a device with lenses that would allow him to see the heavens as if they were mere yards away.'

'Did he?' I felt it best not to admit to knowing anything of Porta's experiments, though his optical device was among the more harmless.

'I hope he does not succeed,' she said, smiling. 'I prefer the heavens to remain a mystery. I find this desire men have to measure and categorise everything to be at odds with awe and beauty. Suppose we could see the stars up close and find they do not look like diamonds on a velvet cloth after all? How disappointing that would be.'

176

'But there is wonder in understanding how the universe works, my lady,' I said, thinking at the same time that I was probably too drunk for a conversation that might stray dangerously close to heresy. 'The knowledge of how to measure and map the oceans has allowed men to discover new worlds over the sea in our lifetime – might the same not be true of the heavens?'

She turned to me and frowned. 'You think there are other worlds in the heavens? I have never heard such an idea.'

But I had. In Porta's secret library I had found books by Nicholas of Cusa and the Polish astronomer Copernicus proposing the theory that the Earth was not the centre of the universe, that it circled the Sun, a star like any other star, and if that were the case, why should every other star we see not also have its own worlds in orbit, just like ours? Those books and their hypotheses were strictly forbidden by the Inquisition; it was pure folly even to hint at them to the sister of a cardinal.

'No. That would be blasphemy,' I said quickly. 'Forgive me, my lady – I talk too much.'

'My sister Lucrezia always says the same of me. By the way – she was looking for you earlier,' Leonora added, giving me a sidelong look. 'She seemed quite determined to find you. Did she?'

I lowered my eyes. I could not think how to answer, though I felt discretion was my best defence. A dull pain throbbed behind my eyes; if I had not been so cold, I might have fallen asleep right there on my feet.

'I see.' She continued to watch me. 'Luigi said he warned you. You turned her down, yes? That's why you've come running out here without your cloak?'

I nodded miserably. She glanced around the yard, then clapped her hands together briskly.

'Then you need to leave immediately. My sister doesn't like to be thwarted – she tends to lash out.'

'How do you mean?' I snapped my head up, alarmed.

'Do as I say. Get yourself away from here while her anger is hot, so none of her poison darts can land. By tomorrow she'll probably have forgotten the whole thing. I'll have your cloak sent on.' She called over one of the grooms. 'You, sirrah – take one of the cardinal's horses and see this young friar safely back to Santa Maria sopra Minerva, quick as you can. Go the back way.

'Merry Christmas to you, Fra Giordano,' Leonora said, as I mounted behind the servant and the gates were opened for us. 'May the Christ child and His Holy Mother bless your audience with His Holiness tomorrow. And don't worry about my sister. I will speak in your defence.'

I thanked her with a tight bow from the saddle, but all I could think was: defence against what? I feared that, of the two impossible choices put before me in that small, firelit chamber, I had made the wrong one.

I woke abruptly into grainy grey light, to find myself shaken by the officious novice from the day before.

'Fra Agostino sent me to fetch you,' he said. 'You've over-slept.' He seemed pleased but unsurprised by this most basic shortcoming.

I sat up gingerly, touching my fingers to my temples. My skull felt like the shell of an egg that might fracture with the slightest unexpected movement. I did not remember much about how I got home; I recalled the horse, the solid bulk of the cardinal's servant as I clung to him through twisting back streets; the knowing nod of the old gatekeeper at Santa Maria as he unlocked the door for me. I had no idea what time that might have been, or any recollection of how I had found my way to my bed.

'Can I get some hot water?' I asked the boy. 'I would like to wash before I see Fra Agostino.'

178

'No time for that,' the boy said, smirking. 'He's waiting for you to go to early Mass at San Pietro.'

Madonna porca. I managed to keep the curse under my breath. I stood, steadying myself as waves of dizziness blurred my vision and the pain threatened to split my head in two. I felt as if I had barely closed my eyes. Never again, I thought, furious with myself; it was all I could do to remember my own name, never mind swathes of scripture.

'What time is it?' I asked.

'Six.' He opened the door and held it for me. Somewhere beyond the cloister a bell was ringing. 'I heard you didn't get back until four.'

I passed a hand through my hair. I didn't want to think about what I looked like. It was then that I realised my habit was trailing on the floor.

'Can I borrow your belt?' I said.

'What?' He looked me up and down. 'No. Don't you have one?'

'I lost it. Come on – I can't go to San Pietro like this. It would reflect badly on our order.'

He hesitated, his cheeks primly sucked in, as if he couldn't imagine how someone could be such a hopeless mess. After a moment, he rolled his eyes and unfastened the cord around his waist. 'This is only so you don't make Santa Maria look bad,' he said. 'Although from what I hear it will take more than a belt.'

I decided not to give him the satisfaction of asking what he meant by that.

'Dear God in Heaven.' Fra Agostino assessed me from head to foot and shook his head in dismay. 'Your face is actually green. Are you going to be sick?'

'I think it must have been something I ate,' I mumbled. 'Probably the wrong season for shellfish.'

179

He gave me a long look. 'I don't think it's what you ate. You reek of wine. I hope you didn't do anything to disgrace yourself?'

'Of course not.' Jagged shards of memory jabbed uncomfortably at me; my hand on Lucrezia's breast; punching Renzo in the stomach; suggesting to the lady Leonora that I believed in other worlds. 'It was all quite uneventful.'

'You can tell me all about it on the way. Oh, and this was sent for you by messenger from the Este house early this morning.' He held up my cloak. 'You must have left in a hurry. Like Joseph fleeing from Potiphar's wife.' He raised an eyebrow.

'No, nothing like that. I just forgot it.'

'Really? I thought you were the memory expert.'

I shrugged the cloak around my shoulders and avoided his eye.

We walked to the Vatican with other senior brothers from Santa Maria, accompanied by several armed servants; Fra Agostino had brought with him a purse from which he distributed Christmas alms to the beggars and workless men who lined the streets with their hands out, hoping for a scrap of seasonal charity from those on their way to Mass at San Pietro. Agostino quizzed me all the way about what I had seen and heard at Cardinal d'Este's the night before; he was disappointed with my claim that I had been seated at a far end of the table among persons of no note and had overheard little of interest.

'No rumours at all that Este is trying to raise a faction against the Pope in the Sacred College?'

'Nothing of that nature,' I said. 'Everyone spoke most respectfully of His Holiness.' As we passed through a small piazza the smell of fresh bread drifted from a tavern; I was at once ravenous and nauseous.

'Hm. And did you see any suggestion of fornication or lewd behaviour?'

180

His eagerness on this point was off-putting. I could not shake the image of Lucrezia unlacing her bodice and reaching under my habit. 'Not in my presence. There was dancing, but it did not seem improper.'

'So you failed to observe anything that might be of value to Cardinal Rebiba,' Agostino said with a sniff as we crossed the Ponte Sant'Angelo. The dark walls of the castle prison loomed ahead and I thought of Cardinal Rebiba locked up there for months on a pope's whim, while his colleague was strangled in the dark. 'Whatever other gifts you may have, you are sadly lacking the skills for spying.'

'I never claimed any such talent,' I said, pulling my cloak tight against the cold. 'That was your idea.' The bridge was crowded and I could see a greater throng of people ahead, pressing towards the Piazza San Pietro for a glimpse of the Holy Father.

'If you hope for a future in Rome,' Agostino said with chilly contempt, 'you would do well to learn that intelligence is the most versatile currency here. Tell me – what did you make of Cardinal d'Este's sisters?'

'Oh – I only saw them from a distance. I found them to be modest, gracious women.'

'Then you are more naïve than I thought. The elder is a notorious Jezebel. Never happier than when she has young men duelling to the death over her. And they say when she tires of her lovers, she finds a way to be rid of them. More than one has found himself on the wrong end of false charges. Those of lower birth don't even get the courtesy of a trial.'

'What?' I turned to him, staring, then quickly dropped my gaze, hoping he had not seen the panic in my eyes.

'Last year, a groom from the Este household washed up dead on the banks of the Tiber. Supposedly an altercation in a tavern over a bet, but rumour said he had been the lover of Lucrezia and she wanted him silenced.' There was a

181

particular malicious pleasure in his tone, or perhaps the lack of sleep made me imagine that.

'Rumour may say much,' I muttered.

'But rarely without cause, where women are concerned,' he said smoothly. 'You must be relieved you only saw her from a distance.'

'Greatly relieved.' For a moment I thought I might be sick on the steps.

Papal guards ushered us into the great draughty basilica of San Pietro and escorted us through the crowd of citizens to the front benches, where the dignitaries of the city's religious houses were seated, their orders marked by the colours of their habits. Ahead of us, closer to the altar, scarlet robes rippled as the members of the Sacred College of Cardinals took their places. I wished I had been in better shape to appreciate the magnificence of my surroundings; though the dome was unfinished and the roof covering temporary, the sheer size of the basilica made it a marvel of art, geometry and engineering, a bold assertion of Rome's primacy as the beating heart of the Christian faith. If I had been feeling less delicate I might have experienced a moment of pride at this religious life I had chosen, or paused to ponder the ineffable mysteries of divine grace as we celebrated the incarnation of God in the Nativity. But as the choir's first clear notes ascended to the heights and I craned around to see the papal procession advancing up the nave, all I could think about were the stories I had just heard concerning Lucrezia d'Este.

After the Mass was over and the Holy Father had left to dispense his blessings from the balcony to the waiting crowd in the piazza, one red-robed figure detached from the flock of cardinals and moved towards us. I saw Fra Agostino's eyes light up like a girl awaiting her sweetheart, and guessed that

182

this must be his patron, to whom I was expected to show my gratitude.

Cardinal Scipione Rebiba was a tall, broad-chested man, with a full beard still more black than grey despite his sixty years. His rectangular slab of a face looked as if it had been carved from one solid block of marble. He did not smile, and his expression when he looked at me was that of a man who expects to be disappointed.

I lowered my eyes in deference. He held out his hand and Fra Agostino bent to kiss the gold ring he offered.

'So this is the talented Fra Giordano Bruno?' He made it sound as if I had given myself the accolade. He stretched his hand to me and then withdrew it hastily. 'What's wrong with him, Agostino? He looks like he's coming down with the plague.'

I was glad I could not see myself in a glass; I was conscious of the sweat glazing my skin.

'I assure you he's perfectly well, Your Eminence,' Fra Agostino said, before I could speak, with an oily little bow. 'It may be that something disagreed with him last night at Cardinal d'Este's feast.'

'Ha. Este disagrees with everyone – it wouldn't surprise me if his food followed suit. Come on, then, don't waste my time.' Rebiba set off down the nave in long strides, cracking a smile at his own wit. Agostino chivvied me along in his wake.

He led us through a side entrance, across a small courtyard and into a chapel that seemed unassuming from the outside, but caused me to cry out as we entered.

'What?' Rebiba, halfway across the chapel, turned impatiently to find me rooted to the spot, staring in amazement at the ceiling. 'Oh, this. Yes, I always forget how it renders people speechless the first time they see it. Bit gaudy for my taste, but he had an eye for spectacle, that Buonarroti.'

'I've never seen anything like it.' I felt as if the breath had been knocked out of my body. I wanted to lie on the floor for a day and take it all in. On every wall, biblical scenes exploded into vivid colour, characters of flesh and muscle, their coiled energy captured as if the master had painted them from life, in the midst of their private dramas. Naples had beautiful churches, but until that moment I had not encountered art possessed by genius. 'It's as if his brush was touched by the hand of God.'

'He certainly thought so,' Rebiba said drily. 'Stubborn old goat.'

'You knew him?' I stared.

'He died only five years ago. Nearly ninety, and still arguing with everyone. I never met a man so sure of his own brilliance. Thought his gifts gave him some kind of divine singularity that permitted him to defy popes.' He pointed a finger in my direction. 'Don't take any lessons from him, if you know what's good for you.'

But I crossed the chapel with my head craned back and my eyes fixed on the ceiling, on the hand of God stretched out to Adam, privately thinking that no pope or cardinal could be closer to the divine mind than the man who had given life to those pictures from his own imagination.

We were accompanied by soldiers from the Papal Guard up a flight of stairs and through a series of rooms no less astonishing in their decoration, until we were shown into a chamber known as the Stanza della Segnatura, and I understood with a tightening of my throat that we were now in the very heart of the Apostolic Palace.

'This is the Holy Father's official study,' Agostino hissed. 'Where he signs the papal bulls that must be obeyed throughout Christendom. Quite a thought, is it not?'

I nodded. I wondered if this was where he would sign

the order of excommunication against Elizabeth of England. Though the high-backed wooden throne at the far end of the room was empty, the setting demanded hushed voices. We were not the only ones waiting for an audience with His Holiness; perhaps a dozen men stood about in small groups, some in silk doublets and fur collars, others in clerical robes or religious habits, heads bent, conferring in whispers. At our arrival they fell silent, looked from me to Cardinal Rebiba and fell back to their murmuring, eyes still fixed on us.

'Who are all these people?' I asked Agostino.

He shrugged. 'Ambassadors. Papal legates. Courtiers. Perhaps other young men gifted in the art of memory, also invited to impress him, who knows.' He looked at me sidelong with a finely honed sneer. My mouth dried; I had not anticipated an audience. I was already regretting the waste of my best performance on Cardinal d'Este and his sisters the night before, and would have given anything for a cup of the coca tea from the New World that Porta served at the meetings of his secret Academy. To ward off the waves of dizziness I concentrated on the painting opposite, fixing my eyes on the receding arches through which the figures of Plato and Aristotle strolled, books in hand, deep in conversation. Imagine walking into that picture and eavesdropping on their debate! You'd have to step over Diogenes to reach them, but it would be worth it just to—

'Don't try to be clever with His Holiness,' Rebiba muttered suddenly, making me jump, his breath hot in my ear. 'He won't appreciate it.'

'Yes, Your Eminence,' I said. 'And my prior warned me not to be stupid, so I will aim somewhere between the two.'

He sucked in air through his teeth.

'The Holy Father wants to see evidence of your memory, not your wit,' he said. 'No one is interested in that. His

Holiness is skilled at asking difficult questions, as I'm sure you know. You would do well to concentrate all your attention on making sure you give him the right answers.'

He drifted away, and I was left staring at the philosophers, my hands clenched into fists and my bowels turned to water.

A ripple of shuffling and straightening in the room brought me back to myself; Agostino nudged me and I followed his gaze to the door. The onlookers sank to their knees as the papal party entered, and I raised my eyes enough to take a look at Christ's vicar on earth. Pope Pius V was unassuming in appearance, a crabbed little man in white robes with a red velvet cape and hat, scowl lines etched into his brow above small dark eyes that swept the room with suspicion, as if there might be heretics lurking behind the furniture. He walked stiffly; though I knew him to be in his mid-sixties, his long white beard and awkward gait aged him. Flanked by two cardinals, he took his seat and arranged his skirts fussily, like an old dowager. I fixed my eyes on the rings flashing from his bony fingers and wondered how many people those hands had tortured to death, directly or indirectly.

'Get up, then.' He sounded irritated, but he spoke with a commanding voice for such a pinched-looking man. The assembled guests straightened and the Pope peered over their heads. 'Well, Cardinal Rebiba. Where is this boy from Naples you insist I see?'

Rebiba shoved me forward with a hand in my back; the rest of the crowd withdrew a few paces and I stumbled into the holy presence.

He held out his hand and I bent to kiss the ring he offered.

'Stand up. Let me look at you.' Though I kept my eyes down, I could feel the force of his scrutiny. 'They tell me you are unnaturally gifted in the art of memory.'

186

Was that an accusation? I cleared my throat, but my words still came out in a squeak.

'Such gifts as I have, Your Holiness, are quite natural, I assure you, and the result of diligent study.'

'I see. So you do not credit God for them?'

'I – well, yes, of course – I thank Him for whatever modest talents He has allowed me to refine.' My palms had grown sticky with sweat. All I could think was don't let him corner you; don't say anything heretical; don't for God's sake pass out.

'Let's hear you, then. Apparently you have the psalms by heart.' He folded his hands in his lap.

'Which would you like to hear, Your Holiness?' I wished I could summon the verve and confidence I had felt the night before, when I was trying to impress Cardinal d'Este's guests and sisters.

The Pope considered. We watched one another and under his gaze my throat tightened; he had the eyes of a crow.

'I think,' he said at length, 'I should like to hear something seasonal. Give us Psalm 110, which foretells the coming of Christ.'

I took a deep breath. On occasion, I had hung about the Commedia Vecchia in Naples, talking to the actors, and had learned from them that the secret to a successful performance was to banish all other thoughts and immerse yourself entirely in the moment on stage.

'The Lord said unto my Lord, Sit thou at my right hand,' I began, in Latin, more confidently than I felt, 'until I make thine enemies thy footstool.' I hesitated, my mouth drying. What was next? All I could summon was an image of Lucrezia d'Este in firelight, her breasts spilling over her bodice.

'Every schoolboy learns that scripture,' muttered one of the cardinals.

Pope Pius merely blinked and gestured for me to continue.

I closed my eyes, banished Lucrezia and turned inwards, through the rooms of my memory palace, through the concentric circles of the system I had adapted from the mystic Ramon Llull, to seek out the words I knew were hidden in the depths of my mind's inner rooms. When I had finished, I opened my eyes to silence.

'And now – what if I ask you to recite it backwards?' the Pope leaned forward, crow eyes fastened on me.

I darted a swift glance at Cardinal Rebiba, whose face gave nothing away.

'If you wish, Your Holiness.' When he said nothing, I began, but after a few lines he held up a hand as if to ward off an attack.

'Stop! I will not have this blasphemy in the Apostolic Palace.'

'But you asked—' I caught Cardinal Rebiba's warning glance just in time.

'When I was Inquisitor in Como,' the Pope said, with a regretful expression that suggested he missed those days, 'it was my sad duty to prosecute witches who among their devilish incantations would recite the Pater Noster backwards to summon demons.'

A gasp of horror susurrated around the room; one of the cardinals crossed himself. I felt as if all the blood had left my body. 'There is no blasphemy here, Your Holiness,' I managed, though the words emerged hoarse and panicked.

'No? Why else would you learn to say the psalms backwards? How can that possibly show respect for the scriptures? It is a well-known trick of witches and magicians in their spells, this deliberate perversion of holy rites.'

'No – it's just a . . .' I dried.

'Just what, my son?' The gentleness of his tone made the look in his eyes even worse.

'A bit of fun,' I said lamely.

188

'*Fun?*'

'You know. A game. To demonstrate the art. To show off, if you like.' I smiled eagerly, as if that would make him like me.

'To show off? Did you hear that, brothers?' He turned to the audience with a mild expression of shock. 'This young man thinks the word of God is a toy to buy cheap applause, like the flaming torches the jongleurs throw and catch in the marketplace, no doubt. And when you defended the heresies of the Protestants, was that also a bit of *fun*, to show off to your friends?'

My hands had begun to shake; I gripped them together but I could feel every man in the room looking at me, relishing the fact that he was not the one squirming on the end of a hook.

'I do not defend the heresies of the Protestants, Your Holiness.'

'I have it on good authority that in' – he leaned across and muttered something to Cardinal Rebiba, who whispered in return – 'September of this year, 1569, during a disputation at the convent of San Domenico Maggiore in Naples, you called Fra Agostino da Montalcino a fool for saying the Protestants were ignorant. Do you deny it?'

I glanced over my shoulder at Fra Agostino. His expression was sombre, except for the tiniest twitch at the corners of his lips. So this was why I was here; so that he could have his petty revenge. The treachery of it stung so sharply that defiance overruled good sense. I drew myself up and looked directly at the Pope.

'Yes, I do.' Another sharp intake of breath from the crowd behind me – they sensed sport – but I spoke firmly. 'I didn't call him a fool. I said his argument was ignorant.'

'Foolish, ignorant – what is the difference?'

'An intelligent man may make an ignorant point, if he

189

speaks without due consideration,' I said. 'I believed, on that occasion, that it was ignorant and reductive for Fra Agostino to dismiss all the Protestant thinkers as stupid, when many of them are learned scholars.'

The room had fallen silent, but I could feel the held breath of the crowd behind me, could almost hear the rustle of silk as they gripped their neighbour's sleeve in apprehension.

'Do you say so? Then you do not believe the Protestants are wrong?' He was looking at me as if we were the only two people in the room.

'Naturally, they are wrong, Your Holiness. But I don't think they are stupid. And I do not believe that dismissing our enemies as ignorant is the most effective way to persuade them of the rightness of our faith.'

'So you think we should give credence to the beliefs of the Protestants? We should engage with their heretical arguments?'

'We should perhaps at least try to understand why men of undeniable learning and scholarship have come to believe as they do, and why their arguments carry so many people with them.'

'Interesting. There are many supposedly great scholars among the Jews and the Infidels – no doubt you admire their work, and think we should seek enlightenment from their writings too?'

'I do not, Your Holiness.' I did, and had even read some in Porta's secret library. 'We have to draw a line somewhere.'

'Oh, do we? And you have appointed yourself to decide where? Perhaps you consider yourself better qualified to judge than the Holy Office?' Before I could answer, he continued, 'So tell me, boy – which of the Protestant theologians do you favour?' His black eyes glittered.

'I did not say I favour them—'

'Whose learned writings do you most admire? Luther?

190

Calvin? John Knox? Philip Melanchthon? Don't gape at me, boy – I have read a few books. Or did you think you would find me a goatherd still?'

'No, I—'

'Do not presume to lecture me on the need to understand our enemies' beliefs,' he said, his voice low. 'It was a distasteful but necessary part of my duty as Grand Inquisitor to read and parse those books, the better to refute their heretical theses. But I find myself curious about how a humble friar of— what age are you?'

'Twenty-one, Your Holiness,' I said faintly.

'—a mere youth, should be so well acquainted with the Protestant writers that he feels emboldened to defend their learning to a superior of his order. It is unusual – or at least it was in my day – that someone of your age and station should have access to such works, since they are all on the Index of Forbidden Books. So I ask again – which of them do you find most persuasive?'

He allowed a narrow smile then, and the look in his eye was that of a chess player whose opponent has proved a disappointingly easy conquest. I watched him, trying to steady my breath. It was checkmate, and everyone in the room could see it. If I acknowledged that I had read any of the Protestant theologians whose work I had defended, I would be questioned in the Castel Sant'Angelo until I told them who had supplied me with forbidden books; Porta and my prior would be implicated in my heresy. And if I said that I had not read them, I would be publicly shamed as a stupid, arrogant youth who disrespects his seniors for a cheap laugh. It would not be pleasant to watch Agostino revelling in my humiliation, but it was clear that I only had one option.

'I have not read them, Your Holiness.'

'What? But you defended them in front of all your brothers

in the basilica of San Domenico! Tell me – does your prior give you licence to study such material?'

'No, Your Holiness. He is strict with us. I spoke out of turn only to—'

'Yes?'

'To appear clever in front of my brothers. To make them laugh.'

'I see. A bit of *fun*, I suppose, at the expense of Fra Agostino. Why, what harm had he done you?'

I kept my eyes on the ground. Did you never, at twenty-one, I wanted to ask him, find mischief in mocking a pompous, puffed-up buffoon twice your age, or were you already tearing people's fingernails out for Jesus?

'I disliked his manner of arguing,' I said. 'I felt it lacked sophistication.'

The Pope sat back and exchanged a glance with Cardinal Rebiba; shocked laughter murmured around the room and was quickly silenced, though I was sure not all of it was disapproving.

'Listen to me, boy,' the Holy Father said, craning towards me again. 'Sophistication is not a mark of godliness. Quite the reverse, often. Truth and error are simple concepts, as I was frequently obliged to explain to those who tried to excuse their heresies with sub-clauses and nuance. So simple even a goatherd or a soldier's son can grasp them. Intellectual pride is the oldest sin, you know this. In the garden of Paradise, our father Adam broke God's only commandment because he lusted after knowledge that was set outside his sphere. I see the same weakness in you.' He left a long pause; I raised my head and met his gaze. 'You owe Fra Agostino an apology, I think. Prostrate yourself here before me and kiss his feet, so that everyone can witness how you have chosen to humble yourself.'

Agostino stepped forward, his expression pure triumph. I

lay face down on the cold marble tiles, kissed each of his leather shoes in turn and mumbled,

'Forgive me, Brother, for my insolence and my lack of respect.'

I could hear the sniggering from the onlookers; my only consolation was that no one in the room appeared to know who I was. After daring to imagine this audience as the moment that would make my name in Rome, I found myself praying that I could slink out of the city without anyone remembering it.

'Get up,' Pope Pius said, when I had abased myself to his satisfaction. 'You deserve a more severe punishment, but I see that you are young and foolish, and you are a fellow Dominican. You may yet mend your ways, with the right guidance. Give thanks that in this holy season of our Saviour's birth, I am inclined to clemency.'

'Your Holiness—' Cardinal Rebiba leaned down as if to intervene, but the Pope held up a hand.

'Peace, My Lord Cardinal. You have what you wanted. If Fra Agostino forgives the boy, I see no need for further measures. I have more important matters to attend to. But hear this, Fra Giordano Bruno of Nola.' I raised my eyes; he pointed a bony finger in my direction. 'I too have been blessed with a prodigious memory, and I take care to make a note of everything. Be sure I will not forget your name. I will write to the Prior of San Domenico instructing him to keep you on a tighter leash. Go back to Naples and serve your order in quiet obedience. Take care who you consort with. If I ever hear word that you have shown an interest in forbidden books, or gone about touting yourself like a side-show reciting holy writ backwards, I will have you arrested on the instant. Do you understand me?'

I inclined my head and Christ's vicar flicked his fingers, as if shooing away a fly. As I was ushered out, I heard him say,

'That boy is headed for the pyre, sooner or later. But let him walk there with his own two feet.'

Fra Agostino strode ahead of me across the Piazza San Pietro, hands tucked in his sleeves, his expression tight. I sensed that he was disappointed to see me let off so lightly. We were halfway across the Ponte Sant'Angelo before I could trust myself to speak.

'*You have what you wanted?*' I repeated.

'What?' He snapped the word over his shoulder without slowing his pace.

'That's what the Pope said to Cardinal Rebiba. After he had me kiss your feet. Was that your intention all along – to have me questioned for heresy and then abase myself for you?'

'I am not responsible for your beliefs, Fra Giordano. If it pleases you to make grandiose public statements, you should be prepared to defend them to the highest authority. You are fortunate he was in a generous frame of mind – that could have gone a lot worse for you.'

'I know – you let him accuse me of witchcraft!'

'He didn't accuse you – if he had, you'd be in there.' He indicated the castle prison. 'He merely pointed out the similarities between your memory tricks and the obscene practices of magicians – something that has struck many of us who have watched you peacocking around, seeking attention. I pray this experience teaches you humility. You're being watched now.'

I slowed my pace and let him put some distance between us so that I could swallow all the curses I wanted to yell at him. This is how it would be from now on: biting back my thoughts, censoring myself, not daring to speak my mind for fear of how my words might be twisted. My prior would be furious; no doubt the Pope's letter would make clear

194

that any further misdemeanour on my part would be taken as evidence of his slack authority. He would feel obliged to tighten discipline; he would make me an example to my brothers of a new, stricter regime. I would be watched at every turn; it would be almost impossible for me to sneak out at night to the Academy of Secrets, and if I were to lose that community, I would be like a man starved of light. I wished I could talk to Porta; he was the only one who would understand, but I was wary of returning to Cardinal d'Este's house after what Leonora had told me about Lucrezia's tendency to lash out when she was thwarted. I felt like Adam, banished from the garden, with no place to call home.

As I passed through the gatehouse of Santa Maria, the old gatekeeper whistled for my attention.

'Message for you, Brother,' he said, reaching into his cloak and drawing out a folded letter. 'Private. Your man gave me a coin to keep it between me and you. Which I have, so far.' He fixed me with a meaningful look.

I reached into the purse beneath my habit and found another. 'Appreciated,' I said. The letter was sealed with blank wax. 'What did he look like, the man who paid you?'

The gatekeeper shrugged. 'Like a servant. No livery though.'

I thanked him again, and tore the paper open on the way to my cell, too upset and impatient to consider discretion.

The message came from Porta.

I need to speak to you urgently. Accusations have been made against you. Best that you leave Rome tonight – I will help you, but I can't get away until later. Meet me at 10 by the Theatre of Marcellus with your bag and I will see you safely on the road.

GdP

For the second time that day, I felt the ground tremble under my feet, as if I could no longer trust it to hold me. Accusations: it could only mean that the lady Lucrezia, to cover her pride, had given out that I had tried to force myself on her. I would have laughed, if my position had not been so precarious. I had already fallen foul of the Pope; if Lucrezia accused me of assaulting her, Cardinal d'Este might feel obliged to act, even if he didn't believe her. Leonora had said she would speak for me, but would anyone listen? Thank God for Porta, I thought, and how far-sighted of Gennaro to know that I would need a friend like him to defend me, in a city where even cardinals could be strangled to death while everyone looked the other way.

I sat alone at supper on the end of a long table, trying to ignore the open laughter and behind-the-hand muttering directed at me from the other brothers; when we stood for the benediction, I heard the word 'witch' whispered among the novices like wind through a copse, accompanied by sniggers. Agostino had clearly wasted no time in spreading the story of my papal audience through the convent. At vespers he preached a sermon about the example of Christ's humility in the Nativity, and how fitting it was this Christmas that one of our number should have been taught a valuable lesson about humility by our Holy Father himself; how, by this example, the community should guard itself against the sin of intellectual pride. I endured this and the office of compline in silence, making sure no one could fault my piety, and when the convent retired to bed, I packed my bag and lay on my bed, waiting for the bells to count out the hours.

Shortly after half-past nine, I crept out of the cell and into the rear courtyard with Porta's knife strapped to my belt under my cloak. Since the discretion of the gatekeeper was clearly for sale to the highest bidder, I decided it was best to give him nothing to trade with; I checked to see that the courtyard was empty, slung my bag over the wall, knotted my habit above my knees and shinned up after it.

A silver half-moon gave enough light to stumble through the streets, its edge sharp against the dark. I glanced up at the stars, regretting my careless comments to the lady Leonora about the possibility of other worlds. What if she should mention that to her brother, when I had already narrowly dodged an accusation of heresy by the Pope? When I paused to consider, I regretted most of what I'd said since arriving in Rome. At least the cold air had finally dispelled the fog in my head.

I remembered the Theatre of Marcellus; Porta's coachman had pointed it out as we entered the city. I found my way to the river and followed it south, one hand under my cloak ready to grasp the knife, but the only people abroad were Christmas revellers still on the right side of festive good cheer, and my habit seemed to afford me some protection; if anyone looked at me for too long, I made the sign of the cross and offered a Christmas blessing, at which they usually dipped their heads, mumbled their thanks and scurried off with a guilty expression. No one wants to be reminded of God when they're indulging in festive pleasures.

I arrived early, and took my place beneath the great arches of the ruined amphitheatre, looking towards the lights of the city. At my back, beyond the Theatre of Marcellus, lay the open wasteland of the Forum with its ancient pillars and tumbled walls; nothing but layers of darkness and the occasional glint that might be a watchful eye or a blade. I drew Porta's knife and held it tight at my side. In the dark spaces between the columns, shadows moved; I guessed the recesses provided shelter for vagrants, and I could not have been more conspicuous in my white robe, with a travelling pack on my back just asking to be stolen by desperate men.

After ten minutes the waiting began to chafe at me. Dogs slunk around my feet, sniffing; I kicked at them, muttering threats, and they scattered to snarl from a distance before creeping back. I needed to move; again that uneasy sensation that I was being observed from the shadows crawled up my neck. I made a circuit of the walls, watching for movement, gripping the knife with freezing fingers. It was only as I progressed slowly past the arches, peering into blackness, that it occurred to me to doubt the message. It had not been Porta's writing, but I had been so distracted earlier by my brush with the Pope and the effects of the night before that I had assumed he must have dictated it. As my chest tightened with the cold realisation that I might have blundered directly into an ambush, I heard a hiss from the shadows of an entrance.

'Porta?' I clutched the knife.

'This way,' a voice said; I caught the flicker of a lantern before it disappeared into the depths. I followed the light through a passageway, and emerged into the vast inner space of the amphitheatre. I had lost sight of the lantern; I stubbed my foot against a lump of rubble and cursed. The place was silent, but it was the silence of held breath; I felt eyes on me. I began to back away, towards the passage through the banks of tiered seating. God, what a fool I had been! Porta would never have dragged me out here and left me stumbling in the dark; the best I could hope for now was to run. It took a moment for my legs to catch up with the command; in the instant I turned to flee, I felt the cold edge of a blade against my throat from behind and hot breath against my hair, the barest hint of a laugh.

Instinct took over; blindly I thrust back my right arm and plunged the knife; I felt it sink, deep, and in my ear I heard

198

a gasp, muted, intimate, as if in shock rather than pain. The steel at my neck clattered to the ground; I looked down and saw the silver sheen of a sword, a gentleman's weapon. I pulled out the knife with one firm tug, my hand came away hot and wet as the man behind me emitted a sound almost like pleasure as he staggered back, hands pressed to his stomach. I turned to see Renzo Arduino doubled over, staring at me, eyes bright with amazement, his mouth working to speak.

'You have killed me,' he said, as if he could hardly believe the audacity, and crumpled to his knees.

Even in that moment, God forgive me, I experienced a flash of impatience. 'Of course I haven't,' I said. 'Lie down. Press hard on the wound. Jesus' sake – what did you expect? You put a sword to a man's throat in the dark, he's going to fight back.'

'I didn't think you'd be armed,' he said weakly.

I flattened my hands over the wound; Gennaro had shown me how to staunch bleeding, but on that occasion I had been furnished with lights, clean linen and hot water. It was too dark in the shadows of the amphitheatre to judge the damage, but I could feel the force of Renzo's blood coursing over my hands as I pressed and I began to shake; my impatience with him ebbed away as the blood pumped faster. The knife had gone deep into his gut; I had felt it.

'I only meant to frighten you,' he croaked.

'I don't believe you.' I spoke with anger, but it was directed at myself. 'You lure me out to this godforsaken place in the middle of the night for what – a chat? You threatened to cut me and dump me in the river. You wouldn't even fight like a man – you were going to slit my throat from behind.'

'I just wanted to see you piss yourself. My lady said you made an attempt on her honour.'

'It's not true.' Even in my panic I had time to think: Jesus,

199

who talks like that? Bleeding to death and he's still pretending he's in a tale of chivalry. 'I didn't touch her.' Not strictly true, but the spirit of it was close enough.

'Thought you needed to be taught a lesson. Neapolitan dog.' He struggled to sit up, and cried out with the pain.

'Shh, shh – don't move.' I eased him down. I could feel a rage boiling up in me, at all of them – him, her, Agostino, the Pope – for everything that had led to this. 'Why did you have to sneak up on me?' I pushed harder against the wound, but I could see it was having no effect.

'Why did you have a knife? You're meant to be a friar.'

I folded his hands under mine. 'Here, you press. I'm going for a doctor.'

There would be an infirmarian at Santa Maria, but I knew I would not make it there and back in time. If I could find a religious house closer at hand, it was possible a physician might be found, but that would be as good as confessing to murder.

'No. Don't leave me alone,' he said, clutching at my wrist. I glanced around; I could see nothing but shadows, though the sense of being watched had only intensified.

'*Are* you alone?' I asked. 'No servants with you?'

'Didn't want witnesses.' His voice was growing fainter. I could hear my own blood thudding in my ears. Was that a confession that he had meant to kill me after all? I supposed I would never know now.

'Get a priest,' he said urgently. He had begun to shiver violently. 'I am afraid.'

I wanted to tell him to stop making a fuss, he'd be fine in a minute, but in my heart I knew he was right.

'I'm a priest,' I said, and was surprised to find that I was crying. This was also not strictly true; I was not yet ordained, but I had taken vows and that had to count for something.

He mumbled something that sounded like 'absolve me',

and fell silent; I stammered my way through the last rites as I felt his grip slacken. He took ten more minutes to die, his breath rattling and gurgling in his throat, until I saw his eyes glass over, fixed past my shoulder to the stars and whatever lay beyond them.

In the moments after he died, the world seemed to have stopped with him. The city had fallen silent; no dogs barked, no owls cried; the only sound was my own breathing, quick and shallow. I stayed there, unable to move, until a distant church bell chimed the half hour and brought me back to myself. I sat up on my haunches and looked around.

I had killed a man, and now I had to work out what to do about it. My mind thrashed like a pigeon trapped in a room, hurtling into walls; I forced myself to slow my breathing as I did when I was about to perform my memory tricks, trying to order my thoughts more clearly. Though I could still see no sign of movement, I knew the amphitheatre must be full of vagrants; some of them might even be sober enough to recall what they had witnessed and repeat it to a magistrate. They would certainly remember the man in a Dominican habit. I picked up Porta's knife – I could not leave that, decorated with his emblem, at the scene – and wiped it clean on the dead man's clothes before tucking it into my belt. The white cloth of my habit was soaked with his blood, but it hardly showed on my black cloak; if I pulled it tight around me, I could hide the worst of the damage in dark streets until I had a chance to change, though I would need to wash first and I had no idea how to go about that – even the lowest inn would think twice before admitting a man covered in gore.

I grabbed Renzo under his arms and dragged his body out of the main arena, laying him down behind a pile of fallen masonry. I knew that my best hope was to delay discovery of the body while I put some distance between myself and

Rome. I returned to pick up his sword and swung it speculatively back and forth; I had never held such an expensive weapon. Briefly I considered throwing it in the river, but the sight of a friar hurling a sword into the water would be memorable for anyone who happened to be passing. As I stood, testing its weight, the silence was broken by a scattering of stones from beneath the arches, as if someone had fled in a hurry. I whipped around, but could make out nothing in the shadows; dogs, perhaps. I decided to leave the sword by the body. I smeared it with blood from Renzo's side and placed it by his right hand, so that whoever found him might think he had taken his life for love.

I hurtled through the streets, holding my habit above my knees, as if the Devil were at my heels, blindly running for the Este palazzo. Porta was the only person who could help me now; I was not sure he would be willing to dirty his hands with this situation, but beneath his genial good manners there was a ruthlessness, and I knew that he had experience in making bodies disappear. I followed the river until I began to recognise landmarks, and after a few wrong turns, found myself at the entrance to the rear courtyard where I had been shown out the night before. If the guards on the gate recognised me, they gave no sign; breathless, wild-eyed and bloodied as I appeared, I could hardly blame them.

When I asked for Porta, I saw the guards exchange a glance, before they informed me that the family had retired for the night and were not admitting visitors. I pulled my cloak tight around me to hide the blood on my habit, but I suspected there was plenty smeared across my face. I insisted that it was urgent; one of the men raised his pikestaff, but to my great good fortune a servant arrived at the gate leading a horse and I saw that it was the groom who had taken me home the night before.

'This man knows me,' I cried, lunging at him so that the horse reared its head back, white-eyed, and whinnied. The groom steadied her, cast a glance at me and nodded reluctantly to the guards to let me in. I followed him into the courtyard and saw the lady Leonora walking by herself, gazing up at the stars, fur cape tight around her shoulders. At the commotion, she turned her head and her mouth dropped open at the sight of me. I rushed across; she was far more likely to find Porta for me than any servant.

'You should not be here,' she hissed, darting a glance behind her to the house. 'My sister has accused you of trying to rape her. She has your belt as proof.'

'I didn't, I swear. I turned her down.'

'I believe you. But I did warn you. Luigi does not intend to do anything about it, she'll calm down eventually – but you can't be seen here while she's still insisting you attacked her. That does seem needlessly provocative.'

'I'll go, but I must see Don Giambattista – please, it's urgent.'

She took in my appearance for the first time. '*Madonna santa*, what has happened to you? Is that blood on your face?'

'I – I was assaulted,' I said. It was the first thing that came to mind. 'In the street.'

'How dreadful. Are you hurt?' She pressed her hands to her face. 'Should we call for the watch?'

'No,' I said, too quickly. 'I'm fine – I just – I must speak with Porta, this minute.'

'You're shaking. Come with me.' She looked back at the house again, then led me across to the stable block, where she pushed open the door of an empty stall. 'Stay in here. Don't let anyone see you – if Lucrezia finds out you're in the grounds, she'll clamour for your arrest and that will put my brother the cardinal in a very difficult position. Here.'

203

She pulled a handkerchief out of her sleeve, licked it and rubbed a spot on my cheek. 'That's better. You look like you've come from the battlefield.' She smiled and dropped her gaze, as if suddenly shy. I found myself thinking that she was not as obviously beautiful as her sister, but she had kind eyes. 'I was looking at the stars again,' she said, as if I had asked for an explanation. 'I've been pondering what you said about other worlds.'

'Please don't repeat that,' I said. 'I'm in enough trouble as it is.'

'Yes, I had heard. The Holy Father accused you of witch-craft.'

'He didn't— how did you know?'

'Oh, you're quite the centre of attention among the cardinals. They're saying it's a Christmas miracle you got out in one piece. Rebiba will be terribly disappointed.' She laughed. 'Well, I will fetch Porta to you.'

I sat down on a bale of straw and a wave of exhaustion crashed over me; Leonora was right, I was trembling all over like someone in the grip of a fever. It was not the first time I had seen a man die. I had been assisting Fra Gennaro in the infirmary since I was sixteen; every autumn, when the fogs rolling in off the Bay of Naples brought the influenza, it always took a few of the elderly brothers. I had watched others die of tumours, agues, infected wounds or, in one case, from falling off a roof. Once or twice I even thought I could pinpoint the moment when the soul left the body, as I stood by the bed with a fumigation while one of the senior brothers gave extreme unction. But I had never, until today, watched a man die at my hands. I stretched them out in front of me and examined my bloodstained palms. I was a murderer. Self-defence, accident; call it what you will, I had taken the life of a young man, barely older than me, who should have had decades left to live. Not only that, he was related to a prince. I thought of the *strappado*, the torture device I had seen in the Campo dei Fiori. I was a dead man. I put my head in my hands and began to cry.

'Hey, hey – none of that.' Porta's voice, almost fatherly, cut through my self-pity. The flame of his lantern sent a wavering light up the wall. 'No one believes Lucrezia, not even her brother. If anything, they feel sorry for you – they think she probably jumped on you. But it was not a good idea to come here. Lie low till she's forgotten about it.'

'It's not that.' I stood and opened my cloak to show him my blood-spattered habit. 'It's worse.'

He kept a hand pressed over his mouth as I told my story, nodding at intervals until I hiccupped my way to the end. He was silent for a long time, his eyes fixed on my clothes, while he made his calculations. Eventually he started to laugh softly.

'What?' I stared at him, incredulous.

'You've been here two days, Bruno, and already you're accused of rape by a cardinal's sister, the Pope has called you a witch, and now you've killed a man in a duel. Such havoc has not been wrought in the city since the Sack of Rome forty years ago. Imagine if you stayed a week.'

'Jesus, Porta – it's not *funny*. And it wasn't a duel. I told you – he ambushed me.'

'Well,' he said, folding his arms, 'Renzo Arduino is no great loss to Italy, I assure you. You know he had the French pox? He would have died young anyway, in exquisite agony, after his nose and cock rotted off – in many ways you've done him a favour.'

'I don't think the law will see it like that. Or his family.'

'Oh, I can't imagine the Prince of Piombino will stir himself. The boy was chronically in debt and constantly begging for money. That's why he was courting Lucrezia so frantically, not that he had any hope of marrying her.'

'Still, he didn't deserve to die.'

'Sounds like he was going to cut your throat.'

'What if he wasn't?'

'Well, it's done,' he said, with a brisk sniff. 'No point wallowing in guilt. The thing now is to tidy up after you. Did anyone see you leave Santa Maria?'

'I don't think so. I went over the wall.'

'Good. How long till they notice you're gone?'

'They'll call at my cell when I don't show up for matins at two.'

He nodded. 'That gives us almost three hours. And will they go in search of you, when they realise you've left the convent?'

I had no idea; I had not discussed with Fra Agostino anything beyond my audience with the Pope. I had assumed I would stay in Rome until Porta was ready to leave. Fra Agostino might be offended at my sudden departure, but I did not suppose he would regret it, unless he was still entertaining hopes of further punishment. 'I doubt it. Oh, but – Renzo left a message with the gatekeeper there, asking to meet. He signed it from you.'

'Ah. Well, I can take responsibility for it, if anyone asks. I'll claim I helped you slink away in shame after your audience with the Pope today.' He smiled. 'I wish I could have seen that, truly. I said you'd be the talk of the town, didn't I?'

'This was not what I imagined.'

'Life never is, Bruno. Get used to it. Now – make yourself comfortable in this stable, as Our Lord did at Christmas, and I'll send Tito to you. We'll meet again in Naples, but not for a while. Not until you're less notorious.'

'But—' I stretched out a hand to him. 'Am I still part of the Academy?'

He pressed a finger to his lips. 'Always. But all of us in

the Academy are sworn to protect one another's secrets, and you and I have rather a lot of those between us. You will be watched closely when you return to Naples, and I don't want that to mean they start watching me. Now – trust me, do everything Tito tells you, and you'll come out of this in one piece. Unlike Renzo.'

'Thank you.' I held out my arms to embrace him, but he stepped back.

'You look like you've come from a slaughterhouse.' He paused and turned in the doorway, his expression serious. 'Bruno. Listen to me. You did what any man would have done with a blade to his throat – you defended yourself. It was his life or yours.'

'What if that's not true?'

'Tell yourself it is. Oh, and – better give me that knife back, just in case.'

After he left, I knelt down in the straw to pray. Even at twenty-one, great cracks had already formed in the foundation of my faith and only continued to widen; the more theology and philosophy I studied, the more I saw only the gaps in their explanations, and my association with Porta and the Academy had opened my eyes to the vast scope of all that was still unknown to man, but might one day be encompassed. I was no longer willing to accept that we had reached the limit of the knowledge that was permitted to us when it came to the universe and its workings, nor could I call that imperfect understanding 'faith'. But I still had a fierce sense of right and wrong, and I could not share Porta's cold dismissal of Renzo Arduino as unworthy of regret. True, he had been brash, arrogant and swaggering, but I had been all those things myself at one time or another. He was young; he might have grown into less of an entitled prick in time, but my blade had robbed him of time, and I couldn't shake the knowledge that God was watching, and had made a note of it in His great book, even if I were to escape the law. No point wallowing in guilt, Porta said, but my conscience was not so easily appeased. Could I be absolved of a sin I could never confess? There was no one to whom I might even put the question.

My prayers were interrupted by a discreet cough; I snapped my head up to see Porta's bodyguard Tito, his broad shoulders filling the doorway. He carried a pail in one hand, steam rising from the lid, and in the other a lantern; under each arm a bundle of cloth.

'Here.' He set the pail down and handed me a sack and a towel. 'Do you have a change of clothes?'

'In here.' I patted my travelling bag. 'But—'

'Good. Save it. You'll need it when you get back to Naples. Wash yourself, put your soiled clothes in the sack with the towel. Then dress in these.' He placed a pile on the straw bale and I saw that it was a servant's brown tunic and breeches, with a rough woollen cloak and cheap boots. 'And take this,' he added, drawing from inside his jacket a silver flask. 'From my master. He says you'll need it. I'll be back in ten minutes.'

I unscrewed the flask, sniffed it, and tipped half its contents down my throat; aqua vitae, fierce and burning, making me cough. While I waited for its heat to lend me courage I stripped, shivering so hard that I had to clench my jaw to keep my teeth from rattling, and sluiced myself head to foot with the hot water. In the dim lamplight I could not see whether I had rid my skin of all traces of blood, but the linen towel came away smeared with dark streaks. I stuffed it in the sack with my stained habit and cloak, tucked the flask inside my tunic, and when Tito returned I appeared like any groom or serving man, complete with a wool cap that I pulled down low over my eyes, and thick gloves. He assessed me with a practised glance and nodded.

'Go out there,' he instructed, checking that the courtyard was empty and indicating a small door in the wall, 'round to the courtyard gate and wait for me in the street.'

When I reached the wide entrance to the stable yard, I saw Porta's coach parked in the street, the horses in harness and Tito holding their bridle, a kerchief tied around his mouth and nose. Black cloth had been draped over the windows and the sides of the coach to hide Porta's insignia.

'Get in.' Tito motioned to the door. I noticed he was carrying a heavy sword at his belt. 'And don't look out. Those drapes are there for a reason.'

Distant sounds of late revellers carried through the night air as the carriage lurched through the streets and I rattled around inside it in the dark, fearing at every turn that we would be stopped and questioned. The aqua vitae burned in my guts. As we pulled to a halt I feared I might be sick with nerves, but when Tito opened the door I saw, to my relief, that he was alone. The great semi-circular wall of the amphitheatre towered over us. A wave of nausea rose in my throat again.

'Come on, then,' Tito said. He carried a lantern and a blanket over his shoulder.

'What about the horses?'

'They'll stay put. If anyone comes near them, they'll let us know. This needs two pairs of hands.'

He handed me the lantern and I led the way. I need not have worried about finding Renzo's body again in the vast darkness of the amphitheatre; the pack of dogs huddled by the fallen wall, yelping wildly in their frenzy for blood, would have led anyone to him. Tito drew his sword and shouted at them; most fled at our approach, and he swiped at the last determined stragglers until the corpse was visible in the dim light. Renzo's naked skin gleamed white against the dark ground, pale as a marble statue, except for the gash in his stomach and the marks where the dogs had gnawed him. I froze, and could only stare in horror.

'What did you do with his clothes?' Tito hissed, unfolding the blanket over his shoulder.

'I didn't. I mean – he was dressed when I left him.' My voice had risen to a panicked squeak.

'Huh.' Tito glanced around. 'Suppose a homeless man doesn't care if a jerkin is covered in gore, long as it's good cloth.'

'His sword is gone too,' I said, disbelieving. I had been gone less than an hour and those unseen figures who sheltered in the theatre's shadows had stripped him completely; even his earring had been taken. I looked down at him. His body was athletic and finely muscled, his skin smooth and pale, with a furze of hair running from his chest to his groin. I wondered if Porta had told the truth about the pox, or if he had said that to make me feel better.

'It's all to the good,' Tito whispered. 'Any of his stuff turns up on a vagrant's back, they'll be the ones questioned.'

'What if any of them saw me?'

'You think the word of a drunk beggar would count for anything, even if they remember? No, it's best if they have his clothes. Saves me getting rid of them. It'll look like he fell foul of robbers.'

'He was going to cut my throat,' I said, defensive.

Tito held up a hand. 'I don't need to know the detail, sir. Give me a hand to shift him.'

He spread the blanket on the ground and we gracelessly rolled Renzo's body on to it, wrapped him in it and took an end each. He was surprisingly heavy and every few minutes one of his limbs would loll out of the blanket as if he had turned over in his sleep, but between us we managed to haul him to the carriage. Tito shoved the body on to the floor inside and motioned for me to get in.

210

'What? In there? With him?'

'Well, he can't sit up front with me, can he?'

'But I—'

'What did you think we were going to do with him?'

'Put him in the river?'

He shook his head brusquely. 'Too dangerous. Too many of them bob back to the surface to tell their tales. Someone would recognise him. Get in, he can't hurt you now.'

He closed the door after me and I pulled my feet up on to the seat so they would not touch the corpse. I had been too panicked to close Renzo's eyes when I first realised he was dead, and Tito was too much of a soldier to bother with such delicacies, so the dead man continued to stare at the roof of the carriage. The jolting of the road caused the blanket to slip off, and every time we bounced over a rut his head would jerk upwards as if he meant to sit up; I could not bring myself to touch his face now, and had to bite my sleeve to stop myself crying out every time he seemed to look at me. It was barely three days since Porta had joked that I would have to get my own carriage if I wanted to take corpses home for Gennaro; I wondered if one day we would be able to laugh at the irony.

The coach smelled thickly of blood. I had considered myself a man of science and reason, but after an hour trapped in that dark, lurching space, avoiding a dead man's accusing stare, I could think only of my grandmother's stories about vengeful wandering souls; in the rattling of the wheels and the buffeting of the wind I was sure I heard voices whispering. When at last we stopped and Tito opened the door, I shot out like a hunting dog, gulping down cold air that did not reek of death.

His lantern concentrated the darkness around us. Overhead, the sky was a velvet cloth stitched with diamonds. Only the cries of night birds and the distant howl of wolves broke the silence. I could make out the silhouette of mountains on the horizon, and the broken shapes of boulders all around. There was no sign of movement anywhere.

Tito lugged Renzo's body out of the carriage and once again we grappled him between us in his blanket. We must have carried him for near ten minutes before I dropped my end; my arms ached with the weight and sweat stood out on my forehead.

'Not much further,' Tito said, trying to sound encouraging, though I could only guess at how much he must resent me for all this.

I wiped my face on my sleeve. 'I can't go on.'

'You can and you will,' he said sharply. 'Nearly there. Come on.'

I bent my legs to take the weight and we dragged him a few yards more, until Tito motioned for me to set him down. He held up the lantern and looked around.

'Are we going to bury him?'

He shook his head. 'Ground's too hard. Keep back here, it's a long way down with some vicious rocks at the bottom.'

I followed the direction of his finger and saw that we were close to the edge of a gulley where the ground fell away. He unrolled Renzo from the blanket, then wandered off with the light, searching for something at his feet. I crouched by Renzo's body, trying to examine him.

'Do you think he had the pox?' I asked, as Tito's shadow fell across the body. 'I can't see any scars, but the light isn't good. Porta said—'

'I don't think it much matters now,' Tito cut in gently, setting down the lantern. 'You might want to look away for this part, sir.'

I glanced up and saw that he held a heavy rock in his right hand. 'What are you going to do?'

'I'm going to make sure his own father wouldn't recognise

212

him. Just to be on the safe side.' He pulled up his sleeve and adjusted his gloves.

'I don't think his own father ever did,' I said, half to myself, as I turned to walk back towards the coach. 'That was his problem.'

At my back I heard the wet crunch of splintering bone. I paused by a boulder and heaved up the contents of my stomach, spat hard, wiped my mouth and finished the aqua vitae in Porta's flask. There came a dragging sound, a scattering of loose rocks, and silence. Tito returned peeling off his gloves, which he dropped into the sack containing my bloodstained clothes.

'Let's get you home then, sir,' he said briskly. 'Try and sleep, if you can.'

I must have slept; I had no idea how long we had been travelling, but the next time the carriage door opened I could see the faintest sheen of dawn light along the horizon. When I unfolded my stiff limbs and climbed out, I could smell the sea and hear the cries of gulls.

'Where are we?'

'Port of Ostia. Stay here with the horses.'

I leaned back against the side of the coach and breathed in the cold air. At length, Tito returned to inform me that he had arranged a berth on a boat bound for the Bay of Naples; I was not to give my real name. He pointed me towards the quayside.

'Tito,' I said, as he turned to go. 'Have you killed a man?'

He gave a worldly laugh. 'I was a soldier, sir.'

I nodded. 'My father's a soldier.'

'Well, then. Ask him. The first one's the worst.'

'I'm not planning to make a career of it.'

'My master will be relieved to hear that.' He clapped me on the shoulder. 'You'd best get on your way.'

213

'Is it over?'

'As long as you keep your mouth shut. My master says you know how to do that.'

I nodded. Ahead, the stars were fading over the sea, and the salt air had begun to scour the taste of blood from my mouth.

It was the day before Twelfth Night when the boat finally docked, wave-tossed, in the harbour of Naples. Behind an abandoned building at the port, I changed into my spare habit, but I kept the servant's clothes, in case of future need.

I had hoped to avoid attention when I arrived back at San Domenico, but I had been in my cell barely ten minutes when there was a knock on the door, and the prior walked in without waiting for an invitation.

'I did not expect you back so soon, Fra Giordano.'

'I didn't want to outstay my welcome.'

He appraised me with a swift glance. 'You've lost weight.'

'I was fasting,' I said. I could hardly tell him that bad weather had prolonged the journey down the coast, and I felt as if I had not kept a meal down for over a week.

He gave me a sceptical look and folded his arms.

'So?' he asked. It could have meant anything.

'You haven't heard . . . ?'

I had no idea how urgently the Pope would have dispatched his promised letter, nor whether Fra Agostino would have sent any message about my abrupt departure, but I was sure a fast rider could cover the distance between Rome and Naples in half the time my boat had taken.

'I'm asking you.'

I hesitated. 'I think – it could have been worse.'

He pursed his lips. 'Well, at least they didn't burn you. Not yet, anyway. What did you make of Cardinal Rebiba?'

'I don't think he liked me,' I said carefully.

214

The faintest smile stretched the corners of his lips. 'No, Bruno. Cardinal Rebiba doesn't like *me*. He wanted to trip you in order to bring me down. But here we both are, still standing, more or less.'

I stared at him. 'If you knew that, why did you let me go?'

'First, because you don't refuse the Pope, and second, because I trusted you to speak for yourself.' He folded his arms. 'Naples is too small for you, Bruno. I've known that since the day you arrived here. You have a fine mind, and one day it will lead you away from us to greater things. But there is much you need to learn first, and I am not talking about your theology degree. To thrive in this world, you must learn how to talk to men of status. You must learn how to defend your arguments without appearing to think yourself cleverer than your opponents, even when you are. You must learn the arts of flattery and humility as well as plain-speaking, because if you can't temper your views, and keep some of your thoughts to yourself, one day you will talk yourself into the arms of the Inquisition.'

'You're saying I must learn to be a politician. To dissemble.'

'You chose the religious life,' he said. 'What else did you expect? I hoped Rome might give you a sharp lesson in those skills.'

I shook my head. 'I am content to stay in Naples,' I said, with some force. 'I'd be happy if I never saw Rome again.'

'Well, it would certainly be wise to keep your distance for now,' he said, and the look he shot me from under his brows made me wonder how much he knew. 'But Rome has eyes everywhere. It grieves me to say it, but neither you nor I know who among our brothers might be watching.'

'Spying for the Vatican, you mean?' I dropped my voice and glanced at the door, as if someone might have his ear pressed to it at that moment.

'The Vatican, the Inquisition, the Spanish, Cardinal Rebiba,

215

Fra Agostino. It hardly matters. There are plenty of people who would like to see San Domenico in the hands of a prior more easily influenced in their favour, and would gladly use your natural disregard for authority as evidence that I allow heresy to flourish unchecked. So – guard yourself more carefully from now on. Popes do not last for ever, but you have used up your one chance with this one, and we can't always be here to protect you.'

'We?' I said.

'Me. Porta. Fra Gennaro. It is not only yourself you endanger by your recklessness. I see you look surprised,' he said, at my expression. 'Do you really imagine I don't know what goes on in my convent? You do not know how many times I have stood between you and the Inquisition, Bruno, defending you from the rumours that attach to your name. Two of our brothers killed in the last three years, both from good families, and both times it has been said that you knew more than you were telling about what happened. But I cannot speak up for you again without sacrificing my position – not after . . .' He shifted his gaze pointedly away from me and allowed the sentence to hang, unfinished. I would probably never find out exactly what he knew of what had passed in Rome; he was well aware that the threat was more effective if he simply implied that I could have no secrets from him. I thought of all the times I had sensed that presence at my back, watching my every move. Had the prior sent someone after me, to make a report? I would not have put it past him. Or was the spy in the pay of one of the others he had mentioned – Rebiba, Agostino, the Pope himself? There was every chance that I had been followed to the Theatre of Marcellus that night, and that Renzo's corpse would one day surface from that ravine to accuse me. But then, it was equally possible that there was no watcher in the shadows; that he was no more than a ghost conjured by my imagination, and that it was my curse to live with one eye over my shoulder, as all guilty men must.

'You will not have to,' I said, chastened.

'See that I don't. Conduct yourself as if your every move is being reported, because for all you know, it is. No unorthodox writings hidden in your cell.' His gaze travelled almost imperceptibly to the rafters, just long enough to assure me that my hiding place was not as safe as I had believed. 'No forbidden books. No more late-night meetings in the infirmary with Fra Gennaro. No sneaking out at night by the garden door.'

'Not even to the Cerriglio?' I asked.

'Bruno, if I thought you were creeping out in search of women and dice, I would positively rejoice. But your transgressions are of a different nature, and endanger us both. You are excused matins tonight – you look as if you need some sleep.'

'Most Reverend Prior, wait,' I said, lunging at him and grabbing his sleeve as he turned to go. 'Would you hear my confession?'

He jerked his arm away as if I had scalded him.

'No.' He drew himself up to regain his composure. 'No, I do not think that would serve either of us. Go into the church, confess your sins to God alone and find His forgiveness in your heart. He will hear you.'

'Isn't that what the Protestants do?'

He pressed his lips together and raised his eyes as if summoning patience. 'Sometimes, Fra Giordano, I can only assume God sent you here to test my faith.'

'I will pray that you pass,' I said, my eyes fixed on the floor.

'Pray that we all pass,' he muttered. But when I glanced up from under my lashes, it seemed to me that he was trying not to smile.

*

I could not sleep. In the dead hours between compline and matins, while the convent was silent, I took myself to the church of San Domenico as the prior had advised, and knelt in front of the altar, the steps still wreathed with festive branches. My breath fogged in the chill air. I raised my eyes to the great crucifix above me, the wooden Christ with his skin white as milk, the gash in His side almost obscene in its gaping redness; but as I looked at Him, all I could see was Renzo's naked body with its livid wound in the dark of the amphitheatre. It was said that St Thomas Aquinas, when he lived in our convent three hundred years earlier, had heard this painted Christ speak to him; pilgrims came by the dozen to kiss its feet. But if there was any truth in the legend, it seemed He had nothing left to say to me.

I could not blame Him; I had killed a man, and I did not know how to reconcile this truth with the person I had believed myself to be. I found myself longing to speak not to Christ but to my father. I had seen little of him since I left home at fifteen to join the Dominicans, and the education he had wanted for me had only served to widen the distance between us. If I was honest – and it shamed me to think it – I had often dismissed him: what could he have to teach me, this old mercenary with no Greek or Latin? I had left him behind, and looked for substitute fathers whose learning I could emulate, like Gennaro and Porta. Now, I felt Giovanni Bruno was the only person who could understand what I had done, and give me the absolution I needed.

In his absence I tried to pray, and the painted Christ looked mutely down with sorrowful eyes. I wondered how the Protestants managed, without confession and penance; how did they know they were forgiven? Was I forgiven? I recalled Renzo's sword against my throat, and thought how easily I could have bled my life away in the dust of an ancient theatre. I thought of the Pope's final words, clearly intended to carry:

'that boy is headed for the pyre'. At that, I felt a sudden rush of anger. Who did he think he was, that jumped-up goatherd in a tiara, to lay bets on my future? He would not write my story. I would return to Rome one day, and prove him wrong.

I stood and brushed myself down, defiant, tilted my chin at the painted Christ, and recited the Pater Noster backwards, just because I could. He didn't say a word, as I knew He would not.

Turn the page for a short story ...

Turn the page for a sneak peek at *Execution*,
the latest story in S. J. Parris's No. 1 *Sunday Times*
bestselling series following Giordano Bruno . . .

PROLOGUE

17th July 1586

Chartley Manor, Staffordshire

Six gentlemen. Six of them, ready to undertake that tragic execution in her name. She smiles at the euphemism. But then: why not call it that? Elizabeth Tudor is a heretic, a traitor and a thief, occupying a throne she has stolen; dispatching her would be no regicide, but a just and deserved punishment under the law. Not the law of England, to be sure, but God's law, which is greater.

Mary sits at the small table in her room, in her prison, thinking, thinking, turning over and over in her mind the pages of the great ledger of injustices heaped against her. Eventually, she dips her quill in the inkpot. She wears gloves with the fingers cut off, because it is always cold here, in Staffordshire; the summer so far has been bleak and grey, or at least what she can see of it from her casement, since she is not permitted to walk outside. She flexes her fingers and hears the knuckles crack; she rubs the sore and swollen joints. A pool of weak light falls on the paper before her; she has havered so long over this reply that the candle has almost burned down, and she only has one left until Paulet, her keeper, brings the new ration in the morning. Sometimes he pretends to forget, just as he does with the firewood, to see how long she will sit in the cold and dark without protesting. And when she does ask meekly for the little that is her due, he uses it against her; charges her with being demanding, spoilt, needy, and says he will tell her cousin. But should a queen plead meekly with the likes of Sir Amias Paulet, that puffed-up Puritan? Should a queen be starved of sunlight, of liberty, of respect, and endure it with patience? Twenty years of imprisonment has not taught her to bear it any better, nor will she ever accept it. The day she bows to their treatment of her, she is no longer worthy of her royal title.

She sets the quill down; she has worked herself into a fury and her shaking hand has spattered ink drops on the clean page; she will have to begin again, when she is calmer. She pushes back the chair and heaves herself with difficulty to her feet, wincing at the pain in her inflamed legs. Each step to the window hurts more than it did the day before; or perhaps she is imagining that. One imagines so much, cooped up here in these four walls. She smooths her skirts over her broad hips; and there is another injustice, that she should still be fat when she eats so little! She doesn't trust the food they bring; one day, she is certain, she will eat or drink something and not wake up. That would suit her cousin Elizabeth very well, so she will not give her the satisfaction. And yet, Mary thinks, curling her lip at her rippled reflection in the dark of the windowpane, she has grown heavy and lumpen on nothing but air, half-crippled by rheumatism, grey and faded, an old woman at forty-four. No trace left of the famous beauty that once drove men to madness. But Elizabeth is ugly too, she has heard; near-bald, teeth blackened, her skin so eaten away by the ceruse she uses to hide her age that she will not be seen by any except her closest women without a full mask of face-paint. There will be no children for her now; at least that is one contest that Mary can say she won, even if she hasn't seen her son for nearly twenty years.

She cups her hands around her face to peer out at the night, watching a barn owl ghosting over the moat, when there is a soft knock at the door. She starts, hastens back to the table to hide the papers, but it is only Claude Nau, her French secretary. He bobs a brief bow, takes in her guilty expression.

'You are writing him a reply, Your Majesty?'

'I am considering.' She draws herself up, haughty. He is going to tell her off, she knows, and she has had enough of men speaking to her as if she is a child. She is Queen of Scotland, Dowager Queen of France, and rightful Queen of England, and they should not forget it.

'I counsel against that.'

She watches Nau; a handsome man, always quietly spoken, infuriatingly self-contained, even when she works herself into one of her fits of passion.

'I know you do. But I make my own decisions.'

'Majesty.' He inclines his head. 'I smell a trap.'

'Oh, you will see conspiracies everywhere. Did you read what he promises, Claude? He has men to do the deed, and earnest assurance of foreign aid, and riders to take me to liberty. Everything is in place.' She allows herself to imagine it, as she has so many times, crossing back to the window. 'See, I have an idea' – she taps the glass, excited – 'if we know the exact date to expect him, we can have one of the servants start a fire in the stables. Everyone will rush out and in the commotion, Anthony Babington and his friends can break down my chamber door and whisk me away.' She spins around, a wide, girlish smile on her face that fades the instant she sees his look. 'What? You do not like my plan?'

'It is a very good plan, Majesty. Only . . .' He folds his hands.

'Speak.'

'We have heard such promises before. This Babington is proposing an assassination.'

'*Execution.*'

He waves a hand. 'Call it what you will. But your own cousin. England's queen. In your name.'

'She is no queen.'

He adopts the patient, pained expression that so irritates her. 'Of course not. But if you agree to their proposal, if you so much as acknowledge it in writing, you make yourself an accessory to treason, and there is only one punishment for that offence.'

'My royal cousin loves me too much to allow that.'

'She loves you.' Nau does not contradict her outright, but he allows his gaze to travel pointedly around the room in which she is held captive.

Mary's eyes flash; he has overstepped the mark. 'Leave me.' She flaps a hand to the door. 'I have my letter to write. Come back in an hour and you can encrypt it.'

'I implore you not to put anything on paper which would implicate you in this reckless business. Babington and his friends are impetuous boys. We would do better to proceed with caution, keep our options open.'

'And I order you to get out. There is no *we* here, Claude. They are *my* options, and *I* will choose. Obey your queen.'

Nau sighs audibly, bows, and backs out of the royal presence. When the door clicks shut behind him, Mary smiles, pleased with herself. She sits again at the table and dips her quill, but she cannot think how to begin. She wants Elizabeth to love her, it's true. She wants Elizabeth dead. She wants only her freedom; she wants the throne of England. She is ill, and desperate, and ready to clutch at any straw Providence tosses her way.

She glances up and sees her embroidered cloth of state hanging on the wall over her bed. Every time the snake Paulet comes into the room, he rips it down – she is not permitted the trappings of a queen, he says. And every time he leaves, her women patiently gather it up, mend the tears and hang it again. Now, this Babington is offering her the real prospect of seeing it where it belongs, above her throne at last. She has waited long enough. She is done with caution. What she wants at this moment, more than anything, is to win.

She takes a fresh sheet of paper and writes the date: 17th July 1586. It is a letter that will kill a queen.

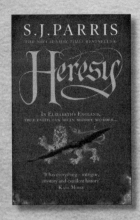

In Elizabeth's England, true faith can mean bloody murder…

Oxford, 1583. A place of learning. And murderous schemes.

The country is rife with plots to assassinate Queen Elizabeth and return the realm to the Catholic faith. Giordano Bruno is recruited by the queen's spymaster and sent undercover to expose a treacherous conspiracy in Oxford – but his own secret mission must remain hidden at all costs.

A spy under orders. A coveted throne under threat.

When a series of hideous murders ruptures close-knit college life, Bruno is compelled to investigate. And what he finds makes it brutally clear that the Tudor throne itself is at stake…

Autumn, 1583. Under Elizabeth's rule, loyalty is bought with blood…

An astrological phenomenon heralds the dawn of a new age and Queen Elizabeth's throne is in peril. As Mary Stuart's supporters scheme to usurp the rightful monarch, a young maid of honour is murdered, occult symbols carved into her flesh.

The Queen's spymaster, Francis Walsingham, calls on maverick agent Giordano Bruno to infiltrate the plotters and secure the evidence that will condemn them to death.

Bruno is cunning, but so are his enemies. His identity could be exposed at any moment. The proof he seeks is within his grasp. But the young woman's murder could point to an even more sinister truth…

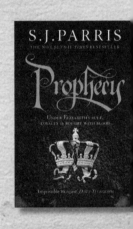

London, 1584. Giordano Bruno travels to Canterbury for love. But finds only murder …

Giordano Bruno is being followed by the woman he once loved – Sophia Underhill, accused of murder and on the run. With the leave of the Queen's spymaster, he sets out to clear Sophia's name. But when more brutal killings occur a far deadlier plot emerges.

A city rife with treachery. A relic steeped in blood.

His hunt for the real killer leads to the shadows of the Cathedral – England's holiest shrine – and the heart of a sinister and powerful conspiracy …

August, 1585. England is on the brink of war…

Sir Francis Drake is preparing to launch a daring expedition against the Spanish when a murder aboard his ship changes everything.

**A relentless enemy.
A treacherous conspiracy.**

Giordano Bruno agrees to hunt the killer down, only to find that more than one deadly plot is brewing in Plymouth's murky underworld. And as he tracks a murderer through its dangerous streets, he uncovers a conspiracy that threatens the future of England itself.

A king without an heir

Heretic-turned-spy Giordano Bruno arrives in Paris to find a city on the edge of catastrophe. King Henri III lives in fear of a coup by the Duke of Guise and his fanatical Catholic League, and another massacre on the streets.

A court at war with God

When Bruno's old rival, Father Paul Lefèvre, is found murdered, Bruno is drawn into a dangerous web of religious politics and court intrigue. And watching over his shoulder is the King's mother, Catherine de Medici, with her harem of beautiful spies.

A deadly conspiracy in play

When murder strikes at the heart of the Palace, Bruno finds himself on the trail of a killer who is protecting a terrible secret. With the royal houses of France and England under threat, Bruno must expose the truth – or be silenced for good…

A treasonous conspiracy

Giordano Bruno, a heretic turned spy, arrives in England with shocking information for spymaster Sir Francis Walsingham. A band of Catholic Englishmen are plotting to kill Queen Elizabeth and spring Mary, Queen of Scots, from prison to take the English throne in her place.

A deadly trap

Bruno is surprised to find that Walsingham is aware of the plot and is allowing it to progress. He hopes that Mary will put her support in writing – and condemn herself to a traitor's death.

A queen in mortal danger

Bruno is tasked with going undercover to join the conspirators. Can he stop them before he is exposed? Either way a queen will die; Bruno must make sure it is the right one…